The
Pagan
Rabbi

and
Other
Stories

Cynthia Ozick

The Pagan Rabbi

—◆—

and Other Stories

Syracuse University Press

First Syracuse University Press Edition 1995

97 98 99 00   6 5 4 3 2

Originally published in 1971.
Reprinted by arrangement with Alfred A. Knopf, Inc.

"The Pagan Rabbi" was originally published in *The Hudson Review*, Autumn 1966;
"Envy; or, Yiddish in America," in *Commentary*, November 1969;
"The Butterfly and the Traffic Light," in *The Literary Review*, Autumn 1961;
"Virility," in *Anon.*, February 1971; "The Doctor's Wife," in *Midstream*, February 1971.

The paper used in this publication meets the minimum requirements
of American National Standard for Information Sciences—Permanence
of Paper for Printed Library Materials, ANSI Z39.48-1984. ∞™

Library of Congress Cataloging-in-Publication Data

Ozick, Cynthia.
The pagan rabbi, and other stories / Cynthia Ozick. — 1st
Syracuse University Press ed.
p.   cm. — (The library of modern Jewish literature)
ISBN 0-8156-0351-7 (pbk : alk. paper)
1. Jews—Social life and customs—Fiction. I. Title.
II. Series.
PS3565.Z5P34   1995
813'.54—dc20   95-18819

Manufactured in the United States of America

For
Bernard

This book (and a part of my life) is
owed to David I. Segal (1928–1970).

Grateful acknowledgment

is made

To Carolyn Kizer and the National Endowment
for the Arts, for faith and works;
And to Norman Podhoretz: *ba'al hanifla'ot.*

Contents

The
Pagan
Rabbi

Rabbi Jacob said: "He who is walking along
and studying, but then breaks off to remark,
'How lovely is that tree!' or 'How beautiful is that
fallow field!'—Scripture regards such a one
as having hurt his own being."
—from The Ethics of the Fathers

WHEN I HEARD that Isaac Kornfeld, a man of piety and brains, had hanged himself in the public park, I put a token in the subway stile and journeyed out to see the tree.

We had been classmates in the rabbinical seminary. Our fathers were both rabbis. They were also friends, but only in a loose way of speaking: in actuality our fathers were enemies. They vied with one another in demonstrations of charitableness, in the captious glitter of their scholia, in the number of their adherents. Of the two, Isaac's father was the milder. I was afraid of my father; he had a certain disease of the larynx, and if he even uttered something so trivial as "Bring the tea" to my mother, it came out splintered, clamorous, and vindictive.

Neither man was philosophical in the slightest. It was the one thing they agreed on. "Philosophy is an abomination," Isaac's father used to say. "The Greeks were philosophers, but they remained children playing with their dolls. Even Socrates, a monotheist, nevertheless sent money down to the temple to pay for incense to their doll."

"Idolatry is the abomination," Isaac argued, "not philosophy."

"The latter is the corridor to the former," his father said.

My own father claimed that if not for philosophy I would never have been brought to the atheism which finally led me to withdraw, in my second year, from the seminary.

The trouble was not philosophy—I had none of Isaac's talent: his teachers later said of him that his imagination was so remarkable he could concoct holiness out of the fine line of a serif. On the day of his funeral the president of his college was criticized for having commented that although a suicide could not be buried in consecrated earth, whatever earth enclosed Isaac Kornfeld was ipso facto consecrated. It should be noted that Isaac hanged himself several weeks short of his thirty-sixth birthday; he was then at the peak of his renown; and the president, of course, did not know the whole story. He judged by Isaac's reputation, which was at no time more impressive than just before his death.

I judged by the same, and marveled that all that holy genius and intellectual surprise should in the end be raised no higher than the next-to-lowest limb of a delicate young oak, with burly roots like the toes of a gryphon exposed in the wet ground.

The tree was almost alone in a long rough meadow, which sloped down to a bay filled with sickly clams and a bad smell. The place was called Trilham's Inlet, and I knew what the smell meant: that cold brown water covered half the city's turds.

On the day I came to see the tree the air was bleary with fog. The weather was well into autumn and, though it was Sunday, the walks were empty. There was something historical about the park just then, with its rusting grasses and deserted monuments. In front of a soldiers' cenotaph a plastic wreath left behind months before by some civic parade stood propped against a stone frieze of identical marchers in the costume of an old war. A banner across the wreath's belly explained that the purpose of war is peace. At the margins of the park they were building a gigantic highway. I felt I was making my way across a battlefield silenced by the victory of the peace machines. The bulldozers had bitten far into the park, and the rolled carcasses of the sacrificed trees were already cut up into logs. There were dozens of felled maples, elms, and oaks. Their moist inner wheels breathed out a fragrance of barns, countryside, decay.

In the bottommost meadow fringing the water I recognized the tree which had caused Isaac to sin against his own life. It looked curiously like a photograph—not only like that newspaper photograph I carried warmly in my pocket, which showed the field and its markers—the drinking-fountain a few yards off, the ruined brick wall of an old estate behind. The caption-writer had particularly remarked on the "rope." But the rope was no longer there; the widow had claimed it. It was his own prayer shawl that Isaac, a short man, had thrown over the comely neck of the next-to-lowest limb. A Jew is buried in his prayer shawl; the police had handed it over to Sheindel. I observed that the bark was rubbed at that spot. The tree lay back against the sky like a licked postage stamp. Rain began to beat it flatter yet. A stench of sewage came up like a veil in the nostril. It seemed to me I was a man in a photograph standing next to a gray blur of tree. I would stand through eternity beside Isaac's guilt if I did not run, so I ran that night to Sheindel herself.

I loved her at once. I am speaking now of the first time I saw her, though I don't exclude the last. The last—the last together with Isaac—was soon after my divorce; at one stroke I left my wife and my cousin's fur business to the small upstate city in which both had repined. Suddenly Isaac and Sheindel and two babies appeared in the lobby of my hotel—they were passing through: Isaac had a lecture engagement in Canada. We sat under scarlet neon and Isaac told how my father could now not speak at all.

"He keeps his vow," I said.

"No, no, he's a sick man," Isaac said. "An obstruction in the throat."

"I'm the obstruction. You know what he said when I left the seminary. He meant it, never mind how many years it is. He's never addressed a word to me since."

"We were reading together. He blamed the reading, who can blame *him*? Fathers like ours don't know how to love. They live too much indoors."

It was an odd remark, though I was too much preoccupied with my own resentments to notice. "It wasn't what we read," I objected. "Torah tells that an illustrious man doesn't have an illustrious son. Otherwise he wouldn't be humble like other people. This much scholarly stuffing I retain. Well, so my father always believed he was more illustrious than anybody, especially more than your father. *There*fore," I delivered in Talmudic cadence, "what chance did I have? A nincompoop and no *sitzfleish*. Now you, you could answer questions that weren't even invented yet. Then you invented them."

"Torah isn't a spade," Isaac said. "A man should have a livelihood. You had yours."

"The pelt of a dead animal isn't a living either, it's an indecency."

All the while Sheindel was sitting perfectly still; the babies, female infants in long stockings, were asleep in her arms. She wore a dark thick woolen hat—it was July—that covered every part of her hair. But I had once seen it in all its streaming black shine.

"And Jane?" Isaac asked finally.

"Speaking of dead animals. Tell my father—he won't answer a letter, he won't come to the telephone—that in the matter of the marriage he was right, but for the wrong reason. If you share a bed with a Puritan you'll come into it cold and you'll go out of it cold. Listen, Isaac, my father calls me an atheist, but between the conjugal sheets every Jew is a believer in miracles, even the lapsed."

He said nothing then. He knew I envied him his Sheindel and his luck. Unlike our fathers, Isaac had never condemned me for my marriage, which his father regarded as his private triumph over my father, and which my father, in his public defeat, took as an occasion for declaring me as one dead. He rent his clothing and sat on a stool for eight days, while Isaac's father came to watch him mourn, secretly satisfied, though aloud he grieved for all apostates. Isaac did not like my wife.

He called her a tall yellow straw. After we were married he never said a word against her, but he kept away.

I went with my wife to his wedding. We took the early train down especially, but when we arrived the feast was well under way, and the guests far into the dancing.

"Look, look, they don't dance together," Jane said.

"Who?"

"The men and the women. The bride and the groom."

"Count the babies," I advised. "The Jews are also Puritans, but only in public."

The bride was enclosed all by herself on a straight chair in the center of a spinning ring of young men. The floor heaved under their whirl. They stamped, the chandeliers shuddered, the guests cried out, the young men with linked arms spiraled and their skullcaps came flying off like centrifugal balloons. Isaac, a mist of black suit, a stamping foot, was lost in the planet's wake of black suits and emphatic feet. The dancing young men shouted bridal songs, the floor leaned like a plate, the whole room teetered.

Isaac had told me something of Sheindel. Before now I had never seen her. Her birth was in a concentration camp, and they were about to throw her against the electrified fence when an army mobbed the gate; the current vanished from the terrible wires, and she had nothing to show for it afterward but a mark on her cheek like an asterisk, cut by a barb. The asterisk pointed to certain dry footnotes: she had no mother to show, she had no father to show, but she had, extraordinarily, God to show—she was known to be, for her age and sex, astonishingly learned. She was only seventeen.

"What pretty hair she has," Jane said.

Now Sheindel was dancing with Isaac's mother. All the ladies made a fence, and the bride, twirling with her mother-in-law, lost a shoe and fell against the long laughing row. The ladies lifted their glistering breasts in their lacy dresses and laughed; the young men, stamping two by two, went on shout-

ing their wedding songs. Sheindel danced without her shoe, and
the black river of her hair followed her.

"After today she'll have to hide it all," I explained.

Jane asked why.

"So as not to be a temptation to men," I told her, and
covertly looked for my father. There he was, in a shadow,
apart. My eyes discovered his eyes. He turned his back and
gripped his throat.

"It's a very anthropological experience," Jane said.

"A wedding is a wedding," I answered her, "among us
even more so."

"Is that your father over there, that little scowly man?"

To Jane all Jews were little. "My father the man of the
cloth. Yes."

"A wedding is not a wedding," said Jane: we had had only
a license and a judge with bad breath.

"Everybody marries for the same reason."

"No," said my wife. "Some for love and some for spite."

"And everybody for bed."

"Some for spite," she insisted.

"I was never cut out for a man of the cloth," I said. "My
poor father doesn't see that."

"He doesn't speak to you."

"A technicality. He's losing his voice."

"Well, he's not like you. He doesn't do it for spite," Jane
said.

"You don't know him," I said.

He lost it altogether the very week Isaac published his
first remarkable collection of responsa. Isaac's father crowed
like a passionate rooster, and packed his wife and himself off
to the Holy Land to boast on the holy soil. Isaac was a little
relieved; he had just been made Professor of Mishnaic History, and his father's whims and pretenses and foolish rivalries
were an embarrassment. It is easy to honor a father from afar,
but bitter to honor one who is dead. A surgeon cut out my
father's voice, and he died without a word.

Isaac and I no longer met. Our ways were too disparate. Isaac was famous, if not in the world, certainly in the kingdom of jurists and scholars. By this time I had acquired a partnership in a small book store in a basement. My partner sold me his share, and I put up a new sign: "The Book Cellar"; for reasons more obscure than filial (all the same I wished my father could have seen it) I established a department devoted especially to not-quite-rare theological works, chiefly in Hebrew and Aramaic, though I carried some Latin and Greek. When Isaac's second volume reached my shelves (I had now expanded to street level), I wrote him to congratulate him, and after that we corresponded, not with any regularity. He took to ordering all his books from me, and we exchanged awkward little jokes. "I'm still in the jacket business," I told him, "but now I feel I'm where I belong. Last time I went too fur." "Sheindel is well, and Naomi and Esther have a sister," he wrote. And later: "Naomi, Esther, and Miriam have a sister." And still later: "Naomi, Esther, Miriam, and Ophra have a sister." It went on until there were seven girls. "There's nothing in Torah that prevents an illustrious man from having illustrious daughters," I wrote him when he said he had given up hope of another rabbi in the family. "But where do you find seven illustrious husbands?" he asked. Every order brought another quip, and we bantered back and forth in this way for some years.

I noticed that he read everything. Long ago he had inflamed my taste, but I could never keep up. No sooner did I catch his joy in Saadia Gaon than he had already sprung ahead to Yehudah Halevi. One day he was weeping with Dostoyevski and the next leaping in the air over Thomas Mann. He introduced me to Hegel and Nietzsche while our fathers wailed. His mature reading was no more peaceable than those frenzies of his youth, when I would come upon him in an abandoned classroom at dusk, his stocking feet on the windowsill, the light already washed from the lowest city clouds, wearing the look of a man half-sotted with print.

But when the widow asked me—covering a certain excess of alertness or irritation—whether to my knowledge Isaac had lately been ordering any books on horticulture, I was astonished.

"He bought so much," I demurred.

"Yes, yes, yes," she said. "How could you remember?" She poured the tea and then, with a discreetness of gesture, lifted my dripping raincoat from the chair where I had thrown it and took it out of the room. It was a crowded apartment, not very neat, far from slovenly, cluttered with dolls and tiny dishes and an array of tricycles. The dining table was as large as a desert. An old-fashioned crocheted lace runner divided it into two nations, and on the end of this, in the neutral zone, so to speak, Sheindel had placed my cup. There was no physical relic of Isaac: not even a book.

She returned. "My girls are all asleep, we can talk. What an ordeal for you, weather like this and going out so far to that place."

It was impossible to tell whether she was angry or not. I had rushed in on her like the rainfall itself, scattering drops, my shoes stuck all over with leaves.

"I comprehend exactly why you went out there. The impulse of a detective," she said. Her voice contained an irony that surprised me. It was brilliantly and unmistakably accented, and because of this jaggedly precise. It was as if every word emitted a quick white thread of great purity, like hard silk, which she was then obliged to bite cleanly off. "You went to find something? An atmosphere? The sadness itself?"

"There was nothing to see," I said, and thought I was lunatic to have put myself in her way.

"Did you dig in the ground? He might have buried a note for goodbye."

"Was there a note?" I asked, startled.

"He left nothing behind for ordinary humanity like yourself."

I saw she was playing with me. "Rebbetzin Kornfeld," I said, standing up, "forgive me. My coat, please, and I'll go."

"Sit," she commanded. "Isaac read less lately, did you notice that?"

I gave her a civil smile. "All the same he was buying more and more."

"Think," she said. "I depend on you. You're just the one who might know. I had forgotten this. God sent you perhaps."

"Rebbetzin Kornfeld, I'm only a bookseller."

"God in his judgment sent me a bookseller. For such a long time Isaac never read at home. Think! Agronomy?"

"I don't remember anything like that. What would a Professor of Mishnaic History want with agronomy?"

"If he had a new book under his arm he would take it straight to the seminary and hide it in his office."

"I mailed to his office. If you like I can look up some of the titles—"

"You were in the park and you saw nothing?"

"Nothing." Then I was ashamed. "I saw the tree."

"And what is that? A tree is nothing."

"Rebbetzin Kornfeld," I pleaded, "it's a stupidity that I came here. I don't know myself why I came, I beg your pardon, I had no idea—"

"You came to learn why Isaac took his life. Botany? Or even, please listen, even mycology? He never asked you to send something on mushrooms? Or having to do with herbs? Manure? Flowers? A certain kind of agricultural poetry? A book about gardening? Forestry? Vegetables? Cereal growing?"

"Nothing, nothing like that," I said excitedly. "Rebbetzin Kornfeld, your husband was a rabbi!"

"I know what my husband was. Something to do with

vines? Arbors? Rice? Think, think, think! Anything to do
with land—meadows—goats—a farm, hay—anything at all,
anything rustic or lunar—"

"Lunar! My God! Was he a teacher or a nurseryman?
Goats! Was he a furrier? Sheindel, are you crazy? *I* was the
furrier! What do you want from the dead?"

Without a word she replenished my cup, though it was
more than half full, and sat down opposite me, on the other
side of the lace boundary line. She leaned her face into
her palms, but I saw her eyes. She kept them wide.

"Rebbetzin Kornfeld," I said, collecting myself, "with
a tragedy like this—"

"You imagine I blame the books. I don't blame the books,
whatever they were. If he had been faithful to his books he
would have lived."

"He lived," I cried, "in books, what else?"

"No," said the widow.

"A scholar. A rabbi. A remarkable Jew!"

At this she spilled a furious laugh. "Tell me, I have always been very interested and shy to inquire. Tell me about
your wife."

I intervened: "I haven't had a wife in years."

"What are they like, those people?"

"They're exactly like us, if you can think what we would
be if we were like them."

"We are not like them. Their bodies are more to them
than ours are to us. Our books are holy, to them their bodies
are holy."

"Jane's was so holy she hardly ever let me get near it,"
I muttered to myself.

"Isaac used to run in the park, but he lost his breath too
quickly. Instead he read in a book about runners with hats
made of leaves."

"Sheindel, Sheindel, what did you expect of him? He
was a student, he sat and he thought, he was a Jew."

She thrust her hands flat. "He was not."

I could not reply. I looked at her merely. She was thinner now than in her early young-womanhood, and her face had an in-between cast, poignant still at the mouth and jaw, beginning to grow coarse on either side of the nose.

"I think he was never a Jew," she said.

I wondered whether Isaac's suicide had unbalanced her.

"I'll tell you a story," she resumed. "A story about stories. These were the bedtime stories Isaac told Naomi and Esther: about mice that danced and children who laughed. When Miriam came he invented a speaking cloud. With Ophra it was a turtle that married a blade of withered grass. By Leah's time the stones had tears for their leglessness. Rebecca cried because of a tree that turned into a girl and could never grow colors again in autumn. Shiphrah, the littlest, believes that a pig has a soul."

"My own father used to drill me every night in sacred recitation. It was a terrible childhood."

"He insisted on picnics. Each time we went farther and farther into the country. It was a madness. Isaac never troubled to learn to drive a car, and there was always a clumsiness of baskets to carry and a clutter of buses and trains and seven exhausted wild girls. And he would look for special places— we couldn't settle just here or there, there had to be a brook or such-and-such a slope or else a little grove. And then, though he said it was all for the children's pleasure, he would leave them and go off alone and never come back until sunset, when everything was spilled and the air freezing and the babies crying."

"I was a grown man before I had the chance to go on a picnic," I admitted.

"I'm speaking of the beginning," said the widow. "Like you, wasn't I fooled? I was fooled, I was charmed. Going home with our baskets of berries and flowers we were a romantic huddle. Isaac's stories on those nights were full of dark invention. May God preserve me, I even begged him to write them down. Then suddenly he joined a club, and Sunday mornings he was up and away before dawn."

"A club? So early? What library opens at that hour?" I said, stunned that a man like Isaac should ally himself with anything so doubtful.

"Ah, you don't follow, you don't follow. It was a hiking club, they met under the moon. I thought it was a pity, the whole week Isaac was so inward, he needed air for the mind. He used to come home too fatigued to stand. He said he went for the landscape. I was like you, I took what I heard, I heard it all and never followed. He resigned from the hikers finally, and I believed all that strangeness was finished. He told me it was absurd to walk at such a pace, he was a teacher and not an athlete. Then he began to write."

"But he always wrote," I objected.

"Not this way. What he wrote was only fairy tales. He kept at it and for a while he neglected everything else. It was the strangeness in another form. The stories surprised me, they were so poor and dull. They were a little like the ideas he used to scare the girls with, but choked all over with notes, appendices, prefaces. It struck me then he didn't seem to understand he was only doing fairy tales. Yet they were really very ordinary—full of sprites, nymphs, gods, everything ordinary and old."

"Will you let me see them?"

"Burned, all burned."

"Isaac burned them?"

"You don't think I did! I see what you think."

It was true that I was marveling at her hatred. I supposed she was one of those born to dread imagination. I was overtaken by a coldness for her, though the sight of her small hands with their tremulous staves of fingers turning and turning in front of her face like a gate on a hinge reminded me of where she was born and who she was. She was an orphan and had been saved by magic and had a terror of it. The coldness fled. "Why should you be bothered by little stories?" I inquired. "It wasn't the stories that killed him."

"No, no, not the stories," she said. "Stupid corrupt things. I was glad when he gave them up. He piled them in the bathtub and lit them with a match. Then he put a notebook in his coat pocket and said he would walk in the park. Week after week he tried all the parks in the city. I didn't dream what he could be after. One day he took the subway and rode to the end of the line, and this was the right park at last. He went every day after class. An hour going, an hour back. Two, three in the morning he came home. 'Is it exercise?' I said. I thought he might be running again. He used to shiver with the chill of night and the dew. 'No, I sit quite still,' he said. 'Is it more stories you do out there?' 'No, I only jot down what I think.' 'A man should meditate in his own house, not by night near bad water,' I said. Six, seven in the morning he came home. I asked him if he meant to find his grave in that place."

She broke off with a cough, half artifice and half resignation, so loud that it made her crane toward the bedrooms to see if she had awakened a child. "I don't sleep any more," she told me. "Look around you. Look, look everywhere, look on the windowsills. Do you see any plants, any common house plants? I went down one evening and gave them to the garbage collector. I couldn't sleep in the same space with plants. They are like little trees. Am I deranged? Take Isaac's notebook and bring it back when you can."

I obeyed. In my own room, a sparse place, with no ornaments but a few pretty stalks in pots, I did not delay and seized the notebook. It was a tiny affair, three inches by five, with ruled pages that opened on a coiled wire. I read searchingly, hoping for something not easily evident. Sheindel by her melancholy innuendo had made me believe that in these few sheets Isaac had revealed the reason for his suicide. But it was all a disappointment. There was not a word of any importance. After a while I concluded that, whatever her

motives, Sheindel was playing with me again. She meant to
punish me for asking the unaskable. My inquisitiveness
offended her; she had given me Isaac's notebook not to en-
lighten but to rebuke. The handwriting was recognizable
yet oddly formed, shaky and even senile, like that of a man
outdoors and deskless who scribbles in his palm or on his
lifted knee or leaning on a bit of bark; and there was no
doubt that the wrinkled leaves, with their ragged corners,
had been in and out of someone's pocket. So I did not mistrust
Sheindel's mad anecdote; this much was true: a park, Isaac,
a notebook, all at once, but signifying no more than that a
professor with a literary turn of mind had gone for a walk.
There was even a green stain straight across one of the quotations, as if the pad had slipped grassward and been trod on.

I have forgotten to mention that the notebook, though
scantily filled, was in three languages. The Greek I could not
read at all, but it had the shape of verse. The Hebrew was
simply a miscellany, drawn mostly from Leviticus and Deuter-
onomy. Among these I found the following extracts, tran-
scribed not quite verbatim:

Ye shall utterly destroy all the places of the gods, upon the
high mountains, and upon the hills, and under every green
tree.

And the soul that turneth after familiar spirits to go a-whoring
after them, I will cut him off from among his people.

These, of course, were ordinary unadorned notes, such
as any classroom lecturer might commonly make to remind
himself of the text, with a phrase cut out here and there for
the sake of speeding his hand. Or I thought it possible that
Isaac might at that time have been preparing a paper on the
Talmudic commentaries for these passages. Whatever the case,
the remaining quotations, chiefly from English poetry, interested me only slightly more. They were the elegiac favorites
of a closeted Romantic. I was repelled by Isaac's Nature:

it wore a capital letter, and smelled like my own Book Cellar.
It was plain to me that he had lately grown painfully academic: he could not see a weed's tassel without finding a
classical reference for it. He had put down a snatch of Byron,
a smudge of Keats (like his Scriptural copyings, these too
were quick and fragmented), a pair of truncated lines from
Tennyson, and this unmarked and clumsy quatrain:

> *And yet all is not taken. Still one Dryad*
> *Flits through the wood, one Oread skims the hill;*
> *White in the whispering stream still gleams a Naiad;*
> *The beauty of the earth is haunted still.*

All of this was so cloying and mooning and ridiculous, and
so pedantic besides, that I felt ashamed for him. And yet there
was almost nothing else, nothing to redeem him and nothing
personal, only a sentence or two in his rigid self-controlled
scholar's style, not unlike the starched little jokes of our
correspondence. "I am writing at dusk sitting on a stone in
Trilham's Inlet Park, within sight of Trilham's Inlet, a bay
to the north of the city, and within two yards of a slender
tree, *Quercus velutina*, the age of which, should one desire
to measure it, can be ascertained by (God forbid) cutting
the bole and counting the rings. The man writing is thirty-
five years old and aging too rapidly, which may be ascertained by counting the rings under his poor myopic eyes."
Below this, deliberate and readily more legible than the rest,
appeared three curious words:

Great Pan lives.

That was all. In a day or so I returned the notebook to
Sheindel. I told myself that she had seven orphans to worry
over, and repressed my anger at having been cheated.
    She was waiting for me. "I am so sorry, there was a letter
in the notebook, it had fallen out. I found it on the carpet
after you left."

"Thank you, no," I said. "I've read enough out of Isaac's pockets."

"Then why did you come to see me to begin with?"

"I came," I said, "just to see you."

"You came for Isaac." But she was more mocking than distraught. "I gave you everything you needed to see what happened and still you don't follow. Here." She held out a large law-sized paper. "Read the letter."

"I've read his notebook. If everything I need to fathom Isaac is in the notebook I don't need the letter."

"It's a letter he wrote to explain himself," she persisted.

"You told me Isaac left you no notes."

"It was not written to me."

I sat down on one of the dining room chairs and Sheindel put the page before me on the table. It lay face up on the lace divider. I did not look at it.

"It's a love letter," Sheindel whispered. "When they cut him down they found the notebook in one pocket and the letter in the other."

I did not know what to say.

"The police gave me everything," Sheindel said. "Everything to keep."

"A love letter?" I repeated.

"That is what such letters are commonly called."

"And the police—they gave it to you, and that was the first you realized what"—I floundered after the inconceivable —"what could be occupying him?"

"What could be occupying him," she mimicked. "Yes. Not until they took the letter and the notebook out of his pocket."

"My God. His habit of life, his mind . . . I can't imagine it. You never guessed?"

"No."

"These trips to the park—"

"He had become aberrant in many ways. I have described them to you."

"But the park! Going off like that, alone—you didn't think he might be meeting a woman?"

"It was not a woman."

Disgust like a powder clotted my nose. "Sheindel, you're crazy."

"I'm crazy, is that it? Read his confession! Read it! How long can I be the only one to know this thing? Do you want my brain to melt? Be my confidant," she entreated so unexpectedly that I held my breath.

"You've said nothing to anyone?"

"Would they have recited such eulogies if I had? Read the letter!"

"I have no interest in the abnormal," I said coldly.

She raised her eyes and watched me for the smallest space. Without any change in the posture of her suppliant head her laughter began; I have never since heard sounds like those—almost mouselike in density for fear of waking her sleeping daughters, but so rational in intent that it was like listening to astonished sanity rendered into a cackling fugue. She kept it up for a minute and then calmed herself. "Please sit where you are. Please pay attention. I will read the letter to you myself."

She plucked the page from the table with an orderly gesture. I saw that this letter had been scrupulously prepared; it was closely written. Her tone was cleansed by scorn.

" 'My ancestors were led out of Egypt by the hand of God,' " she read.

"Is this how a love letter starts out?"

She moved on resolutely. "We were guilty of so-called abominations well-described elsewhere. Other peoples have been nourished on their mythologies. For aeons we have been weaned from all traces of the same."

I felt myself becoming impatient. The fact was I had returned with a single idea: I meant to marry Isaac's widow when enough time had passed to make it seemly. It was my intention to court her with great subtlety at first, so that

I would not appear to be presuming on her sorrow. But she
was possessed. "Sheindel, why do you want to inflict this
treatise on me? Give it to the seminary, contribute it to a
symposium of professors."

"I would sooner die."

At this I began to attend in earnest.

" 'I will leave aside the wholly plausible position of so-
called animism within the concept of the One God. I will
omit a historical illumination of its continuous but covert
expression even within the Fence of the Law. Creature, I
leave these aside—' "

"What?" I yelped.

" 'Creature,' " she repeated, spreading her nostrils.
" 'What is human history? What is our philosophy? What is
our religion? None of these teaches us poor human ones that
we are alone in the universe, and even without them we
would know that we are not. At a very young age I understood that a foolish man would not believe in a fish had he not
had one enter his experience. Innumerable forms exist and
have come to our eyes, and to the still deeper eye of the
lens of our instruments; from this minute perception of what
already is, it is easy to conclude that further forms are possible, that all forms are probable. God created the world
not for Himself alone, or I would not now possess this con-
sciousness with which I am enabled to address thee, Loveliness.' "

"Thee," I echoed, and swallowed a sad bewilderment.

"You must let me go on," Sheindel said, and grimly went
on. " 'It is false history, false philosophy, and false religion
which declare to us human ones that we live among Things.
The arts of physics and chemistry begin to teach us differently, but their way of compassion is new, and finds few to
carry fidelity to its logical and beautiful end. The molecules
dance inside all forms, and within the molecules dance the
atoms, and within the atoms dance still profounder sources of
divine vitality. There is nothing that is Dead. There is no

Non-life. Holy life subsists even in the stone, even in the bones of dead dogs and dead men. Hence in God's fecundating Creation there is no possibility of Idolatry, and therefore no possibility of committing this so-called abomination.' "

"My God, my God," I wailed. "Enough, Sheindel, it's more than enough, no more—"

"There is more," she said.

"I don't want to hear it."

"He stains his character for you? A spot, do you think? You will hear." She took up in a voice which all at once reminded me of my father's: it was unforgiving. " 'Creature, I rehearse these matters though all our language is as breath to thee; as baubles for the juggler. Where we struggle to understand from day to day, and contemplate the grave for its riddle, the other breeds are born fulfilled in wisdom. Animal races conduct themselves without self-investigations; instinct is a higher and not a lower thing. Alas that we human ones —but for certain pitifully primitive approximations in those few reflexes and involuntary actions left to our bodies—are born bare of instinct! All that we unfortunates must resort to through science, art, philosophy, religion, all our imaginings and tormented strivings, all our meditations and vain questionings, all!—are expressed naturally and rightly in the beasts, the plants, the rivers, the stones. The reason is simple, it is our tragedy: our soul is included in us, it inhabits us, we contain it, when we seek our soul we must seek in ourselves. To *see* the soul, to confront it—that is divine wisdom. Yet how can we see into our dark selves? With the other races of being it is differently ordered. The soul of the plant does not reside in the chlorophyll, it may roam if it wishes, it may choose whatever form or shape it pleases. Hence the other breeds, being largely free of their soul and able to witness it, can live in peace. To see one's soul is to know all, to know all is to own the peace our philosophies futilely envisage. Earth displays two categories of soul: the free and the indwelling. We human ones are cursed with the indwelling—' "

"Stop!" I cried.

"I will not," said the widow.

"Please, you told me he burned his fairy tales."

"Did I lie to you? Will you say I lied?"

"Then for Isaac's sake why didn't you? If this isn't a fairy tale what do you want me to think it could be?"

"Think what you like."

"Sheindel," I said, "I beg you, don't destroy a dead man's honor. Don't look at this thing again, tear it to pieces, don't continue with it."

"I don't destroy his honor. He had none."

"Please! Listen to yourself! My God, who was the man? Rabbi Isaac Kornfeld! Talk of honor! Wasn't he a teacher? Wasn't he a scholar?"

"He was a pagan."

Her eyes returned without hesitation to their task. She commenced: " 'All these truths I learned only gradually, against my will and desire. Our teacher Moses did not speak of them; much may be said under this head. It was not out of ignorance that Moses failed to teach about those souls that are free. If I have learned what Moses knew, is this not because we are both men? He was a man, but God addressed him; it was God's will that our ancestors should no longer be slaves. Yet our ancestors, being stiff-necked, would not have abandoned their slavery in Egypt had they been taught of the free souls. They would have said: "Let us stay, our bodies will remain enslaved in Egypt, but our souls will wander at their pleasure in Zion. If the cactus-plant stays rooted while its soul roams, why not also a man?" And if Moses had replied that only the world of Nature has the gift of the free soul, while man is chained to his, and that a man, to free his soul, must also free the body that is its vessel, they would have scoffed. "How is it that men, and men alone, are different from the world of Nature? If this is so, then the condition of men is evil and unjust, and if this condition of ours is evil and unjust in general, what does it matter whether we are slaves in Egypt or citizens in Zion?" And they would not have done God's will and abandoned their slavery. Therefore Moses never spoke to them of the free souls, lest the people not do God's will and go out from Egypt.'"

In an instant a sensation broke in me—it was entirely obscure, there was nothing I could compare it with, and yet I was certain I recognized it. And then I did. It hurtled me into childhood—it was the crisis of insight one experiences when one has just read out, for the first time, that conglomeration of figurines which makes a word. In that moment I penetrated beyond Isaac's alphabet into his language. I saw that he was on the side of possibility: he was both sane and inspired. His intention was not to accumulate mystery but to dispel it.

"All that part is brilliant," I burst out.

Sheindel meanwhile had gone to the sideboard to take a sip of cold tea that was standing there. "In a minute," she said, and pursued her thirst. "I have heard of drawings surpassing Rembrandt daubed by madmen who when released from the fit couldn't hold the chalk. What follows is beautiful, I warn you."

"The man was a genius."

"Yes."

"Go on," I urged.

She produced for me her clownish jeering smile. She read: "'Sometimes in the desert journey on the way they would come to a watering place, and some quick spry boy would happen to glimpse the soul of the spring (which the wild Greeks afterward called naiad), but not knowing of the existence of the free souls he would suppose only that the moon had cast a momentary beam across the water. Loveliness, with the same innocence of accident I discovered thee. Loveliness, Loveliness.'"

She stopped.

"Is that all?"

"There is more."

"Read it."

"The rest is the love letter."

"Is it hard for you?" But I asked with more eagerness than pity.

"I was that man's wife, he scaled the Fence of the Law. For this God preserved me from the electric fence. Read it for yourself."

Incontinently I snatched the crowded page.

" 'Loveliness, in thee the joy, substantiation, and supernal succor of my theorem. How many hours through how many years I walked over the cilia-forests of our enormous aspiring vegetable-star, this light rootless seed that crawls in its single furrow, this shaggy mazy unimplanted cabbage-head of our earth!—never, all that time, all those days of unfulfillment, a white space like a desert thirst, never, never to grasp. I thought myself abandoned to the intrigue of my folly. At dawn, on a hillock, what seemed the very shape and seizing of the mound's nature—what was it? Only the haze of the sunball growing great through hoarfrost. The oread slipped from me, leaving her illusion; or was never there at all; or was there but for an instant, and ran away. What sly ones the free souls are! They have a comedy we human ones cannot dream: the laughing drunkard feels in himself the shadow of the shadow of the shadow of their wit, and only because he has made himself a vessel, as the two banks and the bed of a rivulet are the naiad's vessel. A naiad I may indeed have viewed whole: all seven of my daughters were once wading in a stream in a compact but beautiful park, of which I had much hope. The youngest being not yet two, and fretful, the older ones were told to keep her always by the hand, but they did not obey. I, having passed some way into the woods behind, all at once heard a scream and noise of splashes, and caught sight of a tiny body flying down into the water. Running back through the trees I could see the others bunched together, afraid, as the baby dived helplessly, all these little girls frozen in a garland—when suddenly one of them (it was too quick a movement for me to recognize which) darted to the struggler, who was now underwater, and pulled her up, and put an arm around her to soothe her. The arm was blue—blue. As blue as a lake. And fiercely, from my spot on the bank, panting, I began to count the little girls. I counted eight, thought myself not mad but delivered, again counted, counted seven, knew I had counted well before, knew I counted well even now. A blue-armed girl had come to wade among them. Which is to say the shape of a girl. I questioned my daughters: each in her fright believed one of the others had gone to pluck up the tiresome baby. None wore a dress with blue sleeves.' "

"Proofs," said the widow. "Isaac was meticulous, he used to account for all his proofs always."

"How?" My hand in tremor rustled Isaac's letter; the paper bleated as though whipped.

"By eventually finding a principle to cover them," she finished maliciously. "Well, don't rest even for me, you don't oblige me. You have a long story to go, long enough to make a fever."

"Tea," I said hoarsely.

She brought me her own cup from the sideboard, and I believed as I drank that I swallowed some of her mockery and gall.

"Sheindel, for a woman so pious you're a great skeptic." And now the tremor had command of my throat.

"An atheist's statement," she rejoined. "The more piety, the more skepticism. A religious man comprehends this. Superfluity, excess of custom, and superstition would climb like a choking vine on the Fence of the Law if skepticism did not continually hack them away to make freedom for purity."

I then thought her fully worthy of Isaac. Whether I was worthy of her I evaded putting to myself; instead I gargled some tea and returned to the letter.

" 'It pains me to confess,' " I read, " 'how after that I

moved from clarity to doubt and back again. I had no trust in
my conclusions because all my experiences were evanescent.
Everything certain I attributed to some other cause less certain. Every voice out of the moss I blamed on rabbits and
squirrels. Every motion among leaves I called a bird, though
there positively was no bird. My first sight of the Little People struck me as no more than a shudder of literary delusion,
and I determined they could only be an instantaneous crop of
mushrooms. But one night, a little after ten o'clock at the
crux of summer—the sky still showed strings of light—I was
wandering in this place, this place where they will find my
corpse—' "

"Not for my sake," said Sheindel when I hesitated.

"It's terrible," I croaked, "terrible."

"Withered like a shell," she said, as though speaking of
the cosmos; and I understood from her manner that she had a
fanatic's acquaintance with this letter, and knew it nearly by
heart. She appeared to be thinking the words faster than I
could bring them out, and for some reason I was constrained
to hurry the pace of my reading.

" '—where they will find my corpse withered like the shell
of an insect,' " I rushed on. " 'The smell of putrefaction lifted
clearly from the bay. I began to speculate about my own
body after I was dead—whether the soul would be set free
immediately after the departure of life; or whether only gradually, as decomposition proceeded and more and more of the
indwelling soul was released to freedom. But when I considered how a man's body is no better than a clay pot, a fact
which none of our sages has ever contradicted, it seemed to
me then that an indwelling soul by its own nature would be
obliged to cling to its bit of pottery until the last crumb and
grain had vanished into earth. I walked through the ditches
of that black meadow grieving and swollen with self-pity. It
came to me that while my poor bones went on decaying at
their ease, my soul would have to linger inside them, waiting,
despairing, longing to join the free ones. I cursed it for its

gravity-despoiled, slow, interminably languishing purse of flesh; better to be encased in vapor, in wind, in a hair of a coconut! Who knows how long it takes the body of a man to shrink into gravel, and the gravel into sand, and the sand into vitamin? A hundred years? Two hundred, three hundred? A thousand perhaps! Is it not true that bones nearly intact are constantly being dug up by the paleontologists two million years after burial?'—Sheindel," I interrupted, "this is death, not love. Where's the love letter to be afraid of here? I don't find it."

"Continue," she ordered. And then: "You see I'm not afraid."

"Not of love?"

"No. But you recite much too slowly. Your mouth is shaking. Are you afraid of death?"

I did not reply.

"Continue," she said again. "Go rapidly. The next sentence begins with an extraordinary thought."

" 'An extraordinary thought emerged in me. It was luminous, profound, and practical. More than that, it had innumerable precedents; the mythologies had documented it a dozen dozen times over. I recalled all those mortals reputed to have coupled with gods (a collective word, showing much common sense, signifying what our philosophies more abstrusely call Shekhina), and all that poignant miscegenation represented by centaurs, satyrs, mermaids, fauns, and so forth, not to speak of that even more famous mingling in Genesis, whereby the sons of God took the daughters of men for brides, producing giants and possibly also those abortions, leviathan and behemoth, of which we read in Job, along with unicorns and other chimeras and monsters abundant in Scripture, hence far from fanciful. There existed also the example of the succubus Lilith, who was often known to couple in the mediaeval ghetto even with pre-pubescent boys. By all these evidences I was emboldened in my confidence that I was surely not the first man to conceive such a desire in the his-

tory of our earth. Creature, the thought that took hold of me
was this: if only I could couple with one of the free souls, the
strength of the connection would likely wrest my own soul
from my body—seize it, as if by a tongs, draw it out, so to
say, to its own freedom. The intensity and force of my desire
to capture one of these beings now became prodigious. I
avoided my wife—' "

Here the widow heard me falter.

"Please," she commanded, and I saw creeping in her face
the completed turn of a sneer.

" '—lest I be depleted of potency at that moment (which
might occur in any interval, even, I assumed, in my own bedroom) when I should encounter one of the free souls. I was
borne back again and again to the fetid viscosities of the Inlet,
borne there as if on the rising stink of my own enduring and
tedious putrefaction, the idea of which I could no longer
shake off—I envisaged my soul as trapped in my last granule,
and that last granule itself perhaps petrified, never to dissolve,
and my soul condemned to minister to it throughout eternity!
It seemed to me my soul must be released at once or be lost
to sweet air forever. In a gleamless dark, struggling with this
singular panic, I stumbled from ditch to ditch, strained like a
blind dog for the support of solid verticality; and smacked
my palm against bark. I looked up and in the black could not
fathom the size of the tree—my head lolled forward, my
brow met the trunk with all its gravings. I busied my fingers
in the interstices of the bark's cuneiform. Then with forehead
flat on the tree, I embraced it with both arms to measure it.
My hands united on the other side. It was a young narrow
weed, I did not know of what family. I reached to the lowest
branch and plucked a leaf and made my tongue travel meditatively along its periphery to assess its shape: oak. The taste
was sticky and exaltingly bitter. A jubilation lightly carpeted
my groin. I then placed one hand (the other I kept around
the tree's waist, as it were) in the bifurcation (disgustingly
termed crotch) of that lowest limb and the elegant and de-

voutly firm torso, and caressed that miraculous juncture with a certain languor, which gradually changed to vigor. I was all at once savagely alert and deeply daring: I chose that single tree together with the ground near it for an enemy which in two senses would not yield: it would neither give nor give in. "Come, come," I called aloud to Nature. A wind blew out a braid of excremental malodor into the heated air. "Come," I called, "couple with me, as thou didst with Cadmus, Rhoecus, Tithonus, Endymion, and that king Numa Pompilius to whom thou didst give secrets. As Lilith comes without a sign, so come thou. As the sons of God came to copulate with women, so now let a daughter of Shekhina the Emanation reveal herself to me. Nymph, come now, come now."

" 'Without warning I was flung to the ground. My face smashed into earth, and a flaky clump of dirt lodged in my open mouth. For the rest, I was on my knees, pressing down on my hands, with the fingernails clutching dirt. A superb ache lined my haunch. I began to weep because I was certain I had been ravished by some sinewy animal. I vomited the earth I had swallowed and believed I was defiled, as it is written: "Neither shalt thou lie with any beast." I lay sunk in the grass, afraid to lift my head to see if the animal still lurked. Through some curious means I had been fully positioned and aroused and exquisitely sated, all in half a second, in a fashion impossible to explain, in which, though I performed as with my own wife, I felt as if a preternatural rapine had been committed upon me. I continued prone, listening for the animal's breathing. Meanwhile, though every tissue of my flesh was gratified in its inmost awareness, a marvelous voluptuousness did not leave my body; sensual exultations of a wholly supreme and paradisal order, unlike anything our poets have ever defined, both flared and were intensely satisfied in the same moment. This salubrious and delightful perceptiveness excited my being for some time: a conjoining not dissimilar (in metaphor only; in actuality it cannot be described) from the magical contradiction of the tree and its issuance-of-branch at the point of bifurcation. In me were linked, *in the same instant*, appetite and fulfillment, delicacy and power, mastery and submissiveness, and other paradoxes of entirely remarkable emotional import.

" 'Then I heard what I took to be the animal treading through the grass quite near my head, all cunningly; it withheld its breathing, then snored it out in a cautious and wisplike whirr that resembled a light wind through rushes. With a huge energy (my muscular force seemed to have increased) I leaped up in fear of my life; I had nothing to use for a weapon but—oh, laughable!—the pen I had been writing with in a little notebook I always carried about with me in those days (and still keep on my person as a self-shaming souvenir of my insipidness, my bookishness, my pitiable conjecture and wishfulness in a time when, not yet knowing thee, I knew nothing). What I saw was not an animal but a girl no older than my oldest daughter, who was then fourteen. Her skin was as perfect as an eggplant's and nearly of that color. In height she was half as tall as I was. The second and third fingers of her hands—this I noticed at once—were peculiarly fused, one slotted into the other, like the ligula of a leaf. She was entirely bald and had no ears but rather a type of gill or envelope, one only, on the left side. Her toes displayed the same oddity I had observed in her fingers. She was neither naked nor clothed—that is to say, even though a part of her body, from hip to just below the breasts (each of which appeared to be a kind of velvety colorless pear, suspended from a very short, almost invisible stem), was luxuriantly covered with a flossy or spore-like material, this was a natural efflorescence in the manner of, with us, hair. All her sexual portion was wholly visible, as in any field flower. Aside from these express deviations, she was commandingly human in aspect, if unmistakably flowerlike. She was, in fact, the reverse of our hackneyed euphuism, as when we say a young girl blooms like a flower—she, on the contrary, seemed a flower transfigured into the shape of the most stupendously lovely child I

had ever seen. Under the smallest push of wind she bent at
her superlative waist; this, I recognized, and not the exhala-
tions of some lecherous beast, was the breathlike sound that
had alarmed me at her approach: these motions of hers made
the blades of grass collide. (She herself, having no lungs, did
not "breathe.") She stood bobbing joyfully before me, with a
face as tender as a morning-glory, strangely phosphorescent:
she shed her own light, in effect, and I had no difficulty in
confronting her beauty.

" 'Moreover, by experiment I soon learned that she was
not only capable of language, but that she delighted in playing with it. This she literally could do—if I had distinguished
her hands before anything else, it was because she had held
them out to catch my first cry of awe. She either caught my
words like balls or let them roll, or caught them and then
darted off to throw them into the Inlet. I discovered that
whenever I spoke I more or less pelted her; but she liked this,
and told me ordinary human speech only tickled and amused,
whereas laughter, being highly plosive, was something of an
assault. I then took care to pretend much solemnity, though
I was lightheaded with rapture. Her own "voice" I appre-
hended rather than heard—which she, unable to imagine how
we human ones are prisoned in sensory perception, found
hard to conceive. Her sentences came to me not as a series of
differentiated frequencies but (impossible to develop this idea
in language) as a diffused cloud of field fragrances; yet to say
that I assimilated her thought through the olfactory nerve
would be a pedestrian distortion. All the same it was clear that
whatever she said reached me in a shimmer of pellucid per-
fumes, and I understood her meaning with an immediacy of
glee and with none of the ambiguities and suspiciousness of
motive that surround our human communication.

" 'Through this medium she explained that she was a dryad
and that her name was Iripomoňoéià (as nearly as I can ren-
der it in our narrowly limited orthography, and in this dunce's
alphabet of ours which is notoriously impervious to odorifer-

ous categories). She told me what I had already seized: that she had given me her love in response to my call.

" ' "Wilt thou come to any man who calls?" I asked.

" ' "All men call, whether realizing it or not. I and my sisters sometimes come to those who do not realize. Almost never, unless for sport, do we come to that man who calls knowingly—he wishes only to inhabit us out of perversity or boastfulness or to indulge a dreamed-of disgust."

" ' "Scripture does not forbid sodomy with the plants," I exclaimed, but she did not comprehend any of this and lowered her hands so that my words would fly past her uncaught. "I too called thee knowingly, not for perversity but for love of Nature."

" ' "I have caught men's words before as they talked of Nature, you are not the first. It is not Nature they love so much as Death they fear. So Corylylyb my cousin received it in a season not long ago coupling in a harbor with one of your kind, one called Spinoza, one that had catarrh of the lung. I am of Nature and immortal and so I cannot pity your deaths. But return tomorrow and say Iripomoňoéià." Then she chased my last word to where she had kicked it, behind the tree. She did not come back. I ran to the tree and circled it diligently but she was lost for that night.

" 'Loveliness, all the foregoing, telling of my life and meditations until now, I have never before recounted to thee or any other. The rest is beyond mean telling: those rejoicings from midnight to dawn, when the greater phosphorescence of the whole shouting sky frightened thee home! How in a trance of happiness we coupled in the ditches, in the long grasses, behind a fountain, under a broken wall, once recklessly on the very pavement, with a bench for roof and trellis! How I was taught by natural arts to influence certain chemistries engendering explicit marvels, blisses, and transports no man has slaked himself with since Father Adam pressed out the forbidden chlorophyll of Eden! Loveliness, Loveliness, none like thee. No brow so sleek, no elbow-crook so fine, no eye so green, no waist so pliant, no limbs so pleasant and acute. None like immortal Iripomoňoéià.

" 'Creature, the moon filled and starved twice, and there was still no end to the glorious archaic newness of Iripomoňoéià.

" 'Then last night. Last night! I will record all with simplicity.

" 'We entered a shallow ditch. In a sweet-smelling voice of extraordinary redolence—so intense in its sweetness that even the barbaric stinks and wind-lifted farts of the Inlet were overpowered by it—Iripomoňoéià inquired of me how I felt without my soul. I replied that I did not know this was my condition. "Oh yes, your body is now an empty packet, that is why it is so light. Spring." I sprang in air and rose effortlessly. "You have spoiled yourself, spoiled yourself with confusions," she complained, "now by morning your body will be crumpled and withered and ugly, like a leaf in its sere hour, and never again after tonight will this place see you." "Nymph!" I roared, amazed by levitation. "Oh, oh, that damaged," she cried, "you hit my eye with that noise," and she wafted a deeper aroma, a leeklike mist, one that stung the mucous membranes. A white bruise disfigured her petally lid. I was repentant and sighed terribly for her injury. "Beauty marred is for our kind what physical hurt is for yours," she reproved me. "Where you have pain, we have ugliness. Where you profane yourselves by immorality, we are profaned by ugliness. Your soul has taken leave of you and spoils our pretty game." "Nymph!" I whispered, "heart, treasure, if my soul is separated how is it I am unaware?"

" ' "Poor man," she answered, "you have only to look and you will see the thing." Her speech had now turned as acrid as an herb, and all that place reeked bitterly. "You know I am a spirit. You know I must flash and dart. All my sisters flash and dart. Of all races we are the quickest. Our very religion is all-of-a-sudden. No one can hinder us, no one may delay us. But yesterday you undertook to detain me in your embrace, you stretched your kisses into years, you called me your treasure and your heart endlessly, your soul in its slow greed kept me close and captive, all the while knowing well how a spirit cannot stay and will not be fixed. I made to leap from you, but your obstinate soul held on until it was snatched straight from your frame and escaped with me. I saw it hurled out onto the pavement, the blue beginning of day was already seeping down, so I ran away and could say nothing until this moment."

" ' "My soul is free? Free entirely? And can be seen?"

" ' "Free. If I could pity any living thing under the sky I would pity you for the sight of your soul. I do not like it, it conjures against me."

" ' "My soul loves thee," I urged in all my triumph, "it is freed from the thousand-year grave!" I jumped out of the ditch like a frog, my legs had no weight; but the dryad sulked in the ground, stroking her ugly violated eye. "Iripomoňoéià, my soul will follow thee with thankfulness into eternity."

" ' "I would sooner be followed by the dirty fog. I do not like that soul of yours. It conjures against me. It denies me, it denies every spirit and all my sisters and every nereid of the harbor, it denies all our multiplicity, and all gods diversiform, it spites even Lord Pan, it is an enemy, and you, poor man, do not know your own soul. Go, look at it, there it is on the road."

" 'I scudded back and forth under the moon.

" ' "Nothing, only a dusty old man trudging up there."

" ' "A quite ugly old man?"

" ' "Yes, that is all. My soul is not there."

" ' "With a matted beard and great fierce eyebrows?"

" ' "Yes, yes, one like that is walking on the road. He is half bent over under the burden of a dusty old bag. The bag is stuffed with books—I can see their raveled bindings sticking out."

" ' "And he reads as he goes?"

" ' "Yes, he reads as he goes."

" ' "What is it he reads?"

" ' "Some huge and terrifying volume, heavy as a stone."
I peered forward in the moonlight. "A Tractate. A Tractate
of the Mishnah. Its leaves are so worn they break as he turns
them, but he does not turn them often because there is much
matter on a single page. He is so sad! Such antique weariness
broods in his face! His throat is striped from the whip. His
cheeks are folded like ancient flags, he reads the Law and
breathes the dust."

" ' "And are there flowers on either side of the road?"

" ' "Incredible flowers! Of every color! And noble shrubs
like mounds of green moss! And the cricket crackling in the
field. He passes indifferent through the beauty of the field.
His nostrils sniff his book as if flowers lay on the clotted page,
but the flowers lick his feet. His feet are bandaged, his
notched toenails gore the path. His prayer shawl droops on
his studious back. He reads the Law and breathes the dust and
doesn't see the flowers and won't heed the cricket spitting in
the field."

" ' "That," said the dryad, "is your soul." And was gone
with all her odors.

" 'My body sailed up to the road in a single hop. I
alighted near the shape of the old man and demanded whether
he were indeed the soul of Rabbi Isaac Kornfeld. He trembled but confessed. I asked if he intended to go with his
books through the whole future without change, always with
his Tractate in his hand, and he answered that he could do
nothing else.

" ' "Nothing else! You, who I thought yearned for the
earth! You, an immortal, free, and caring only to be bound
to the Law!"

" 'He held a dry arm fearfully before his face, and with
the other arm hitched up his merciless bag on his shoulder.
"Sir," he said, still quavering, "didn't you wish to see me with
your own eyes?"

" ' "I know your figure!" I shrieked. "Haven't I seen that

figure a hundred times before? On a hundred roads? It is not mine! I will not have it be mine!"

" ' "If you had not contrived to be rid of me, I would have stayed with you till the end. The dryad, who does not exist, lies. It was not I who clung to her but you, my body. Sir, all that has no real existence lies. In your grave beside you I would have sung you David's songs, I would have moaned Solomon's voice to your last grain of bone. But you expelled me, your ribs exile me from their fate, and I will walk here alone always, in my garden"—he scratched on his page— "with my precious birds"—he scratched at the letters—"and my darling trees"—he scratched at the tall side-column of commentary.

" 'He was so impudent in his bravery—for I was all flesh-liness and he all floppy wraith—that I seized him by the collar and shook him up and down, while the books on his back made a vast rubbing one on the other, and bits of shredding leather flew out like a rain.

" ' "The sound of the Law," he said, "is more beautiful than the crickets. The smell of the Law is more radiant than the moss. The taste of the Law exceeds clear water."

" 'At this nervy provocation—he more than any other knew my despair—I grabbed his prayer shawl by its tassels and whirled around him once or twice until I had unwrapped it from him altogether, and wound it on my own neck and in one bound came to the tree.

" ' "Nymph!" I called to it. "Spirit and saint! Iripomoňoéià, come! None like thee, no brow so sleek, no elbow-crook so fine, no eye so green, no waist so pliant, no limbs so pleasant and acute. For pity of me, come, come."

" 'But she does not come.

" ' "Loveliness, come."

" 'She does not come.

" 'Creature, see how I am coiled in the snail of this shawl as if in a leaf. I crouch to write my words. Let soul call thee lie, but body . . .

"'...body...

"'... fingers twist, knuckles dark as wood, tongue dries like grass, deeper now into silk ...

"'... silk of pod of shawl, knees wilt, knuckles wither, neck ...' "

Here the letter suddenly ended.

"You see? A pagan!" said Sheindel, and kept her spiteful smile. It was thick with audacity.

"You don't pity him," I said, watching the contempt that glittered in her teeth.

"Even now you don't see? You can't follow?"

"Pity him," I said.

"He who takes his own life does an abomination."

For a long moment I considered her. "You don't pity him? You don't pity him at all?"

"Let the world pity me."

"Goodbye," I said to the widow.

"You won't come back?"

I gave what amounted to a little bow of regret.

"I told you you came just for Isaac! But Isaac"—I was in terror of her cough, which was unmistakably laughter—"Isaac disappoints. 'A scholar. A rabbi. A remarkable Jew!' Ha! He disappoints you?"

"He was always an astonishing man."

"But not what you thought," she insisted. "An illusion."

"Only the pitiless are illusory. Go back to that park, Rebbetzin," I advised her.

"And what would you like me to do there? Dance around a tree and call Greek names to the weeds?"

"Your husband's soul is in that park. Consult it." But her low derisive cough accompanied me home: whereupon I remembered her earlier words and dropped three green house plants down the toilet; after a journey of some miles through conduits they straightway entered Trilham's Inlet, where they decayed amid the civic excrement.

Envy;
or,
Yiddish
in
America

EDELSHTEIN, an American for forty years, was a ravenous reader of novels by writers "of"—he said this with a snarl—"Jewish extraction." He found them puerile, vicious, pitiable, ignorant, contemptible, above all stupid. In judging them he dug for his deepest vituperation—they were, he said, "*Amerikaner-geboren.*" Spawned in America, pogroms a rumor, *mamaloshen* a stranger, history a vacuum. Also many of them were still young, and had black eyes, black hair, and red beards. A few were blue-eyed, like the *cheder-yinglach* of his youth. Schoolboys. He was certain he did not envy them, but he read them like a sickness. They were reviewed and praised, and meanwhile they were considered Jews, and knew nothing. There was even a body of Gentile writers in reaction, beginning to show familiarly whetted teeth: the Jewish Intellectual Establishment was misrepresenting American letters, coloring it with an alien dye, taking it over, and so forth. Like Berlin and Vienna in the twenties. *Judenrein ist Kulturrein* was Edelshtein's opinion. Take away the Jews and where, O so-called Western Civilization, is your literary culture?

For Edelshtein Western Civilization was a sore point. He had never been to Berlin, Vienna, Paris, or even London. He had been to Kiev, though, but only once, as a young boy. His father, a *melamed*, had traveled there on a tutoring job and had taken him along. In Kiev they lived in the cellar of

a big house owned by rich Jews, the Kirilovs. They had
been born Katz, but bribed an official in order to Russify
their name. Every morning he and his father would go up a
green staircase to the kitchen for a breakfast of coffee and
stale bread and then into the schoolroom to teach *chumash*
to Alexei Kirilov, a red-cheeked little boy. The younger
Edelshtein would drill him while his father dozed. What had
become of Alexei Kirilov? Edelshtein, a widower in New
York, sixty-seven years old, a Yiddishist (so-called), a poet,
could stare at anything at all—a subway car-card, a garbage
can lid, a streetlight—and cause the return of Alexei Kirilov's
face, his bright cheeks, his Ukraine-accented Yiddish, his
shelves of mechanical toys from Germany—trucks, cranes,
wheelbarrows, little colored autos with awnings overhead.
Only Edelshtein's father was expected to call him Alexei—
everyone else, including the young Edelshtein, said Avremeleh. Avremeleh had a knack of getting things by heart. He
had a golden head. Today he was a citizen of the Soviet Union.
Or was he finished, dead, in the ravine at Babi Yar? Edelshtein
remembered every coveted screw of the German toys. With
his father he left Kiev in the spring and returned to Minsk. The
mud, frozen into peaks, was melting. The train carriage reeked
of urine and the dirt seeped through their shoelaces into their
socks.

And the language was lost, murdered. The language—a
museum. Of what other language can it be said that it died
a sudden and definite death, in a given decade, on a given
piece of soil? Where are the speakers of ancient Etruscan?
Who was the last man to write a poem in Linear B? Attrition,
assimilation. Death by mystery not gas. The last Etruscan
walks around inside some Sicilian. Western Civilization, that
pod of muck, lingers on and on. The Sick Man of Europe
with his big globe-head, rotting, but at home in bed. Yiddish,
a littleness, a tiny light—oh little holy light!—dead, vanished.
Perished. Sent into darkness.

This was Edelshtein's subject. On this subject he lec-

tured for a living. He swallowed scraps. Synagogues, com-
munity centers, labor unions underpaid him to suck on the
bones of the dead. Smoke. He traveled from borough to
borough, suburb to suburb, mourning in English the death
of Yiddish. Sometimes he tried to read one or two of his
poems. At the first Yiddish word the painted old ladies of
the Reform Temples would begin to titter from shame, as at
a stand-up television comedian. Orthodox and Conservative
men fell instantly asleep. So he reconsidered, and told jokes:

Before the war there was held a great International Esperanto
Convention. It met in Geneva. Esperanto scholars, doctors of
letters, learned men, came from all over the world to deliver
papers on the genesis, syntax, and functionalism of Esperanto.
Some spoke of the social value of an international language,
others of its beauty. Every nation on earth was represented
among the lecturers. All the papers were given in Esperanto.
Finally the meeting was concluded, and the tired great men
wandered companionably along the corridors, where at last
they began to converse casually among themselves in their
international language: *"Nu, vos macht a yid?"*

After the war a funeral cortège was moving slowly down a
narrow street on the Lower East Side. The cars had left the
parking lot behind the chapel in the Bronx and were on their
way to the cemetery in Staten Island. Their route took them
past the newspaper offices of the last Yiddish daily left in the
city. There were two editors, one to run the papers off the
press and the other to look out the window. The one looking
out the window saw the funeral procession passing by and
called to his colleague: "Hey Mottel, print one less!"

But both Edelshtein and his audiences found the jokes
worthless. Old jokes. They were not the right kind. They
wanted jokes about weddings—spiral staircases, doves flying
out of cages, bashful medical students—and he gave them
funerals. To speak of Yiddish was to preside over a funeral.

He was a rabbi who had survived his whole congregation. Those for whom his tongue was no riddle were specters.

The new Temples scared Edelshtein. He was afraid to use the word *shul* in these palaces—inside, vast mock-bronze Tablets, mobiles of outstretched hands rotating on a motor, gigantic dangling Tetragrammatons in transparent plastic like chandeliers, platforms, altars, daises, pulpits, aisles, pews, polished-oak bins for prayerbooks printed in English with made-up new prayers in them. Everything smelled of wet plaster. Everything was new. The refreshment tables were long and luminous—he saw glazed cakes, snowheaps of egg salad, herring, salmon, tuna, whitefish, gefilte fish, pools of sour cream, silver electric coffee urns, bowls of lemon-slices, pyramids of bread, waferlike teacups from the Black Forest, Indian-brass trays of hard cheeses, golden bottles set up in rows like ninepins, great sculptured butter-birds, Hansel-and-Gretel houses of cream cheese and fruitcake, bars, butlers, fat napery, carpeting deep as honey. He learned their term for their architecture: "soaring." In one place—a flat wall of beige brick in Westchester—he read Scripture riveted on in letters fashioned from 14-karat gold molds: "And thou shalt see My back; but My face shall not be seen." Later that night he spoke in Mount Vernon, and in the marble lobby afterward he heard an adolescent girl mimic his inflections. It amazed him: often he forgot he had an accent. In the train going back to Manhattan he slid into a miniature jogging doze—it was a little nest of sweetness there inside the flaps of his overcoat, and he dreamed he was in Kiev, with his father. He looked through the open schoolroom door at the smoking cheeks of Alexei Kirilov, eight years old. "Avremeleh," he called, "Avremeleh, *kum tsu mir, lebst ts' geshtorben?*" He heard himself yelling in English: Thou shalt see my asshole! A belch woke him to hot fear. He was afraid he might be, unknown to himself all his life long, a secret pederast.

He had no children and only a few remote relations (a

druggist cousin in White Plains, a cleaning store in-law hanging on somewhere among the blacks in Brownsville), so he loitered often in Baumzweig's apartment—dirty mirrors and rusting crystal, a hazard and invitation to cracks, an abandoned exhausted corridor. Lives had passed through it and were gone. Watching Baumzweig and his wife—gray-eyed, sluggish, with a plump Polish nose—it came to him that at this age, his own and theirs, it was the same having children or not having them. Baumzweig had two sons, one married and a professor at San Diego, the other at Stanford, not yet thirty, in love with his car. The San Diego son had a son. Sometimes it seemed that it must be in deference to his childlessness that Baumzweig and his wife pretended a detachment from their offspring. The grandson's photo—a fat-lipped blond child of three or so—was wedged between two wine glasses on top of the china closet. But then it became plain that they could not imagine the lives of their children. Nor could the children imagine their lives. The parents were too helpless to explain, the sons were too impatient to explain. So they had given each other up to a common muteness. In that apartment Josh and Mickey had grown up answering in English the Yiddish of their parents. Mutes. Mutations. What right had these boys to spit out the Yiddish that had bred them, and only for the sake of Western Civilization? Edelshtein knew the titles of their Ph.D. theses: literary boys, one was on Sir Gawain and the Green Knight, the other was on the novels of Carson McCullers.

Baumzweig's lethargic wife was intelligent. She told Edelshtein he too had a child, also a son. "Yourself, yourself," she said. "You remember yourself when you were a little boy, and *that* little boy is the one you love, *him* you trust, *him* you bless, *him* you bring up in hope to a good manhood." She spoke a rich Yiddish, but high-pitched.

Baumzweig had a good job, a sinecure, a pension in disguise, with an office, a part-time secretary, a typewriter with Hebrew characters, ten-to-three hours. In 1910 a laxative manufacturer—a philanthropist—had founded an organization called the Yiddish-American Alliance for Letters and Social Progress. The original illustrious members were all dead— even the famous poet Yehoash was said to have paid dues for a month or so—but there was a trust providing for the group's continuation, and enough money to pay for a biannual periodical in Yiddish. Baumzweig was the editor of this, but of the Alliance nothing was left, only some crumbling brown snapshots of Jews in derbies. His salary check came from the laxative manufacturer's grandson—a Republican politician, an Episcopalian. The name of the celebrated product was LUKEWARM: it was advertised as delightful to children when dissolved in lukewarm cocoa. The name of the obscure periodical was *Bitterer Yam*, Bitter Sea, but it had so few subscribers that Baumzweig's wife called it Invisible Ink. In it Baumzweig published much of his own poetry and a little of Edelshtein's. Baumzweig wrote mostly of Death, Edelshtein mostly of Love. They were both sentimentalists, but not about each other. They did not like each other, though they were close friends.

Sometimes they read aloud among the dust of empty bowls their newest poems, with an agreement beforehand not to criticize: Paula should be the critic. Carrying coffee back and forth in cloudy glasses, Baumzweig's wife said: "Oh, very nice, very nice. But so sad. Gentlemen, life is not that sad." After this she would always kiss Edelshtein on the forehead, a lazy kiss, often leaving stuck on his eyebrow a crumb of Danish: very slightly she was a slattern.

Edelshtein's friendship with Baumzweig had a ferocious secret: it was moored entirely to their agreed hatred for the man they called *der chazer*. He was named Pig because of his extraordinarily white skin, like a tissue of pale ham, and also because in the last decade he had become unbelievably famous. When they did not call him Pig they called him *shed*—Devil. They also called him Yankee Doodle. His name was Yankel Ostrover, and he was a writer of stories.

They hated him for the amazing thing that had happened to him—his fame—but this they never referred to. Instead they discussed his style: his Yiddish was impure, his sentences lacked grace and sweep, his paragraph transitions were amateur, vile. Or else they raged against his subject matter, which was insanely sexual, pornographic, paranoid, freakish —men who embraced men, women who caressed women, sodomists of every variety, boys copulating with hens, butchers who drank blood for strength behind the knife. All the stories were set in an imaginary Polish village, Zwrdl, and by now there was almost no American literary intellectual alive who had not learned to say Zwrdl when he meant lewd. Ostrover's wife was reputed to be a high-born Polish Gentile woman from the "real" Zwrdl, the daughter in fact of a minor princeling, who did not know a word of Yiddish and read her husband's fiction falteringly, in English translation— but both Edelshtein and Baumzweig had encountered her often enough over the years, at this meeting and that, and regarded her as no more impressive than a pot of stale fish. Her Yiddish had an unpleasant gargling Galician accent, her vocabulary was a thin soup—they joked that it was correct to say she spoke no Yiddish—and she mewed it like a peasant, comparing prices. She was a short square woman, a cube with low-slung udders and a flat backside. It was partly Ostrover's mockery, partly his self-advertising, that had converted her into a little princess. He would make her go into their bedroom to get a whip he claimed she had used on her bay, Romeo, trotting over her father's lands in her girlhood. Baumzweig often said this same whip was applied to the earlobes of Ostrover's translators, unhappy pairs of collaborators he changed from month to month, never satisfied.

Ostrover's glory was exactly in this: that he required translators. Though he wrote only in Yiddish, his fame was American, national, international. They considered him a "modern." Ostrover was free of the prison of Yiddish! Out, out—he had burst out, he was in the world of reality.

And how had he begun? The same as anybody, a colum-nist for one of the Yiddish dailies, a humorist, a cheap fast article-writer, a squeezer-out of real-life tales. Like anybody else, he saved up a few dollars, put a paper clip over his stories, and hired a Yiddish press to print up a hundred copies. A book. Twenty-five copies he gave to people he counted as relatives, another twenty-five he sent to enemies and rivals, the rest he kept under his bed in the original cartons. Like anybody else, his literary gods were Chekhov and Tolstoy, Peretz and Sholem Aleichem. From this, how did he come to *The New Yorker*, to *Playboy*, to big lecture fees, invita-tions to Yale and M.I.T. and Vassar, to the Midwest, to Buenos Aires, to a literary agent, to a publisher on Madison Avenue?

"He sleeps with the right translators," Paula said. Edel-shtein gave out a whinny. He knew some of Ostrover's trans-lators—a spinster hack in dresses below the knee, occasionally a certain half-mad and drunken lexicographer, college boys with a dictionary.

Thirty years ago, straight out of Poland via Tel Aviv, Ostrover crept into a toying affair with Mireleh, Edelshtein's wife. He had left Palestine during the 1939 Arab riots, not, he said, out of fear, out of integrity rather—it was a country which had turned its face against Yiddish. Yiddish was not honored in Tel Aviv or Jerusalem. In the Negev it was worthless. In the God-given State of Israel they had no use for the language of the bad little interval between Canaan and now. Yiddish was inhabited by the past, the new Jews did not want it. Mireleh liked to hear these anecdotes of how rotten it was in Israel for Yiddish and Yiddishists. In Israel the case was even lamer than in New York, thank God! There was after all a reason to live the life they lived: it was worse somewhere else. Mireleh was a tragedian. She carried herself according to her impression of how a barren woman should sit, squat, stand, eat and sleep, talked constantly of her six miscarriages, and was vindictive about Edelshtein's sperm-count. Ostrover would arrive in the rain, crunch down on the sofa, complain about the transportation from the Bronx to the West Side, and begin to woo Mireleh. He took her out to supper, to his special café, to Second Avenue vaudeville, even home to his apartment near Crotona Park to meet his little princess Pesha. Edelshtein noticed with self-curiosity that he felt no jealousy whatever, but he thought himself obliged to throw a kitchen chair at Ostrover. Ostrover had very fine teeth, his own; the chair knocked off half a lateral incisor, and Edelshtein wept at the flaw. Immediately he led Ostrover to the dentist around the corner.

The two wives, Mireleh and Pesha, seemed to be falling in love: they had dates, they went to museums and movies together, they poked one another and laughed day and night, they shared little privacies, they carried pencil-box rulers in their purses and showed each other certain hilarious measurements, they even became pregnant in the same month. Pesha had her third daughter, Mireleh her seventh miscarriage. Edelshtein was griefstricken but elated. "*My* sperm-count?" he screamed. "*Your* belly! Go fix the machine before you blame the oil!" When the dentist's bill came for Ostrover's jacket crown, Edelshtein sent it to Ostrover. At this injustice Ostrover dismissed Mireleh and forbade Pesha to go anywhere with her ever again.

About Mireleh's affair with Ostrover Edelshtein wrote the following malediction:

You, why do you snuff out my sons, my daughters?
Worse than Mother Eve, cursed to break waters
for little ones to float out upon in their tiny barks of skin,
you, merciless one, cannot even bear the fruit of sin.

It was published to much gossip in *Bitterer Yam* in the spring of that year—one point at issue being whether "snuff out" was the right term in such a watery context. (Baumzweig, a less oblique stylist, had suggested "drown.") The late

Zimmerman, Edelshtein's cruelest rival, wrote in a letter to
Baumzweig (which Baumzweig read on the telephone to
Edelshtein):

> Who is the merciless one, after all, the barren woman who
> makes the house peaceful with no infantile caterwauling, or
> the excessively fertile poet who bears the fruit of his sin
> —namely his untalented verses? He bears it, but who can
> bear it? In one breath he runs from seas to trees. Like his
> ancestors the amphibians, puffed up with arrogance. Her-
> sheleh Frog! Why did God give Hersheleh Edelshtein an
> unfaithful wife? To punish him for writing trash.

Around the same time Ostrover wrote a story: two
women loved each other so much they mourned because
they could not give birth to one another's children. Both had
husbands, one virile and hearty, the other impotent, with a
withered organ, a *shlimazal*. They seized the idea of making
a tool out of one of the husbands: they agreed to transfer
their love for each other into the man, and bear the child of
their love through him. So both women turned to the virile
husband, and both women conceived. But the woman who
had the withered husband could not bear her child: it
withered in her womb. "As it is written," Ostrover concluded, "Paradise is only for those who have already been
there."

A stupid fable! Three decades later—Mireleh dead of a
cancerous uterus, Pesha encrusted with royal lies in *Time*
magazine (which photographed the whip)—this piece of insignificant mystification, this *pollution*, included also in Ostrover's *Complete Tales* (Kimmel & Segal, 1968), was the
subject of graduate dissertations in comparative literature, as
if Ostrover were Thomas Mann, or even Albert Camus.
When all that happened was that Pesha and Mireleh had gone
to the movies together now and then—and such a long time
ago! All the same, Ostrover was released from the dungeon

of the dailies, from *Bitterer Yam* and even seedier nullities, he was free, the outside world knew his name. And why Ostrover? Why not somebody else? Was Ostrover more gifted than Komorsky? Did he think up better stories than Horowitz? Why does the world outside pick on an Ostrover instead of an Edelshtein or even a Baumzweig? What occult knack, what craft, what crooked convergence of planets drove translators to grovel before Ostrover's naked swollen sentences with their thin little threadbare pants always pulled down? Who had discovered that Ostrover was a "modern"? His Yiddish, however fevered on itself, bloated, was still Yiddish, it was still *mamaloshen*, it still squeaked up to God with a littleness, a familiarity, an elbow-poke, it was still pieced together out of *shtetl* rags, out of a baby *aleph*, a toddler *beys*—so why Ostrover? Why only Ostrover? Ostrover should be the only one? Everyone else sentenced to darkness, Ostrover alone saved? Ostrover the survivor? As if hidden in the Dutch attic like that child. *His* diary, so to speak, the only documentation of what was. Like Ringelblum of Warsaw. Ostrover was to be the only evidence that there was once a Yiddish tongue, a Yiddish literature? And all the others lost? Lost! Drowned. Snuffed out. Under the earth. As if never.

Edelshtein composed a letter to Ostrover's publishers:

Kimmel & Segal
244 Madison Avenue, New York City

My dear Mr. Kimmel, and very honored Mr. Segal:

I am writing to you in reference to one Y. Ostrover, whose works you are the company that places them before the public's eyes. Be kindly enough to forgive all flaws of English Expression. Undoubtedly, in the course of his business with you, you have received from Y. Ostrover, letters in English, even worse than this. (I HAVE NO TRANSLATOR!) We immigrants, no matter how long already Yankified, stay

inside always green and never attain to actual native writing
Smoothness. For one million green writers, one Nabokov,
one Kosinski. I mention these to show my extreme familiar-
ness with American Literature in all Contemporaneous ava-
tars. In your language I read, let us say, wolfishly. I regard
myself as a very Keen critic, esp. concerning so-called
Amer.-Jewish writers. If you would give time I could will-
ingly explain to you many clear opinions I have concerning
these Jewish-Amer. boys and girls such as (not alphabetical)
Roth Philip/ Rosen Norma/ Melammed Bernie/ Friedman
B.J./ Paley Grace/ Bellow Saul/ Mailer Norman. Of the latter having just read several recent works including political
I would like to remind him what F. Kafka, rest in peace,
said to the German-speaking, already very comfortable,
Jews of Prague, Czechoslovakia: "Jews of Prague! You
know more Yiddish than you think!"

Perhaps, since doubtless you do not read the Jewish
Press, you are not informed. Only this month all were taken
by surprise! In that filthy propaganda *Sovietish Heymland*
which in Russia they run to show that their prisoners the
Jews are not prisoners—a poem! By a 20-year-old young
Russian Jewish girl! Yiddish will yet live through our young.
Though I doubt it as do other pessimists. However, this is
not the point! I ask you—what does the following person-
ages mean to you, you who are Sensitive men, Intelligent,
and with closely-warmed Feelings! Lyessin, Reisen, Yehoash! H. Leivik himself! Itzik Manger, Chaim Grade, Aaron
Zeitlen, Jacob Glatshtein, Eliezer Greenberg! Molodowsky
and Korn, ladies, gifted! Dovid Ignatov, Morris Rosenfeld,
Moishe Nadir, Moishe Leib Halpern, Reuven Eisland, Mani
Leib, Zisha Landau! I ask you! Frug, Peretz, Vintchevski,
Bovshover, Edelshtat! Velvl Zhbarzher, Avrom Goldfaden!
A. Rosenblatt! Y.Y. Schwartz, Yoisef Rollnick! These are
all our glorious Yiddish poets. And if I would add to them
our beautiful recent Russian brother-poets that were killed
by Stalin with his pockmarks, for instance Peretz Markish,
would you know any name of theirs? No! THEY HAVE NO
TRANSLATORS!

Esteemed Gentlemen, you publish only one Yiddish

writer, not even a Poet, only a Story-writer. I humbly submit you give serious wrong Impressions. That we have produced nothing else. I again refer to your associate Y. Ostrover. I do not intend to take away from him any possible talent by this letter, but wish to WITH VIGOROUSNESS assure you that others also exist without notice being bothered over them! I myself am the author and also publisher of four tomes of poetry: *N'shomeh un Guf, Zingen un Freyen, A Velt ohn Vint, A Shtundeh mit Shney*. To wit, "Soul and Body," "Singing and Being Happy," "A World with No Wind," "An Hour of Snow," these are my Deep-Feeling titles.

Please inform me if you will be willing to provide me with a translator for these very worthwhile pieces of hidden writings, or, to use a Hebrew Expression, "Buried Light."

Yours very deeply respectful.

He received an answer in the same week.

Dear Mr. Edelstein:

Thank you for your interesting and informative letter. We regret that, unfortunately, we cannot furnish you with a translator. Though your poetry may well be of the quality you claim for it, practically speaking, reputation must precede translation.

Yours sincerely.

A lie! Liars!

Dear Kimmel, dear Segal,

Did YOU, Jews without tongues, ever hear of Ostrover before you found him translated everywhere? In Yiddish he didn't exist for you! For you Yiddish has no existence! A darkness inside a cloud! Who can see it, who can hear it? The world has no ears for the prisoner! You sign yourself "Yours." You're not mine and I'm not Yours!

Sincerely.

He then began to search in earnest for a translator. Expecting little, he wrote to the spinster hack.

Esteemed Edelshtein [she replied]:

To put it as plainly as I can—a plain woman should be as plain in her words—you do not know the world of practicality, of reality. Why should you? You're a poet, an idealist. When a big magazine pays Ostrover $500, how much do I get? Maybe $75. If he takes a rest for a month and doesn't write, what then? Since he's the only one they want to print he's the only one worth translating. Suppose I translated one of your nice little love songs? Would anyone buy it? Foolishness even to ask. And if they bought it, should I slave for the $5? You don't know what I go through with Ostrover anyhow. He sits me down in his dining room, his wife brings in a samovar of tea—did you ever hear anything as pretentious as this—and sits also, watching me. She has jealous eyes. She watches my ankles, which aren't bad. Then we begin. Ostrover reads aloud the first sentence the way he wrote it, in Yiddish. I write it down, in English. Right away it starts. Pesha reads what I put down and says, "That's no good, you don't catch his idiom." Idiom! She knows! Ostrover says, "The last word sticks in my throat. Can't you do better than that? A little more robustness." We look in the dictionary, the thesaurus, we scream out different words, trying, trying. Ostrover doesn't like any of them. Suppose the word is "big." We go through huge, vast, gigantic, enormous, gargantuan, monstrous, etc., etc., etc., and finally Ostrover says—by now it's five hours later, my tonsils hurt, I can hardly stand—"all right, so let it be 'big.' Simplicity above all." Day after day like this! And for $75 is it worth it? Then after this he fires me and gets himself a college boy! Or that imbecile who cracked up over the mathematics dictionary! Until he needs me. However I get a little glory out of it. Everyone says, "There goes Ostrover's translator." In actuality I'm his pig, his stool (I mean that in both senses, I assure you). You write that he has no talent. That's your opinion, maybe you're not wrong, but let me tell you he has a talent for pressure. The way among *them* they write careless novels, hoping they'll be transformed into beautiful movies and sometimes it happens—that's how it is with him. Never mind the quality of his Yiddish, what will it turn into when it becomes English? Transformation is all he cares for—and in English he's a cripple—like, please excuse me, yourself and everyone of your generation. But Ostrover has the sense to be a suitor. He keeps all his translators in a perpetual frenzy of envy for each other, but they're just rubble and offal to him, they aren't the object of his suit. What he woos is *them*. Them! You understand me, Edelshtein? He stands on the backs of hacks to reach. I know you call me hack, and it's all right, by myself I'm what you think me, no imagination, so-so ability (I too once wanted to be a poet, but that's another life)—with Ostrover on my back I'm something else: I'm "Ostrover's translator." You think that's nothing? It's an entrance into *them*. I'm invited everywhere, I go to the same parties Ostrover goes to. Everyone looks at me and thinks I'm a bit freakish, but they say: "It's Ostrover's translator." A marriage. Pesha, that junk-heap, is less married to Ostrover than I am. Like a wife, I have the supposedly passive role. Supposedly: who knows what goes on in the bedroom? An unmarried person like myself becomes good at guessing at these matters. The same with translation. Who makes the language Ostrover is famous for? You ask: what has persuaded *them* that he's a "so-called modern"?—a sneer. Aha. *Who* has read James Joyce, Ostrover or I? I'm fifty-three years old. I wasn't born back of Hlusk for nothing, I didn't go to Vassar for nothing —do you understand me? I got caught in between, so I got squeezed. Between two organisms. A cultural hermaphrodite, neither one nor the other. I have a forked tongue. When I fight for five hours to make Ostrover say "big" instead of "gargantuan," when I take out all the nice homey commas he sprinkles like a fool, when I drink his wife's stupid tea and then go home with a watery belly—*then* he's being turned into a "modern," you see? I'm the one! No one recognizes this, of course, they think it's something in-

side the stories themselves, when actually it's the way I
dress them up and paint over them. It's all cosmetics, I'm a
cosmetician, a painter, the one they pay to do the same
job on the corpse in the mortuary, among *them* . . . don't,
though, bore me with your criticisms. I tell you his Yiddish
doesn't matter. Nobody's Yiddish matters. Whatever's in
Yiddish doesn't matter.

The rest of the letter—all women are long-winded,
strong-minded—he did not read. He had already seen what
she was after: a little bit of money, a little bit of esteem. A
miniature megalomaniac: she fancied herself the *real* Ostrover.
She believed she had fashioned herself a genius out of a rag.
A rag turned into a sack, was that genius? She lived out there
in the light, with *them:* naturally she wouldn't waste her time
on an Edelshtein. In the bleakness. Dark where he was. An
idealist! How had this good word worked itself up in society
to become an insult? A darling word nevertheless. Idealist.
The difference between him and Ostrover was this: Ostrover
wanted to save only himself, Edelshtein wanted to save Yiddish.
　　Immediately he felt he lied.
　　With Baumzweig and Paula he went to the 92nd
Street Y to hear Ostrover read. "Self-mortification," Paula
said of this excursion. It was a snowy night. They had to
shove their teeth into the wind, tears of suffering iced down
their cheeks, the streets from the subway were Siberia. "Two
Christian saints, self-flagellation," she muttered, "with chains
of icicles they hit themselves." They paid for the tickets
with numb fingers and sat down toward the front. Edelshtein felt paralyzed. His toes stung, prickled, then seemed
diseased, grangrenous, furnace-like. The cocoon of his bed at
home, the pen he kept on his night table, the first luminous
line of his new poem lying there waiting to be born—*Oh that
I might like a youth be struck with the blow of belief*—all at
once he knew how to go on with it, what it was about and
what he meant by it, the hall around him seemed preposter-

ous, unnecessary, why was he here? Crowds, huddling, the whine of folding chairs lifted and dropped, the babble, Paula yawning next to him with squeezed and wrinkled eyelids, Baumzweig blowing his flat nose into a blue plaid handkerchief and exploding a great green flower of snot, why was he in such a place at this? What did such a place have in common with what he knew, what he felt?

Paula craned around her short neck inside a used-up skunk collar to read the frieze, mighty names, golden letters, Moses, Einstein, Maimonides, Heine. Heine. Maybe Heine knew what Edelshtein knew, a convert. But these, ushers in fine jackets, skinny boys carrying books (Ostrover's), wearing them nearly, costumed for blatant bookishness, blatant sexuality, in pants crotch-snug, penciling buttocks on air, mustachioed, some hairy to the collarbone, shins and calves menacing as hammers, and girls, tunics, knees, pants, boots, little hidden sweet tongues, black-eyed. Woolly smell of piles and piles of coats. For Ostrover! The hall was full, the ushers with raised tweed wrists directed all the rest into an unseen gallery nearby: a television screen there, on which the little gray ghost of Ostrover, palpable and otherwise white as a washed pig, would soon flutter. The Y. Why? Edelshtein also lectured at Y's—Elmhurst, Eastchester, Rye, tiny platforms, lecterns too tall for him, catalogues of vexations, his sad recitations to old people. Ladies and Gentlemen, they have cut out my vocal cords, the only language I can freely and fluently address you in, my darling *mamaloshen*, surgery, dead, the operation was a success. Edelshtein's Y's were all old people's homes, convalescent factories, asylums. To himself he sang,

Why	*Farvos di Vy?*
the Y?	*Ich reyd*
Lectures	*ohn freyd*
to specters,	*un sheydim tantsen derbei,*

aha! specters, if my tongue has no riddle for you, Ladies and Gentlemen, you are specter, wraith, phantom, I have invented you, you are my imagining, there is no one here at all, an empty chamber, a vacant valve, abandoned, desolate. Everyone gone. *Pust vi dem kalten shul mein harts* (another first line left without companion-lines, fellows, followers), the cold study-house, spooks dance there. Ladies and Gentlemen, if you find my tongue a riddle, here is another riddle: How is a Jew like a giraffe? A Jew too has no vocal cords. God blighted Jew and giraffe, one in full, one by half. And no salve. Baumzweig hawked up again. Mucus the sheen of the sea. In God's Creation no thing without beauty however perverse. *Khrakeh khrakeh.* Baumzweig's roar the only noise in the hall. "Shah," Paula said, "*ot kumt der shed.*"

Gleaming, gleaming, Ostrover stood—high, far, the stage broad, brilliant, the lectern punctilious with microphone and water pitcher. A rod of powerful light bored into his eye sockets. He had a moth-mouth as thin and dim as a chalk line, a fence of white hair erect over his ears, a cool voice.

"A new story," he announced, and spittle flashed on his lip. "It isn't obscene, so I consider it a failure."

"Devil," Paula whispered, "washed white pig, Yankee Doodle."

"Shah," Baumzweig said, "*lomir heren.*"

Baumzweig wanted to hear the devil, the pig! Why should anyone want to hear him? Edelshtein, a little bit deaf, hung forward. Before him, his nose nearly in it, the hair of a young girl glistened—some of the stage light had become enmeshed in it. Young, young! Everyone young! Everyone for Ostrover young! A modern.

Cautiously, slyly, Edelshtein let out, as on a rope, little bony shiverings of attentiveness. Two rows in front of him he glimpsed the spinster hack, Chaim Vorovsky the drunken lexicographer whom too much mathematics had crazed, six unknown college boys.

Ostrover's story:

Satan appears to a bad poet. "I desire fame," says the poet, "but I cannot attain it, because I come from Zwrdl, and the only language I can write is Zwrdlish. Unfortunately no one is left in the world who can read Zwrdlish. That is my burden. Give me fame, and I will trade you my soul for it."

"Are you quite sure," says Satan, "that you have estimated the dimensions of your trouble entirely correctly?" "What do you mean?" says the poet. "Perhaps," says Satan, "the trouble lies in your talent. Zwrdl or no Zwrdl, it's very weak." "Not so!" says the poet, "and I'll prove it to you. Teach me French, and in no time I'll be famous." "All right," says Satan, "as soon as I say Glup you'll know French perfectly, better than de Gaulle. But I'll be generous with you. French is such an easy language, I'll take only a quarter of your soul for it."

And he said Glup. And in an instant there was the poet, scribbling away in fluent French. But still no publisher in France wanted him and he remained obscure. Back came Satan: "So the French was no good, *mon vieux? Tant pis!*" "Feh," says the poet, "what do you expect from a people that kept colonies, they should know what's good in the poetry line? Teach me Italian, after all even the Pope dreams in Italian." "Another quarter of your soul," says Satan, ringing it up in his portable cash register. And Glup! There he was again, the poet, writing *terza rima* with such fluency and melancholy that the Pope would have been moved to holy tears of praise if only he had been able to see it in print —unfortunately every publisher in Italy sent the manuscript back with a plain rejection slip, no letter.

"What? Italian no good either?" exclaims Satan. "*Mamma mia*, why don't you believe me, little brother, it's not the language, it's you." It was the same with Swahili and Armenian, Glup!—failure, Glup!—failure, and by now, having rung up a quarter of it at a time, Satan owned the poet's entire soul, and took him back with him to the Place of

Fire. "I suppose you'll burn me up," says the poet bitterly.
"No, no," says Satan, "we don't go in for that sort of treat-
ment for so silken a creature as a poet. Well? Did you bring
everything? I told you to pack carefully! Not to leave behind a scrap!" "I brought my whole file," says the poet, and
sure enough, there it was, strapped to his back, a big black
metal cabinet. "Now empty it into the Fire," Satan orders.
"My poems! Not all my poems? My whole life's output?"
cries the poet in anguish. "That's right, do as I say," and
the poet obeys, because, after all, he's in hell and Satan owns
him. "Good," says Satan, "now come with me, I'll show
you to your room."

A perfect room, perfectly appointed, not too cold, not too
hot, just the right distance from the great Fire to be comfortable. A jewel of a desk, with a red leather top, a lovely
swivel chair cushioned in scarlet, a scarlet Persian rug on
the floor, nearby a red refrigerator stocked with cheese and
pudding and pickles, a glass of reddish tea already steaming
on a little red table. One window without a curtain. "That's
your Inspiring View," says Satan, "look out and see." Nothing outside but the Fire cavorting splendidly, flecked with
unearthly colors, turning itself and rolling up into unimaginable new forms. "It's beautiful," marvels the poet. "Exactly," says Satan. "It should inspire you to the composition
of many new verses." "Yes, yes! May I begin, your Lord-
ship?" "That's why I brought you here," says Satan. "Now
sit down and write, since you can't help it anyhow. There
is only one stipulation. The moment you finish a stanza you
must throw it out of the window, like this." And to illus-
trate, he tossed out a fresh page.

Instantly a flaming wind picked it up and set it afire, drawing it into the great central conflagration. "Remember that
you are in hell," Satan says sternly, "here you write only
for oblivion." The poet begins to weep. "No difference, no
difference! It was the same up there! O Zwrdl, I curse you
that you nurtured me!" "And still he doesn't see the point!"
says Satan, exasperated. "Glup glup glup glup glup glup

glup! Now write." The poor poet began to scribble, one poem after another, and lo! suddenly he forgot every word of Zwrdlish he ever knew, faster and faster he wrote, he held on to the pen as if it alone kept his legs from flying off on their own, he wrote in Dutch and in English, in German and in Turkish, in Santali and in Sassak, in Lapp and in Kurdish, in Welsh and in Rhaeto-Romanic, in Niasese and in Nicobarese, in Galcha and in Ibanag, in Ho and in Khmer, in Ro and in Volapük, in Jagatai and in Swedish, in Tulu and in Russian, in Irish and in Kalmuck! He wrote in every language but Zwrdlish, and every poem he wrote he had to throw out the window because it was trash anyhow, though he did not realize it. . . .

Edelshtein, spinning off into a furious and alien meditation, was not sure how the story ended. But it was brutal, and Satan was again in the ascendancy: he whipped down aspiration with one of Ostrover's sample aphorisms, dense and swollen as a phallus, but sterile all the same. The terrifying laughter, a sea-wave all around: it broke toward Edelshtein, meaning to lash him to bits. Laughter for Ostrover. Little jokes, little jokes, all they wanted was jokes! "Baumzweig," he said, pressing himself down across Paula's collar (under it her plump breasts), "he does it for spite, you see that?"

But Baumzweig was caught in the laughter. The edges of his mouth were beaten by it. He whirled in it like a bug. "Bastard!" he said.

"Bastard," Edelshtein said reflectively.

"He means *you*," Baumzweig said.

"Me?"

"An allegory. You see how everything fits . . . ."

"If you write letters, you shouldn't mail them," Paula said reasonably. "It got back to him you're looking for a translator."

"He doesn't need a muse, he needs a butt. Naturally it got back to him," Baumzweig said. "That witch herself told him."

"Why me?" Edelshtein said. "It could be you."

"I'm not a jealous type," Baumzweig protested. "What he has you want." He waved over the audience: just then he looked as insignificant as a little bird.

Paula said, "You both want it."

What they both wanted now began. Homage.

Q. Mr. Ostrover, what would you say is the symbolic weight of this story?

A. The symbolic weight is, what you need you deserve. If you don't need to be knocked on the head you'll never deserve it.

Q. Sir, I'm writing a paper on you for my English class. Can you tell me please if you believe in hell?

A. Not since I got rich.

Q. How about God? Do you believe in God?

A. Exactly the way I believe in pneumonia. If you have pneumonia, you have it. If you don't, you don't.

Q. Is it true your wife is a Countess? Some people say she's really only Jewish.

A. In religion she's a transvestite, and in actuality she's a Count.

Q. Is there really such a language as Zwrdlish?

A. You're speaking it right now, it's the language of fools.

Q. What would happen if you weren't translated into English?

A. The pygmies and the Eskimos would read me instead. Nowadays to be Ostrover is to be a worldwide industry.

Q. Then why don't you write about worldwide things like wars?

A. Because I'm afraid of loud noises.

Q. What do you think of the future of Yiddish?

A. What do you think of the future of the Doberman pinscher?

Q. People say other Yiddishists envy you.

A. No, it's I who envy them. I like a quiet life.

Q. Do you keep the Sabbath?

A. Of course, didn't you notice it's gone?—I keep it hidden.

Q. And the dietary laws? Do you observe them?

A. Because of the moral situation of the world I have to. I was heartbroken to learn that the minute an oyster enters my stomach, he becomes an anti-Semite. A bowl of shrimp once started a pogrom against my intestines.

Jokes, jokes! It looked to go on for another hour. The condition of fame, a Question Period: a man can stand up forever and dribble shallow quips and everyone admires him for it. Edelshtein threw up his seat with a squeal and sneaked up the aisle to the double doors and into the lobby. On a bench, half-asleep, he saw the lexicographer. Usually he avoided him —he was a man with a past, all pasts are boring—but when he saw Vorovsky raise his leathery eyelids he went toward him.

"What's new, Chaim?"

"Nothing. Liver pains. And you?"

"Life pains. I saw you inside."

"I walked out, I hate the young."

"You weren't young, no."

"Not like these. I never laughed. Do you realize, at the age of twelve I had already mastered calculus? I practically reinvented it on my own. You haven't read Wittgenstein, Hersheleh, you haven't read Heisenberg, what do you know about the empire of the universe?"

Edelshtein thought to deflect him: "Was it your translation he read in there?"

"Did it sound like mine?"

"I couldn't tell."

"It was and it wasn't. Mine, improved. If you ask that ugly one, she'll say it's hers, improved. Who's really Ostrover's translator? Tell me, Hersheleh, maybe it's you. Nobody knows. It's as they say—by several hands, and all the hands are in Ostrover's pot, burning up. I would like to make a good strong b.m. on your friend Ostrover."

"My friend? He's not my friend."

"So why did you pay genuine money to see him? You can see him for free somewhere else, no?"

"The same applies to yourself."

"Youth, I brought youth."

A conversation with a madman: Vorovsky's *meshugas* was to cause other people to suspect him of normality. Edelshtein let himself slide to the bench—he felt his bones accordion downward. He was in the grip of a mournful fatigue. Sitting eye to eye with Vorovsky he confronted the other's hat—a great Russian-style fur monster. A nimbus of droshky-bells surrounded it, shrouds of snow. Vorovsky had a big head, with big kneaded features, except for the nose, which looked like a doll's, pink and formlessly delicate. The only sign of drunkenness was at the bulbs of the nostrils, where the cartilage was swollen, and at the tip, also swollen. Of actual madness there was, in ordinary discourse, no sign, except a tendency toward elusiveness. But it was known that Vorovsky, after compiling his dictionary, a job of seventeen years, one afternoon suddenly began to laugh, and continued laughing for six months, even in his sleep: in order to rest from laughing he had to be given sedatives, though even these could not entirely·suppress his laughter. His wife died, and then his father, and he went on laughing. He lost control of his bladder, and then discovered the curative potency, for laughter, of drink. Drink cured him, but he still peed publicly, without realizing it; and even his cure was tentative and unreliable, because if he happened to hear a joke that he liked he might laugh at it for a minute or two, or, on occasion, three hours. Apparently none of Ostrover's jokes had struck home with him—he was sober and desolate-looking. Nevertheless Edelshtein noticed a large dark patch near his fly. He had wet himself, it was impossible to tell how long ago. There was no odor. Edelshtein moved his buttocks back an inch. "Youth?" he inquired.

"My niece. Twenty-three years old, my sister Ida's girl. She reads Yiddish fluently," he said proudly. "She writes."

"In Yiddish?"

"Yiddish," he spat out. "Don't be crazy, Hersheleh, who writes in Yiddish? Twenty-three years old, she should write in Yiddish? What is she, a refugee, an American girl like that? She's crazy for literature, that's all, she's like the rest in there, to her Ostrover's literature. I brought her, she wanted to be introduced."

"Introduce me," Edelshtein said craftily.

"She wants to be introduced to someone famous, where do you come in?"

"Translated I'd be famous. Listen, Chaim, a talented man like you, so many languages under your belt, why don't you give me a try? A try and a push."

"I'm no good at poetry. You should write stories if you want fame."

"I don't want fame."

"Then what are you talking about?"

"I want—" Edelshtein stopped. What did he want? "To reach," he said.

Vorovsky did not laugh. "I was educated at the University of Berlin. From Vilna to Berlin, that was 1924. Did I reach Berlin? I gave my whole life to collecting a history of the human mind, I mean expressed in mathematics. In mathematics the final and only poetry possible. Did I reach the empire of the universe? Hersheleh, if I could tell you about reaching, I would tell you this: reaching is impossible. Why? Because when you get where you wanted to reach to, that's when you realize that's not what you want to reach to.—Do you know what a bilingual German-English mathematical dictionary is good for?"

Edelshtein covered his knees with his hands. His knuckles glimmered up at him. Row of white skulls.

"Toilet paper," Vorovsky said. "Do you know what poems are good for? The same. And don't call me cynic, what I say isn't cynicism."

"Despair maybe," Edelshtein offered.

"Despair up your ass. I'm a happy man. I know something about laughter." He jumped up—next to the seated
Edelshtein he was a giant. Fists gray, thumbnails like bone.
The mob was pouring out of the doors of the auditorium.
"Something else I'll tell you. Translation is no equation. If
you're looking for an equation, better die first. There are no
equations, equations don't happen. It's an idea like a two-
headed animal, you follow me? The last time I saw an equation it was in a snapshot of myself. I looked in my own eyes,
and what did I see there? I saw God in the shape of a murderer. What you should do with your poems is swallow your
tongue. There's my niece, behind Ostrover like a tail. Hey
Yankel!" he boomed.

The great man did not hear. Hands, arms, heads enclosed
him like a fisherman's net. Baumzweig and Paula paddled
through eddies, the lobby swirled. Edelshtein saw two little
people, elderly, overweight, heavily dressed. He hid himself,
he wanted to be lost. Let them go, let them go—

But Paula spotted him. "What happened? We thought
you took sick."

"It was too hot in there."

"Come home with us, there's a bed. Instead of your
own place alone."

"Thank you no. He signs autographs, look at that."

"Your jealousy will eat you up, Hersheleh."

"I'm not jealous!" Edelshtein shrieked; people turned to
see. "Where's Baumzweig?"

"Shaking hands with the pig. An editor has to keep up
contacts."

"A poet has to keep down vomit."

Paula considered him. Her chin dipped into her skunk
ruff. "How can you vomit, Hersheleh? Pure souls have no
stomachs, only ectoplasm. Maybe Ostrover's right, you have
too much ambition for your size. What if your dear friend
Baumzweig didn't publish you? You wouldn't know your
own name. My husband doesn't mention this to you, he's a

kind man, but I'm not afraid of the truth. Without him you wouldn't exist."

"With him I don't exist," Edelshtein said. "What is existence?"

"I'm not a Question Period," Paula said.

"That's all right," Edelshtein said, "because I'm an Answer Period. The answer is period. Your husband is finished, period. Also I'm finished, period. We're already dead. Whoever uses Yiddish to keep himself alive is already dead. Either you realize this or you don't realize it. I'm one who realizes."

"I tell him all the time he shouldn't bother with you. You come and you hang around."

"Your house is a gallows, mine is a gas chamber, what's the difference?"

"Don't come any more, nobody needs you."

"My philosophy exactly. We are superfluous on the face of the earth."

"You're a scoundrel."

"Your husband's a weasel, and you're the wife of a weasel."

"Pig and devil yourself."

"Mother of puppydogs." (Paula, such a good woman, the end, he would never see her again!)

He blundered away licking his tears, hitting shoulders with his shoulder, blind with the accident of his grief. A yearning all at once shouted itself in his brain:

EDELSHTEIN: Chaim, teach me to be a drunk!
VOROVSKY: First you need to be crazy.
EDELSHTEIN: Teach me to go crazy!
VOROVSKY: First you need to fail.
EDELSHTEIN: I've failed, I'm schooled in failure, I'm a master of failure!
VOROVSKY: Go back and study some more.

One wall was a mirror. In it he saw an old man crying, dragging a striped scarf like a prayer shawl. He stood and

looked at himself. He wished he had been born a Gentile.
Pieces of old poems littered his nostrils, he smelled the hour
of their creation, his wife in bed beside him, asleep after he
had rubbed her, to compensate her for bitterness. *The sky is
cluttered with stars of David. . . . If everything is something
else, then I am something else. . . . Am I a thing and not a
bird? Does my way fork though I am one? Will God take
back history? Who will let me begin again. . . .*

Ostrover: Hersheleh, I admit I insulted you, but who will
    know? It's only a make-believe story, a game.
Edelshtein: Literature isn't a game! Literature isn't little
    stories!
Ostrover: So what is it, Torah? You scream out loud like a
    Jew, Edelshtein. Be quiet, they'll hear you.
Edelshtein: And you, Mr. Elegance, you aren't a Jew?
Ostrover: Not at all, I'm one of *them.* You too are lured,
    aren't you, Hersheleh? Shakespeare is better than a
    shadow, Pushkin is better than a pipsqueak, hah?
Edelshtein: If you become a Gentile you don't automati-
    cally become a Shakespeare.
Ostrover: Oho! A lot you know. I'll let you in on the facts,
    Hersheleh, because I feel we're really brothers, I feel you
    straining toward the core of the world. Now listen—
    did you ever hear of Velvl Shikkerparev? Never. A
    Yiddish scribbler writing romances for the Yiddish stage
    in the East End, I'm speaking of London, England. He
    finds a translator and overnight he becomes Willie
    Shakespeare. . . .
Edelshtein: Jokes aside, is this what you advise?
Ostrover: I would advise my own father no less. Give it up,
    Hersheleh, stop believing in Yiddish.
Edelshtein: But I don't believe in it!
Ostrover: You do. I see you do. It's no use talking to you,
    you won't let go. Tell me, Edelshtein, what language
    does Moses speak in the world-to-come?
Edelshtein: From babyhood I know this. Hebrew on the
    Sabbath, on weekdays Yiddish.

Ostrover: Lost soul, don't make Yiddish into the Sabbath-tongue! If you believe in holiness, you're finished. Holiness is for make-believe.
Edelshtein: I want to be a Gentile like you!
Ostrover: I'm only a make-believe Gentile. This means that I play at being a Jew to satisfy them. In my village when I was a boy they used to bring in a dancing bear for the carnival, and everyone said, "It's human!"— They said this because they knew it was a bear, though it stood on two legs and waltzed. But it was a bear.

Baumzweig came to him then. "Paula and her temper. Never mind, Hersheleh, come and say hello to the big celebrity, what can you lose?" He went docilely, shook hands with Ostrover, even complimented him on his story. Ostrover was courtly, wiped his lip, let ooze a drop of ink from a slow pen, and continued autographing books. Vorovsky lingered humbly at the rim of Ostrover's circle: his head was fierce, his eyes timid; he was steering a girl by the elbow, but the girl was mooning oven an open flyleaf, where Ostrover had written his name. Edelshtein, catching a flash of letters, was startled: it was the Yiddish version she held.

"Excuse me," he said.

"My niece," Vorovsky said.

"I see you read Yiddish," Edelshtein addressed her. "In your generation a miracle."

"Hannah, before you stands H. Edelshtein the poet."

"Edelshtein?"

"Yes."

She recited, "*Little fathers, little uncles, you with your beards and glasses and curly hair....*"

Edelshtein shut his lids and again wept.

"If it's the same Edelshtein?"

"The same," he croaked.

"My grandfather used to do that one all the time. It was in a book he had, *A Velt ohn Vint*. But it's not possible."

"Not possible?"

"That you're still alive."

"You're right, you're right," Edelshtein said, struck. "We're all ghosts here."

"My grandfather's dead."

"Forgive him."

"*He* used to read you! And he was an old man, he died years ago, and you're still alive—"

"I'm sorry," Edelshtein said. "Maybe I was young then, I began young."

"Why do you say ghosts? Ostrover's no ghost."

"No, no," he agreed. He was afraid to offend. "Listen, I'll say the rest for you. I'll take a minute only, I promise. Listen, see if you can remember from your grandfather—"

Around him, behind him, in front of him Ostrover, Vorovsky, Baumzweig, perfumed ladies, students, the young, the young, he clawed at his wet face and declaimed, he stood like a wanton stalk in the heart of an empty field:

How you spring out of the ground covered with poverty!
In your long coats, fingers rolling wax, tallow eyes.
How can I speak to you, little fathers?
You who nestled me with lyu, lyu, lyu,
lip-lullaby. Jabber of blue-eyed sailors,
how am I fallen into a stranger's womb?

Take me back with you, history has left me out.
You belong to the Angel of Death,
I to you.
Braided wraiths, smoke,
let me fall into your graves,
I have no business being your future.

He gargled, breathed, coughed, choked, tears invaded some false channel in his throat—meanwhile he swallowed up with the seizure of each bawled word this niece, this Hannah, like the rest, boots, rough full hair, a forehead made on a Jewish last, chink eyes—

At the edge of the village a little river.
Herons tip into it pecking at their images
when the waders pass whistling like Gentiles.
The herons hang, hammocks above the sweet summer-water.
Their skulls are full of secrets, their feathers scented.
The village is so little it fits into my nostril.
The roofs shimmer tar,
the sun licks thick as cow.
No one knows what will come.
How crowded with mushrooms the forest's dark floor.

Into his ear Paula said, "Hersheleh, I apologize, come home with us, please, please, I apologize." Edelshtein gave her a push, he intended to finish. "*Littleness*," he screamed,

I speak to you.
We are such a little huddle.
Our little hovels, our grandfathers' hard hands, how little,
our little, little words,
this lullaby
sung at the lip of your grave,

he screamed.

Baumzweig said, "That's one of your old good ones, the best."

"The one on my table, in progress, is the best," Edelshtein screamed, clamor still high over his head; but he felt soft, rested, calm; he knew how patient.

Ostrover said, "That one you shouldn't throw out the window."

Vorovsky began to laugh.

"This is the dead man's poem, now you know it," Edelshtein said, looking all around, pulling at his shawl, pulling and pulling at it: this too made Vorovsky laugh.

"Hannah, better take home your uncle Chaim," Ostrover said: handsome, all white, a public genius, a feather.

Edelshtein discovered he was cheated, he had not examined the girl sufficiently.

He slept in the sons' room—bunk beds piled on each other. The top one was crowded with Paula's storage boxes. He rolled back and forth on the bottom, dreaming, jerking awake, again dreaming. Now and then, with a vomitous taste, he belched up the hot cocoa Paula had given him for reconciliation. Between the Baumzweigs and himself a private violence: lacking him, whom would they patronize? They were moralists, they needed someone to feel guilty over. Another belch. He abandoned his fine but uninnocent dream —young, he was kissing Alexei's cheeks like ripe peaches, he drew away . . . it was not Alexei, it was a girl, Vorovsky's niece. After the kiss she slowly tore the pages of a book until it snowed paper, black bits of alphabet, white bits of empty margin. Paula's snore traveled down the hall to him. He writhed out of bed and groped for a lamp. With it he lit up a decrepit table covered with ancient fragile model airplanes. Some had rubber-band propellers, some were papered over a skeleton of balsa-wood ribs. A game of Monopoly lay under a samite tissue of dust. His hand fell on two old envelopes, one already browning, and without hesitation he pulled the letters out and read them:

Today was two special holidays in one, Camp Day and Sacco and Vanzetti Day. We had to put on white shirts and white shorts and go to the casino to hear Chaver Rosenbloom talk about Sacco and Vanzetti. They were a couple of Italians who were killed for loving the poor. Chaver Rosenbloom cried, and so did Mickey but I didn't. Mickey keeps forgetting to wipe himself in the toilet but I make him.

Paula and Ben: thanks so much for the little knitted suit and the clown rattle. The box was a bit smashed in but the rattle came safe anyhow. Stevie will look adorable in his new blue suit when he gets big enough for it. He already seems to like the duck on the collar. It will keep him good

and warm too. Josh has been working very hard these days
preparing for a course in the American Novel and asks me
to tell you he'll write as soon as he can. We all send love,
and Stevie sends a kiss for Grandma and Pa. *P.S.* Mickey
drove down in a pink Mercedes last week. We all had quite
a chat and told him he should settle down!

Heroes, martyrdom, a baby. Hatred for these letters made his
eyelids quiver. Ordinariness. Everything a routine. Whatever
man touches becomes banal like man. Animals don't con-
taminate nature. Only man the corrupter, the anti-divinity.
All other species live within the pulse of nature. He despised
these ceremonies and rattles and turds and kisses. The point-
lessness of their babies. Wipe one generation's ass for the
sake of wiping another generation's ass: this was his whole
definition of civilization. He pushed back the airplanes,
cleared a front patch of table with his elbow, found his pen,
wrote:

Dear Niece of Vorovsky:

It is very strange to me to feel I become a Smasher, I
who was born to being humane and filled with love for our
darling Human Race.

But nausea for his shadowy English, which he pursued in
dread, passion, bewilderment, feebleness, overcame him. He
started again in his own tongue—

Unknown Hannah:

I am a man writing you in a room of the house of
another man. He and I are secret enemies, so under his roof
it is difficult to write the truth. Yet I swear to you I will
speak these words with my heart's whole honesty. I do not
remember either your face or your body. Vaguely your
angry voice. To me you are an abstraction. I ask whether
the ancients had any physical representation of the Future,
a goddess Futura, so to speak. Presumably she would have

blank eyes, like Justice. It is an incarnation of the Future to whom this letter is addressed. Writing to the Future one does not expect an answer. The Future is an oracle for whose voice one cannot wait in inaction. One must do to be. Although a Nihilist, not by choice but by conviction, I discover in myself an unwillingness to despise survival. Often I have spat on myself for having survived the death-camps—survived them drinking tea in New York!—but today when I heard carried on your tongue some old syllables of mine I was again wheedled into tolerance of survival. The sound of a dead language on a live girl's tongue! That baby should follow baby is God's trick on us, but surely we too can have a trick on God? If we fabricate with our syllables an immortality passed from the spines of the old to the shoulders of the young, even God cannot spite it. If the prayer-load that spilled upward from the mass graves should somehow survive! If not the thicket of lamentation itself, then the language on which it rode. Hannah, youth itself is nothing unless it keeps its promise to grow old. Grow old in Yiddish, Hannah, and carry fathers and uncles into the future with you. Do this. You, one in ten thousand maybe, who were born with the gift of Yiddish in your mouth, the alphabet of Yiddish in your palm, don't make ash of these! A little while ago there were twelve million people—not including babies—who lived inside this tongue, and now what is left? A language that never had a territory except Jewish mouths, and half the Jewish mouths on earth already stopped up with German worms. The rest jabber Russian, English, Spanish, God knows what. Fifty years ago my mother lived in Russia and spoke only broken Russian, but her Yiddish was like silk. In Israel they give the language of Solomon to machinists. Rejoice—in Solomon's time what else did the mechanics speak? Yet whoever forgets Yiddish courts amnesia of history. Mourn—the forgetting has already happened. A thousand years of our travail forgotten. Here and there a word left for vaudeville jokes. Yiddish, I call on you to choose! Yiddish! Choose death or death. Which is to say death through forgetting or death through translation. Who will redeem you? What act of

salvation will restore you? All you can hope for, you tattered, you withered, is translation in America! Hannah, you
have a strong mouth, made to carry the future—

But he knew he lied, lied, lied. A truthful intention is
not enough. Oratory and declamation. A speech. A lecture.
He felt himself an obscenity. What did the death of Jews
have to do with his own troubles? His cry was ego and more
ego. His own stew, foul. Whoever mourns the dead mourns
himself. He wanted someone to read his poems, no one could
read his poems. Filth and exploitation to throw in history.
As if a dumb man should blame the ears that cannot hear
him.

He turned the paper over and wrote in big letters:

EDELSHTEIN GONE,

and went down the corridor with it in pursuit of Paula's
snore. Taken without ridicule a pleasant riverside noise.
Bird. More cow to the sight: the connubial bed, under his
gaze, gnarled and lumped—in it this old male and this old
female. He was surprised on such a cold night they slept
with only one blanket, gauzy cotton. They lay like a pair of
kingdoms in summer. Long ago they had been at war, now
they were exhausted into downy truce. Hair all over Baumzweig. Even his leg-hairs gone white. Nightstands, a pair
of them, on either side of the bed, heaped with papers, books,
magazines, lampshades sticking up out of all that like figurines
on a prow—the bedroom was Baumzweig's second office.
Towers of back issues on the floor. On the dresser a typewriter besieged by Paula's toilet water bottles and face
powder. Fragrance mixed with urinous hints. Edelshtein went
on looking at the sleepers. How reduced they seemed, each
breath a little demand for more, more, more, a shudder
of jowls; how they heaved a knee, a thumb; the tiny blue
veins all over Paula's neck. Her nightgown was stretched

away and he saw that her breasts had dropped sidewise and,
though still very fat, hung in pitiful creased bags of mole-
dappled skin. Baumzweig wore only his underwear: his
thighs were full of picked sores.

He put EDELSHTEIN GONE between their heads. Then
he took it away—on the other side was his real message:
secret enemies. He folded the sheet inside his coat pocket
and squeezed into his shoes. Cowardly. Pity for breathing
carrion. All pity is self-pity. Goethe on his deathbed: more
light!

In the street he felt liberated. A voyager. Snow was still
falling, though more lightly than before, a night-colored
blue. A veil of snow revolved in front of him, turning him
around. He stumbled into a drift, a magnificent bluish pile
slanted upward. Wetness pierced his feet like a surge of cold
blood. Beneath the immaculate lifted slope he struck stone
—the stair of a stoop. He remembered his old home, the hill
of snow behind the study-house, the smoky fire, his father
swaying nearly into the black fire and chanting, one big
duck, the stupid one, sliding on the ice. His mother's neck
too was finely veined and secretly, sweetly, luxuriantly
odorous. Deeply and gravely he wished he had worn galoshes
—no one reminds a widower. His shoes were infernos of
cold, his toes dead blocks. Himself the only life in the street,
not even a cat. The veil moved against him, turning, and
beat on his pupils. Along the curb cars squatted under humps
of snow, blue-backed tortoises. Nothing moved in the road.
His own house was far, Vorovsky's nearer, but he could not
read the street sign. A building with a canopy. Vorovsky's
hat. He made himself very small, small as a mouse, and curled
himself up in the fur of it. To be very, very little and to
live in a hat. A little wild creature in a burrow. Inside warm,
a mound of seeds nearby, licking himself for cleanliness, all
sorts of weather leaping down. His glasses fell from his face
and with an odd tiny crack hit the lid of a garbage can.
He took off one glove and felt for them in the snow. When

he found them he marveled at how the frames burned. Suppose a funeral on a night like this, how would they open the earth? His glasses were slippery as icicles when he put them on again. A crystal spectrum delighted him, but he could not see the passageway, or if there was a canopy. What he wanted from Vorovsky was Hannah.

There was no elevator. Vorovsky lived on the top floor, very high up. From his windows you could look out and see people so tiny they became patterns. It was a different building, not this one. He went down three fake-marble steps and saw a door. It was open: inside was a big black room knobby with baby carriages and tricycles. He smelled wet metal like a toothpain: life! Peretz tells how on a bitter night a Jew outside the window envied peasants swigging vodka in a hovel—friends in their prime and warm before the fire. Carriages and tricycles, instruments of Diaspora. Baumzweig with his picked sores was once also a baby. In the Diaspora the birth of a Jew increases nobody's population, the death of a Jew has no meaning. Anonymous. To have died among the martyrs—solidarity at least, a passage into history, one of the marked ones, *kiddush ha-shem.*—A telephone on the wall. He pulled off his glasses, all clouded over, and took out a pad with numbers in it and dialed.

"Ostrover?"

"Who is this?"

"*Yankel* Ostrover, the writer, or Pisher Ostrover the plumber?"

"What do you want?"

"To leave evidence," Edelshtein howled.

"Never mind! Make an end! Who's there?"

"The Messiah."

"Who is this?—Mendel, it's you?"

"Never."

"Gorochov?"

"That toenail? Please. Trust me."

"Fall into a hole!"

"This is how a man addresses his Redeemer?"

"It's five o'clock in the morning! What do you want? Bum! Lunatic! Cholera! Black year! Plague! Poisoner! Strangler!"

"You think you'll last longer than your shroud, Ostrover? Your sentences are an abomination, your style is like a pump, a pimp has a sweeter tongue—"

"Angel of Death!"

He dialed Vorovsky but there was no answer.

The snow had turned white as the white of an eye. He wandered toward Hannah's house, though he did not know where she lived, or what her name was, or whether he had ever seen her. On the way he rehearsed what he would say to her. But this was not satisfactory, he could lecture but not speak into a face. He bled to retrieve her face. He was in pursuit of her, she was his destination. Why? What does a man look for, what does he need? What can a man retrieve? Can the future retrieve the past? And if retrieve, how redeem? His shoes streamed. Each step was a pond. The herons in spring, red-legged. Secret eyes they have: the eyes of birds—frightening. Too open. The riddle of openness. His feet poured rivers. Cold, cold.

> *Little old man in the cold,*
> *come hop up on the stove,*
> *your wife will give you a crust with jam.*
> *Thank you, muse, for this little psalm.*

He belched. His stomach was unwell. Indigestion? A heart attack? He wiggled the fingers of his left hand: though frozen they tingled. Heart. Maybe only ulcer. Cancer, like Mireleh? In a narrow bed he missed his wife. How much longer could he expect to live? An unmarked grave. Who would know he had ever been alive? He had no descendants, his grandchildren were imaginary. *O my unborn grandson*

. . . Hackneyed. *Ungrandfathered ghost* . . . Too baroque.
Simplicity, purity, truthfulness.
   He wrote:

Dear Hannah:

   You made no impression on me. When I wrote you
before at Baumzweig's I lied. I saw you for a second in a
public place, so what? Holding a Yiddish book. A young
face on top of a Yiddish book. Nothing else. For me this
is worth no somersault. Ostrover's vomit!—that popularizer,
vulgarian, panderer to people who have lost the memory of
peoplehood. A thousand times a pimp. Your uncle Chaim
said about you: "She writes." A pity on his judgment.
Writes! Writes! Potatoes in a sack! Another one! What do
you write? When will you write? How will you write?
Either you'll become an editor of *Good Housekeeping*, or,
if serious, join the gang of so-called Jewish novelists. I've
sniffed them all, I'm intimate with their smell. Satirists they
call themselves. Picking at their crotches. What do they
know, I mean of *knowledge*? To satirize you have to know
something. In a so-called novel by a so-called Jewish novelist
(*"activist-existential"*—listen, I understand, I read everything!)—Elkin, Stanley, to keep to only one example—the
hero visits Williamsburg to contact a so-called "miracle
rabbi." Even the word *rabbi!* No, listen—to me, a descend-
ant of the Vilna Gaon myself, the *guter yid* is a charlatan
and his *chasidim* are victims, never mind if willing or not.
But that's not the point. You have to KNOW SOMETHING!
At least the difference between a *rav* and a *rebbeh!* At
least a *pinteleh* here and there! Otherwise where's the joke,
where's the satire, where's the mockery? American-born!
An ignoramus mocks only himself. *Jewish* novelists! Savages! The allrightnik's children, all they know is to curse
the allrightnik! Their Yiddish! One word here, one word
there. *Shikseh* on one page, *putz* on the other, and that's the
whole vocabulary! And when they give a try at phonetic
rendition! Darling God! If they had mothers and fathers,
they crawled out of the swamps. Their grandparents were

tree-squirrels if that's how they held their mouths. They know ten words for, excuse me, penis, and when it comes to a word for learning they're impotent!

Joy, joy! He felt himself on the right course at last. Daylight was coming, a yellow elephant rocked silently by in the road. A little light burned eternally on its tusk. He let it slide past, he stood up to the knees in the river at home, whirling with joy. He wrote:

TRUTH!

But this great thick word, Truth!, was too harsh, oaken; with his finger in the snow he crossed it out.

I was saying: indifference. I'm indifferent to you and your kind. Why should I think you're another species, something better? Because you knew a shred of a thread of a poem of mine? Ha! I was seduced by my own vanity. I have a foolish tendency to make symbols out of glimpses. My poor wife, peace on her, used to ridicule me for this. Riding in the subway once I saw a beautiful child, a boy about twelve. A Puerto Rican, dusky, yet he had cheeks like pomegranates. I once knew, in Kiev, a child who looked like that. I admit to it. A portrait under the skin of my eyes. The love of a man for a boy. Why not confess it? Is it against the nature of man to rejoice in beauty? "This is to be expected with a childless man"—my wife's verdict. That what I wanted was a son. Take this as a complete explanation: if an ordinary person cannot

The end of the sentence flew like a leaf out of his mind . . . it was turning into a quarrel with Mireleh. Who quarrels with the dead? He wrote:

Esteemed Alexei Yosifovitch:

You remain. You remain. An illumination. More than my own home, nearer than my mother's mouth. Nimbus.

Your father slapped my father. You were never told. Because I kissed you on the green stairs. The shadow-place on the landing where I once saw the butler scratch his pants. They sent us away shamed. My father and I, into the mud.

Again a lie. Never near the child. Lying is like a vitamin, it has to fortify everything. Only through the doorway, looking, looking. The gleaming face: the face of flame. Or would test him on verb-forms: *kal, nifal, piel, pual, hifil, hofal, hispael.* On the afternoons the Latin tutor came, crouched outside the threshold, Edelshtein heard *ego, mei, mihi, me, me.* May may. Beautiful foreign nasal chant of riches. Latin! Dirty from the lips of idolators. An apostate family. Edelshtein and his father took their coffee and bread, but otherwise lived on boiled eggs: the elder Kirilov one day brought home with him the *mashgiach* from the Jewish poorhouse to testify to the purity of the servants' kitchen, but to Edelshtein's father the whole house was *treyf*, the *mashgiach* himself a hired impostor. Who would oversee the overseer? Among the Kirilovs with their lying name money was the best overseer. Money saw to everything. Though they had their particular talent. Mechanical. Alexei Y. Kirilov, engineer. Bridges, towers. Consultant to Cairo. Builder of the Aswan Dam, assistant to Pharaoh for the latest Pyramid. To set down such a fantasy about such an important Soviet brain . . . poor little Alexei, Avremeleh, I'll jeopardize your position in life, little corpse of Babi Yar.

Only focus. Hersh! Scion of the Vilna Gaon! Prince of rationality! Pay attention!

He wrote:

The gait—the prance, the hobble—of Yiddish is not the same as the gait of English. A big headache for a translator probably. In Yiddish you use more words than in English. Nobody believes it but it's true. Another big problem is form. The moderns take the old forms and fill them up with mockery, love, drama, satire, etc. Plenty of play. But

STILL THE SAME OLD FORMS, conventions left over from the
last century even. It doesn't matter who denies this, out of
pride: it's true. Pour in symbolism, impressionism, be com-
plex, be subtle, be daring, take risks, break your teeth—
whatever you do, it still comes out Yiddish. *Mamaloshen*
doesn't produce *Wastelands*. No alienation, no nihilism, no
dadaism. With all the suffering no smashing! No INCOHER-
ENCE! Keep the latter in mind, Hannah, if you expect to
make progress. Also: please remember that when a goy from
Columbus, Ohio, says "Elijah the Prophet" he's not talking
about *Eliohu hanovi*. Eliohu is one of us, a *folksmensh*,
running around in second-hand clothes. Theirs is God knows
what. The same biblical figure, with exactly the same history, once he puts on a name from King James, COMES OUT
A DIFFERENT PERSON. Life, history, hope, tragedy, they don't
come out even. They talk Bible Lands, with us it's *eretz
yisroel*. A misfortune.

Astonished, he struck up against a kiosk. A telephone!
On a street corner! He had to drag the door open, pulling
a load of snow. Then he squeezed inside. His fingers were
sticks. Never mind the pad, he forgot even where the pocket
was. In his coat? Jacket? Pants? With one stick he dialed
Vorovsky's number: from memory.
   "Hello, Chaim?"
   "This is Ostrover."
   "Ostrover! Why Ostrover? What are you doing there?
I want Vorovsky."
   "Who's this?"
   "Edelshtein."
   "I thought so. A persecution, what is this? I could send
you to jail for tricks like before—"
   "Quick, give me Vorovsky."
   "I'll *give* you."
   "Vorovsky's not home?"
   "How do I know if Vorovsky's home? It's dawn, go ask
Vorovsky!"

Edelshtein grew weak: "I called the wrong number."

"Hersheleh, if you want some friendly advice you'll listen to me. I can get you jobs at fancy out-of-town country clubs, Miami Florida included, plenty of speeches your own style, only what they need is rational lecturers not lunatics. If you carry on like tonight you'll lose what you have."

"I don't have anything."

"Accept life, Edelshtein."

"Dead man, I appreciate your guidance."

"Yesterday I heard from Hollywood, they're making a movie from one of my stories. So now tell me again who's dead."

"The puppet the ventriloquist holds in his lap. A piece of log. It's somebody else's language and the dead doll sits there."

"Wit, you want them to make movies in Yiddish now?"

"In Talmud if you save a single life it's as if you saved the world. And if you save a language? Worlds maybe. Galaxies. The whole universe."

"Hersheleh, the God of the Jews made a mistake when he didn't have a son, it would be a good occupation for you."

"Instead I'll be an extra in your movie. If they shoot the *shtetl* on location in Kansas send me expense money. I'll come and be local color for you. I'll put on my *shtreiml* and walk around, the people should see a real Jew. For ten dollars more I'll even speak *mamaloshen*."

Ostrover said, "It doesn't matter what you speak, envy sounds the same in all languages."

Edelshtein said, "Once there was a ghost who thought he was still alive. You know what happened to him? He got up one morning and began to shave and he cut himself. And there was no blood. No blood at all. And he still didn't believe it, so he looked in the mirror to see. And there was no reflection, no sign of himself. He wasn't there. But he still didn't believe it, so he began to scream, but there was no sound, no sound at all—"

There was no sound from the telephone. He let it dangle and rock.

He looked for the pad. Diligently he consulted himself: pants cuffs have a way of catching necessary objects. The number had fallen out of his body. Off his skin. He needed Vorovsky because he needed Hannah. Worthwhile maybe to telephone Baumzweig for Vorovsky's number, Paula could look it up—Baumzweig's number he knew by heart, no mistake. He had singled out his need. Svengali, Pygmalion, Rasputin, Dr. (jokes aside) Frankenstein. What does it require to make a translator? A secondary occupation. Parasitic. But your own creature. Take this girl Hannah and train her. His alone. American-born but she had the advantage over him, English being no worm on her palate; also she could read his words in the original. Niece of a vanquished mind—still, genes are in reality God, and if Vorovsky had a little talent for translation why not the niece?—Or the other. Russia. The one in the Soviet Union who wrote two stanzas in Yiddish. In Yiddish! And only twenty! Born 1948, same year they made up to be the Doctors' Plot, Stalin already very busy killing Jews, Markish, Kvitko, Kushnirov, Hofshtein, Mikhoels, Susskin, Bergelson, Feffer, Gradzenski with the wooden leg. All slaughtered. How did Yiddish survive in the mouth of that girl? Nurtured in secret. Taught by an obsessed grandfather, a crazy uncle: Marranos. The poem reprinted, as they say, in the West. (The West! If a Jew says "the West," he sounds like an imbecile. In a puddle what's West, what's East?) Flowers, blue sky, she yearns for the end of winter: very nice. A zero, and received like a prodigy! An aberration! A miracle! Because composed in the lost tongue. As if some Neapolitan child suddenly begins to prattle in Latin. Not the same. Little verses merely. Death confers awe. Russian: its richness, directness. For "iron" and "weapon" the same word. A *thick* language, a world-language. He visualized himself translated into Russian, covertly, by the Marranos' daughter. To be circulated, in typescript, underground: to be read, read!

Understand me, Hannah—that our treasure-tongue is derived from strangers means nothing. 90 per cent German roots, 10 per cent Slavic: irrelevant. The Hebrew take for granted without percentages. We are a people who have known how to forge the language of need out of the language of necessity. Our reputation among ourselves as a nation of scholars is mostly empty. In actuality we are a mob of working people, laborers, hewers of wood, believe me. Leivik, our chief poet, was a house painter. Today all pharmacists, lawyers, accountants, haberdashers, but tickle the lawyer and you'll see his grandfather sawed wood for a living. That's how it is with us. Nowadays the Jew is forgetful, everybody with a profession, every Jewish boy a professor—justice seems less urgent. Most don't realize this quiet time is only another Interim. Always, like in a terrible Wagnerian storm, we have our interludes of rest. So now. Once we were slaves, now we are free men, remember the bread of affliction. But listen. Whoever cries Justice! is a liberated slave. Whoever honors Work is a liberated slave. They accuse Yiddish literature of sentimentality in this connection. Very good, true. True, so be it! A dwarf at a sewing machine can afford a little loosening of the heart. I return to Leivik. He could hang wallpaper. I once lived in a room he papered—yellow vines. Rutgers Street that was. A good job, no bubbles, no peeling. This from a poet of very morbid tendencies. Mani Leib fixed shoes. Moishe Leib Halpern was a waiter, once in a while a handyman. I could tell you the names of twenty poets of very pure expression who were operators, pressers, cutters. In addition to fixing shoes Mani Leib was also a laundryman. I beg you not to think I'm preaching Socialism. To my mind politics is dung.

What I mean is something else: Work is Work, and Thought
is Thought. Politics tries to mix these up, Socialism especially. The language of a hard-pressed people works under
the laws of purity, dividing the Commanded from the Profane. I remember one of my old teachers. He used to take
attendance every day and he gave his occupation to the tax-
ing council as "attendance-taker"—so that he wouldn't be
getting paid for teaching Torah. This with five pupils, all
living in his house and fed by his wife! Call it splitting a
hair if you want, but it's the hair of a head that distinguished
between the necessary and the merely needed. People who
believe that Yiddish is, as they like to say, "richly inter-
mixed," and that in Yiddishkeit the presence of the Cove-
nant, of Godliness, inhabits humble things and humble
words, are under a delusion or a deception. The slave knows
exactly when he belongs to God and when to the oppressor.
The liberated slave who is not forgetful and can remember
when he himself was an artifact, knows exactly the difference between God and an artifact. A language also knows
whom it is serving at each moment. I am feeling very cold
right now. Of course you see that when I say liberated I
mean self-liberated. Moses not Lincoln, not Franz Josef. Yiddish is the language of auto-emancipation. Theodor Herzl
wrote in German but the message spread in *mamaloshen*—
my God cold. Naturally the important thing is to stick to
what you learned as a slave including language, and not to
speak their language, otherwise you will become like them,
acquiring their confusion between God and artifact and
consequently their taste for making slaves, both of themselves and others.

Slave of rhetoric! This is the trouble when you use God
for a Muse. Philosophers, thinkers—all cursed. Poets have it
better: most are Greeks and pagans, unbelievers except in
natural religion, stones, stars, body. This cube and cell.
Ostrover had already sentenced him to jail, little booth in the
vale of snow; black instrument beeped from a gallows. The
white pad—something white—on the floor. Edelshtein bent

for it and struck his jaw. Through the filth of the glass doors morning rose out of the dark. He saw what he held:

"ALL OF US ARE HUMANS TOGETHER
BUT SOME HUMANS SHOULD DROP DEAD."

DO YOU FEEL THIS?

IF SO CALL TR 5-2530 IF YOU WANT TO
KNOW WHETHER YOU WILL SURVIVE IN
CHRIST'S FIVE-DAY INEXPENSIVE
ELECT-PLAN

*

"AUDITORY PHRENOLOGY"
PRACTICED FREE FREE

*

(PLEASE NO ATHEISTS OR CRANK CALLS
WE ARE SINCERE SCIENTIFIC SOUL-SOCIOLOGISTS)

*

ASK FOR ROSE OR LOU
WE LOVE YOU

He was touched and curious, but withdrawn. The cold lit him unfamiliarly: his body a brilliant hollowness, emptied of organs, cleansed of debris, the inner flanks of him perfect lit glass. A clear chalice. Of small change he had only a nickel and a dime. For the dime he could CALL TR 5-2530 and take advice appropriate to his immaculateness, his transparency. Rose or Lou. He had no satire for their love. How manifold and various the human imagination. The simplicity of an ascent lured him, he was alert to the probability of levitation but disregarded it. The disciples of Reb Moshe of Kobryn also disregarded feats in opposition to nature—they had no awe for their master when he hung in air, but when he slept —the miracle of his lung, his breath, his heartbeat! He lurched from the booth into rushing daylight. The depth of snow sucked off one of his shoes. The serpent too prospers without feet, so he cast off his and weaved on. His arms, particularly his hands, particularly those partners of mind his fingers, he was sorry to lose. He knew his eyes, his tongue, his stinging loins. He was again tempted to ascend. The hillock was profound. He outwitted it by creeping through it, he drilled patiently into the snow. He wanted to stand then, but without legs could not. Indolently he permitted himself to rise. He went only high enough to see the snowy sidewalks, the mounds in gutters and against stoops, the beginning of business time. Lifted light. A doorman fled out of a building wearing earmuffs, pulling a shovel behind him like a little tin cart. Edelshtein drifted no higher than the man's shoulders. He watched the shovel pierce the snow, tunneling down, but there was no bottom, the earth was without foundation.

He came under a black wing. He thought it was the first blindness of Death but it was only a canopy.

The doorman went on digging under the canopy; under the canopy Edelshtein tasted wine and felt himself at a wedding, his own, the canopy covering his steamy gold eyeglasses made blind by Mireleh's veil. Four beings held up the poles: one his wife's cousin the postman, one his own cousin the druggist; two poets. The first poet was a beggar who lived on institutional charity—Baumzweig; the second, Silverman, sold ladies' elastic stockings, the kind for varicose veins. The postman and the druggist were still alive, only one of them retired. The poets were ghosts, Baumzweig picking at himself in bed also a ghost, Silverman long dead, more than twenty years—*lideleh-shreiber* they called him, he wrote for the popular theater. "Song to Steerage": *Steerage, steerage, I remember the crowds, the rags we took with us we treated like shrouds, we tossed them away when we spied out the shore, going re-born through the Golden Door.* . . . Even on Second Avenue 1905 was already stale, but it stopped the show, made fevers, encores, tears, yells. Golden sidewalks. America the bride, under her fancy gown nothing. Poor Silverman, in love with the Statue of Liberty's lifted arm, what did he do in his life besides raise up a post at an empty wedding, no progeny? The doorman dug out a piece of statuary, an urn with a stone wreath. Under the canopy Edelshtein recognized it. Sand, butts, a half-naked angel astride the wreath. Once Edelshtein saw a condom in it. Found! Vorovsky's building. There is no God, yet who brought him here if not the King of the Universe? Not so bad off after all, even in a snowstorm he could find his way, an expert, he knew one block from another in this desolation of a world.

He carried his shoe into the elevator like a baby, an orphan, a redemption. He could kiss even a shoe.

In the corridor laughter, toilets flushing; coffee stabbed him.

He rang the bell.

From behind Vorovsky's door, laughter, laughter!

No one came.

He rang again. No one came. He banged. "Chaim, crazy man, open up!" No one came. "A dead man from the cold knocks, you don't come? Hurry up, open, I'm a stick of ice, you want a dead man at your door? Mercy! Pity! Open up!"

No one came.

He listened to the laughter. It had a form; a method, rather: some principle, closer to physics than music, of arching up and sinking back. Inside the shape barks, howls, dogs, wolves, wilderness. After each fright a crevice to fall into. He made an anvil of his shoe and took the doorknob for an iron hammer and thrust. He thrust, thrust. The force of an iceberg.

Close to the knob a panel bulged and cracked. Not his fault. On the other side someone was unused to the lock.

He heard Vorovsky but saw Hannah.

She said: "What?"

"You don't remember me? I'm the one what recited to

you tonight my work from several years past, I was passing
by in your uncle's neighborhood—"

"He's sick."

"What, a fit?"

"All night. I've been here the whole night. The whole
night—"

"Let me in."

"Please go away. I just told you."

"In. What's the matter with you? I'm sick myself, I'm
dead from cold! Hey, Chaim! Lunatic, stop it!"

Vorovsky was on his belly on the floor, stifling his
mouth with a pillow as if it were a stone, knocking his head
down on it, but it was no use, the laughter shook the pillow
and came yelping out, not muffled but increased, darkened.
He laughed and said "Hannah" and laughed.

Edelshtein took a chair and dragged it near Vorovsky
and sat. The room stank, a subway latrine.

"Stop," he said.

Vorovsky laughed.

"All right, merriment, very good, be happy. You're
warm, I'm cold. Have mercy, little girl—tea. Hannah. Boil
it up hot. Pieces of flesh drop from me." He heard that he
was speaking Yiddish, so he began again for her. "I'm sorry.
Forgive me. A terrible thing to do. I was lost outside, I was
looking, so now I found you, I'm sorry."

"It isn't a good time for a visit, that's all."

"Bring some tea also for your uncle."

"He can't."

"He can maybe, let him try. Someone who laughs like
this is ready for a feast—*flanken, tsimmis, rosselfleysh*—" In
Yiddish he said, "In the world-to-come people dance at parties like this, all laughter, joy. The day after the Messiah
people laugh like this."

Vorovsky laughed and said "Messiah" and sucked the
pillow, spitting. His face was a flood: tears ran upside down
into his eyes, over his forehead, saliva sprang in puddles

around his ears. He was spitting, crying, burbling, he gasped, wept, spat. His eyes were bloodshot, the whites showed like slashes, wounds; he still wore his hat. He laughed, he was still laughing. His pants were wet, the fly open, now and then seeping. He dropped the pillow for tea and ventured a sip, with his tongue, like an animal full of hope—vomit rolled up with the third swallow and he laughed between spasms, he was still laughing, stinking, a sewer.

Edelshtein took pleasure in the tea, it touched him to the root, more gripping on his bowel than the coffee that stung the hall. He praised himself with no meanness, no bitterness: prince of rationality! Thawing, he said, "Give him *schnapps*, he can hold *schnapps*, no question."

"He drank and he vomited."

"Chaim, little soul," Edelshtein said, "what started you off? Myself. I was there. I said it, I said graves, I said smoke. I'm the responsible one. Death. Death, I'm the one who said it. Death you laugh at, you're no coward."

"If you want to talk business with my uncle come another time."

"Death is business?"

Now he examined her. Born 1945, in the hour of the death-camps. Not selected. Immune. The whole way she held herself looked immune—by this he meant American. Still, an exhausted child, straggled head, remarkable child to stay through the night with the madman. "Where's your mother?" he said. "Why doesn't she come and watch her brother? Why does it fall on you? You should be free, you have your own life."

"You don't know anything about families."

She was acute: no mother, father, wife, child, what did he know about families? He was cut off, a survivor. "I know your uncle," he said, but without belief: in the first place Vorovsky had an education. "In his right mind your uncle doesn't want you to suffer."

Vorovsky, laughing, said "Suffer."

"He likes to suffer. He wants to suffer. He admires suffering. All you people want to suffer."

Pins and needles: Edelshtein's fingertips were fevering. He stroked the heat of the cup. He could feel. He said, " 'You people'?"

"You Jews."

"Aha. Chaim, you hear? Your niece Hannah—on the other side already, never mind she's acquainted with *mamaloshen*. In one generation, 'you Jews.' You don't like suffering? Maybe you respect it?"

"It's unnecessary."

"It comes from history, history is also unnecessary?"

"History's a waste."

America the empty bride. Edelshtein said, "You're right about business. I came on business. My whole business is waste."

Vorovsky laughed and said "Hersheleh Frog Frog Frog."

"I think you're making him worse," Hannah said. "Tell me what you want and I'll give him the message."

"He's not deaf."

"He doesn't remember afterward—"

"I have no message."

"Then what do you want from him?"

"Nothing. I want from you."

"Frog Frog Frog Frog Frog."

Edelshtein finished his tea and put the cup on the floor and for the first time absorbed Vorovsky's apartment: until now Vorovsky had kept him out. It was one room, sink and stove behind a plastic curtain, bookshelves leaning over not with books but journals piled flat, a sticky table, a sofa-bed, a desk, six kitchen chairs, and along the walls seventy-five cardboard boxes which Edelshtein knew harbored two thousand copies of Vorovsky's dictionary. A pity on Vorovsky, he had a dispute with the publisher, who turned back half the printing to him. Vorovsky had to pay for two thousand German-English mathematical dictionaries, and now he had to sell them himself, but he did not know what to do, how to go about it. It was his fate to swallow what he first excreted. Because of a mishap in business he owned his life, he possessed what he was, a slave, but invisible. A hungry snake has to eat its tail all the way down to the head until it disappears.

Hannah said: "What could I do for you"—flat, not a question.

"Again 'you.' A distinction, a separation. What I'll ask is this: annihilate 'you,' annihilate 'me.' We'll come to an understanding, we'll get together."

She bent for his cup and he saw her boot. He was afraid of a boot. He said mildly, nicely, "Look, your uncle tells me you're one of us. By 'us' he means writer, no?"

"By 'us' you mean Jew."

"And you're not a Jew, *meydeleh?*"

"Not your kind."

"Nowadays there have to be kinds? Good, bad, old, new—"

"Old and new."

"All right! So let it be old and new, fine, a reasonable beginning. Let old work with new. Listen, I need a collaborator. Not exactly a collaborator, it's not even complicated like that. What I need is a translator."

"My uncle the translator is indisposed."

At that moment Edelshtein discovered he hated irony. He yelled, "Not your uncle. You! You!"

Howling, Vorovsky crawled to a tower of cartons and beat on them with his bare heels. There was an alteration in his laughter, something not theatrical but of the theater—he was amused, entertained, clowns paraded between his legs.

"You'll save Yiddish," Edelshtein said, "you'll be like a Messiah to a whole generation, a whole literature, naturally you'll have to work at it, practice, it takes knowledge, it takes a gift, a genius, a born poet—"

Hannah walked in her boots with his dirty teacup. From

behind the plastic he heard the faucet. She opened the curtain and came out and said: "You old men."

"Ostrover's pages you kiss!"

"You jealous old men from the ghetto," she said.

"And Ostrover's young, a young prince? Listen! You don't see, you don't follow—translate me, lift me out of the ghetto, it's my life that's hanging on you!"

Her voice was a whip. "Bloodsuckers," she said. "It isn't a translator you're after, it's someone's soul. Too much history's drained your blood, you want someone to take you over, a dybbuk—"

"Dybbuk! Ostrover's language. All right, I need a dybbuk, I'll become a golem, I don't care, it doesn't matter! Breathe in me! Animate me! Without you I'm a clay pot!" Bereaved, he yelled, "Translate me!"

The clowns ran over Vorovsky's charmed belly.

Hannah said: "You think I have to read Ostrover in translation? You think translation has anything to do with what Ostrover is?"

Edelshtein accused her, "Who taught you to read Yiddish?—A girl like that, to know the letters worthy of life and to be ignorant! 'You Jews,' 'you people,' you you you!"

"I learned, my grandfather taught me, I'm not responsible for it, I didn't go looking for it, I was smart, a golden head, same as now. But I have my own life, you said it yourself, I don't have to throw it out. So pay attention, Mr. Vampire: even in Yiddish Ostrover's not in the ghetto. Even in Yiddish he's not like you people."

"He's not in the ghetto? Which ghetto, what ghetto? So where is he? In the sky? In the clouds? With the angels? Where?"

She meditated, she was all intelligence. "In the world," she answered him.

"In the marketplace. A fishwife, a *kochleffel*, everything's his business, you he'll autograph, me he'll get jobs, he listens to everybody."

"Whereas you people listen only to yourselves."

In the room something was absent.

Edelshtein, pushing into his snow-damp shoe, said into the absence, "So? You're not interested?"

"Only in the mainstream. Not in your little puddles."

"Again the ghetto. Your uncle stinks from the ghetto? Graduated, 1924, the University of Berlin, Vorovsky stinks from the ghetto? Myself, four God-given books not one living human being knows, I stink from the ghetto? God, four thousand years since Abraham hanging out with Jews, God also stinks from the ghetto?"

"Rhetoric," Hannah said. "Yiddish literary rhetoric. That's the style."

"Only Ostrover doesn't stink from the ghetto."

"A question of vision."

"Better say visions. He doesn't know real things."

"He knows a reality beyond realism."

"American literary babies! And in your language you don't have a rhetoric?" Edelshtein burst out. "Very good, he's achieved it, Ostrover's the world. A pantheist, a pagan, a goy."

"That's it. You've nailed it. A Freudian, a Jungian, a sensibility. No little love stories. A contemporary. He speaks for everybody."

"Aha. Sounds familiar already. For humanity he speaks? Humanity?"

"Humanity," she said.

"And to speak for Jews isn't to speak for humanity? We're not human? We're not present on the face of the earth? We don't suffer? In Russia they let us live? In Egypt they don't want to murder us?"

"Suffer suffer," she said. "I like devils best. They don't think only about themselves and they don't suffer."

Immediately, looking at Hannah—my God, an old man, he was looking at her little waist, underneath it where the little apple of her womb was hidden away—immediately, all

at once, instantaneously, he fell into a chaos, a trance, of truth,
of actuality: was it possible? He saw everything in miraculous
reversal, blessed—everything plain, distinct, understandable,
true. What he understood was this: that the ghetto was the
real world, and the outside world only a ghetto. Because in
actuality who was shut off? Who then was really buried,
removed, inhabited by darkness? To whom, in what little
space, did God offer Sinai? Who kept Terach and who followed Abraham? Talmud explains that when the Jews went
into Exile, God went into Exile also. Babi Yar is maybe
the real world, and Kiev with its German toys, New York
with all its terrible intelligence, all fictions, fantasies. Un-
reality.

An infatuation! He was the same, all his life the same
as this poisonous wild girl, he coveted mythologies, specters,
animals, voices. Western Civilization his secret guilt, he was
ashamed of the small tremor of his self-love, degraded by
being ingrown. Alexei with his skin a furnace of desire, his
trucks and trains! He longed to be Alexei. Alexei with his
German toys and his Latin! Alexei whose destiny was to
grow up into the world-at-large, to slip from the ghetto, to
break out into engineering for Western Civilization! Alexei,
I abandon you! I'm at home only in a prison, history is my
prison, the ravine my house, only listen—suppose it turns out
that the destiny of the Jews is vast, open, eternal, and that
Western Civilization is meant to dwindle, shrivel, shrink
into the ghetto of the world—what of history then? Kings,
Parliaments, like insects, Presidents like vermin, their religion a row of little dolls, their art a cave smudge, their
poetry a lust—Avremeleh, when you fell from the ledge
over the ravine into your grave, for the first time you fell
into reality.

To Hannah he said: "I didn't ask to be born into
Yiddish. It came on me."

He meant he was blessed.

"So keep it," she said, "and don't complain."

With the whole ferocity of his delight in it he hit her mouth. The madman again struck up his laugh. Only now was it possible to notice that something had stopped it before. A missing harp. The absence filled with bloody laughter, bits of what looked like red pimento hung in the vomit on Vorovsky's chin, the clowns fled, Vorovsky's hat with its pinnacle of fur dangled on his chest—he was spent, he was beginning to fall into the quake of sleep, he slept, he dozed, roars burst from him, he hiccuped, woke, laughed, an enormous grief settled in him, he went on napping and laughing, grief had him in its teeth.

Edelshtein's hand, the cushiony underside of it, blazed from giving the blow. "You," he said, "you have no ideas, what are you?" A shred of learning flaked from him, what the sages said of Job ripped from his tongue like a peeling of the tongue itself, *he never was, he never existed*. "You were never born, you were never created!" he yelled. "Let me tell you, a dead man tells you this, at least i had a life, at least I understood something!"

"Die," she told him. "Die now, all you old men, what are you waiting for? Hanging on my neck, him and now you, the whole bunch of you, parasites, hurry up and die."

His palm burned, it was the first time he had ever slapped a child. He felt like a father. Her mouth lay back naked on her face. Out of spite, against instinct, she kept her hands from the bruise—he could see the shape of her teeth, turned a little one on the other, imperfect, again vulnerable. From fury her nose streamed. He had put a bulge in her lip.

"Forget Yiddish!" he screamed at her. "Wipe it out of your brain! Extirpate it! Go get a memory operation! You have no right to it, you have no right to an uncle, a grandfather! No one ever came before you, you were never born! A vacuum!"

"You old atheists," she called after him. "You dead old socialists. Boring! You bore me to death. You hate magic, you hate imagination, you talk God and you hate God, you despise, you bore, you envy, you eat people up with your disgusting old age—cannibals, all you care about is your own youth, you're finished, give somebody else a turn!" This held him. He leaned on the door frame. "A turn at what? I didn't offer you a turn? An opportunity of a life-time? To be published now, in youth, in babyhood, early in life? Translated I'd be famous, this you don't understand. Hannah, listen," he said, kindly, ingratiatingly, reasoning with her like a father, "you don't have to like my poems, do I ask you to *like* them? I don't ask you to like them, I don't ask you to respect them, I don't ask you to love them. A man my age, do I want a lover or a translator? Am I ask-ing a favor? No. Look," he said, "one thing I forgot to tell you. A business deal. That's all. Business, plain and simple. I'll pay you. You didn't think I wouldn't pay, God forbid?"

Now she covered her mouth. He wondered at his need to weep; he was ashamed.

"Hannah, please, how much? I'll pay, you'll see. What-ever you like. You'll buy anything you want. Dresses, shoes—" *Gottenyu*, what could such a wild beast want? "You'll buy more boots, all kinds of boots, whatever you want, books, everything—" He said relentlessly, "You'll have from me money."

"No," she said, "no."

"Please. What will happen to me? What's wrong? My ideas aren't good enough? Who asks you to believe in my beliefs? I'm an old man, used up, I have nothing to say any more, anything I ever said was all imitation. Walt Whitman I used to like. Also John Donne. Poets, masters. We, what have we got? A Yiddish Keats? Never—" He was ashamed, so he wiped his cheeks with both sleeves. "Business. I'll pay you," he said.

"No."

"Because I laid a hand on you? Forgive me, I apologize. I'm crazier than he is, I should be locked up for it—"

"Not because of that."

"Then why not? *Meydeleh*, why not? What harm would it do you? Help out an old man."

She said desolately, "You don't interest me. I would have to be interested."

"I see. Naturally." He looked at Vorovsky. "Goodbye, Chaim, regards from Aristotle. What distinguishes men from the beasts is the power of ha-ha-ha. So good morning, ladies and gentlemen. Be well. Chaim, live until a hundred and twenty. The main thing is health."

In the street it was full day, and he was warm from the tea. The road glistened, the sidewalks. Paths crisscrossed in unexpected places, sleds clanged, people ran. A drugstore was open and he went in to telephone Baumzweig: he dialed, but on the way he skipped a number, heard an iron noise like a weapon, and had to dial again. "Paula," he practiced, "I'll come back for a while, all right? For breakfast maybe," but instead he changed his mind and decided to CALL TR 5-2530. At the other end of the wire it was either Rose or Lou. Edelshtein told the eunuch's voice, "I believe with you about some should drop dead. Pharaoh, Queen Isabella, Haman, that pogromchik King Louis they call in history Saint, Hitler, Stalin, Nasser—" The voice said, "You're a Jew?" It sounded Southern but somehow not Negro— maybe because schooled, polished: "Accept Jesus as your Saviour and you shall have Jerusalem restored." "We already got it," Edelshtein said. *Meshiachtseiten!* "The terrestrial Jerusalem has no significance. Earth is dust. The Kingdom of God is within. Christ released man from Judaic exclusivism." "Who's excluding who?" Edelshtein said. "Christianity is Judaism universalized. Jesus is Moses publicized for ready availability. Our God is the God of Love, your God is the God of Wrath. Look how He abandoned you in Auschwitz." "It wasn't only God who didn't notice." "You people are cowards, you never even tried to defend yourselves. You got a wide streak of yellow, you don't know how to hold

a gun." "Tell it to the Egyptians," Edelshtein said. "Everyone you come into contact with turns into your enemy.
When you were in Europe every nation despised you. When
you moved to take over the Middle East the Arab Nation,
spic faces like your own, your very own blood-kin, began
to hate you. You are a bone in the throat of all mankind."
"Who gnaws at bones? Dogs and rats only." "Even your
food habits are abnormal, against the grain of quotidian delight. You refuse to seethe a lamb in the milk of its mother.
You will not eat a fertilized egg because it has a spot of
blood on it. When you wash your hands you chant. You
pray in a debased jargon, not in the beautiful sacramental
English of our Holy Bible." Edelshtein said, "That's right,
Jesus spoke the King's English." "Even now, after the good
Lord knows how many years in America, you talk with a
kike accent. You kike, you Yid."

Edelshtein shouted into the telephone, "Amalekite!
Titus! Nazi! The whole world is infected by you anti-
Semites! On account of you children become corrupted!
On account of you I lost everything, my whole life! On
account of you I have no translator!"

The
Suitcase

M R. HENCKE, the father of the artist, was a German, an architect, and a traveler—not particularly in that order of importance. He had flown a Fokker for the Kaiser, but there was little of the pilot left in him: he had a rather commonplace military-like snap to his shoulders, especially when he was about to meet someone new. This was not because he had been in the fierce and rigid Air Force, but because he was clandestinely shy. His long grim face, with the mouth running across its lower hem like a slipped thread in a linen sack, was as pitted as a battlefield. Under a magnifying glass his skin would have shown moon-craters. As a boy he had had the smallpox. He lived in a big yellow-brick house in Virginia, and no longer thought of himself as a German. He did not have German thoughts, except in a certain recurring dream, in which he always rode naked on a saddleless horse, holding on to its black moist mane and crying *"Schneller, schneller."* With the slowness of anguish they glided over a meadow he remembered from childhood, past the millhouse, into a green endlessness hazy with buttercups. Sometimes the horse, which he knew was a stallion, nevertheless seemed to be his wife, who was dead. He was sorry he had named his son after himself—what a name for a boy to have come through Yale with! If he had it to do over again he would have called him John.

"Where am I to put my bag?" he asked Gottfried, who was paying the truckmen and did not hear. His father saw a gray-green flash of money. The truckmen began setting up rows of folding chairs, and he guessed that Gottfried had tipped them to do it. Gottfried had organized everything himself—hired the loft, turned it into a gallery, and invited the famous critic to come and speak at the opening. There was even a sign swinging from the loft-window over West Fifty-Third Street: Nobody's Gallery, it said—a metaphysical joke. Gottfried was not Nobody—the proof was he had married Somebody. Somebody had an unearned income of fifty thousand a year: she was a Chicago blueblood, a beautiful girl, long-necked, black-haired, sweetly and irreproachably mannered, with a voice like a bird. Mr. Hencke had spent two whole dinners in her company before he understood that she had no vocabulary, comprehended nothing, exclaimed at nothing, was bored by nothing. She was totally stupid. Since she had nothing to do—there was a cook, a maid, and a governess—she could scarcely improve, and exhausted her summers in looking diaphanous. Mr. Hencke was retired, but his son could never retire because he had never worked. Catherine liked him to stay at home, jiggle the baby now and then, play records, dance, and occasionally fire the governess, whom she habitually suspected of bad morals. All the same he went uptown to Lexington Avenue every day, where he rented an apartment next door to a Mrs. Siebzehnhauer, called it his studio, and painted timidly. Through the wall he could catch the bleatings of Mrs. Siebzehnhauer's Black Forest cuckoo clock. Sometimes he felt tired, so he put in a bed. In this bed he received his Jewish mistress.

The famous critic had already arrived, and was examining Gottfried's paintings. He poked his wheezing scrutiny so close to each canvas that the fashionable point of his beard dusted the bottom of the frame. Gottfried's paintings tramped solidly around the walls, and the famous critic followed them. He was not an art critic; he was a literary critic, a "cultural" critic—he was going to say something about the Meaning of the Work in Terms of the Zeitgeist. His lecture-fee was extremely high; Mr. Hencke hoped his opinion would be half so high. He himself did not know what to think of Gottfried's labors. His canvases were full of hidden optical tricks and were so bewildering to one's routine retinal expectations that, once the eye had turned away, a whirring occurred in the pupil's depth, and the paintings began to speak through their afterimage. Everything was disconcerting, everything seemed pasted down flat—strips, corners, angles, slivers. Mr. Hencke had a perilous sense that Gottfried had simply cut up the plans for an old office building with extraordinarily tiny scissors. All the paintings were in black and white, but there were drawings in brown pencil. The drawings were mostly teasing dots, like notes on a score. They hurtled up and down. The famous critic studied them with heated seriousness, making notes on a paper napkin he had taken from the refreshment table.

"Where am I to put my bag?" Mr. Hencke asked Catherine, who was just then passing by with her arm slung through the arm of Gottfried's mistress.

"Oh, put it anywhere," said Genevieve at once.

"Papa, stay with us this time. You can have the big room upstairs," Catherine said, mustering all her confident politeness.

"I have a reservation at such a very nice hotel," said Mr. Hencke.

"Nothing could be nicer than the big room upstairs. I've just had the curtains changed. Papa, they're all yellow now," Catherine said with her yielding inescapable smile, and through her father-in-law's conventionally gossamer soul, in which he believed as thoroughly as any peasant, there slipped the spider-thread flick of one hair of the horse's mane, as if drawn across his burlap cheek: not for nothing was he the father of an artist, he was susceptible to yellow, he still remembered the yellow buttercups on the slope below the millhouse.

"Kitty, you're hopeless," said Genevieve. "How can you think of shutting up a genuine bachelor at the top of your stuffy old house?"

"Not bachelor, widower," said Mr. Hencke. "Not exactly the same thing."

"The same in the end," said Genevieve. "You can't let them stuff you up, you have to be free to come and go and have people in and out if you want to."

"It's a nice house. It's not stuffy, it's very airy. You can even smell the river. It's an elegant house on an elegant street," Catherine protested.

"A very fine house," Mr. Hencke agreed, though he secretly despised New York brownstone. "Only I feel Gottfried is not comfortable when I am in it. So for family peace I prefer the hotel."

"Papa, Gottfried promised not to have a fight this time."

"What in the world do they find to fight about?" Genevieve asked.

"Papa thinks Gottfried should have a job. It isn't *neces*sary," Catherine said.

"It isn't necessary for Rockefeller either," Mr. Hencke said. "You don't see any of the Rockefellers idle. Every Rockefeller has a job."

"Oh, you Lutherans," Genevieve said. "You awful Lutherans and your awful Protestant Work Ethic."

"Papa, Gottfried's *never* idle. You don't know. You just don't know. He goes to his studio every day."

"And sleeps on the bed."

"My goodness, papa, you don't think Gottfried would be having this whole huge show if he never did any *work*, do you? He's a real worker, papa, he's an artist, so *what* if he has a bed up there."

"Now, now," Genevieve said, "that isn't fair, all the Rockefellers have beds too, Kitty's right."

"I wish you would tell me where to put my bag," Mr. Hencke said.

"Put it over there," Genevieve suggested. "With my things. See that chair behind the bar—where the barman's standing—no, there, that man putting on a white jacket—I left my pocketbook on it, under my coat. See it, it's the coat with all that black-and-white geometry all over it? Someone's liable to think it's one of Gottfried's things and buy it for nine hundred dollars," Genevieve said, and Catherine laughed like a sparrow. "You can lay your suitcase right on top of my nine-hundred-dollar coat, it won't be in the way. God, what a mob already."

"We sent programs to *every*body," Catherine said.

"Don't think they're coming completely for Gottfried," Mr. Hencke said.

"Papa, what do you mean?"

"He means they're coming to hear Creighton Mac-Dougal. Look, there's that whole bunch—not that way, over there, near the stairs—from *Partisan Review*. I can always tell *Partisan Review* people, they have faces like a mackerel after it's been caught, with the hook still in its mouth."

"They might be dealers," Catherine said hopefully. "Or museum people."

"They're MacDougal people. Him and his notes, get a load of that. I can hardly wait to hear him explain how Gottfried represents the existential revolt against Freud."

"Gottfried put in something about Freud in the program. Did you see the program yet, papa? He did a sort of preface for it. It's not really *writing*, it's just quotations. One of them's Freud, I think."

"Not Freud, dear, Jung," Genevieve said.

"Well, I knew it was some famous Jewish psychiatrist anyway," Catherine said. "Come on, Gen, let's go get papa a program."

"I'll get one, don't trouble yourself," Mr. Hencke said. "First I'll put away my bag."

"Jung isn't a Jew," Genevieve said.

"Isn't? Don't you mean wasn't? Isn't he dead?"

"He isn't a Jew," Genevieve said. "That's why he went on staying alive."

"I thought he was dead."

"Everybody dies," Mr. Hencke said, looking into the crowd. It resembled a zoo crowd: it had taken the form of a thick ragged rope and was wandering slowly past the long even array of Gottfried's paintings, peering into each one as though it were a cage containing some unlikely beast.

"Like a concentration camp," Genevieve said. "Everybody staring through the barbed wire hoping for rescue and knowing it's no use. That's what they look like."

Catherine said, "I certainly hope some of them are dealers."

"You don't want me to put my bag *on* your overcoat, Genevieve," Mr. Hencke said. "I must not crush your things. I'll put the bag just there behind the chair, that will be best."

"You know what Gottfried's stuff reminds me of?" Genevieve said.

Mr. Hencke perceived that she was provoking him. Her earlier reference to why he chose a hotel over his son's house—what she had said about his having people in and out—clearly meant prostitutes. He was stupendously offended. He never frequented prostitutes, though he knew Gottfried sometimes did. But Gottfried was still a young man—in America, curiously, to be past thirty-seven, and even a little bald in the back, like Gottfried, hardly interfered with the intention to go on being young. Gottfried, then, was not only a very young man, but gave every sign of continuing that way for years and years, while poor Catherine, though socially and financially Somebody, was surely—at sex—a Nobody. Her little waist was undoubtedly charming, her stretched-forward neck (perhaps she was nearsighted and didn't realize it?) was fragrant with hygiene.

Her whole body was exceptionally mannerly, even the puppet-motion of her immaculate thighs under her white dress: so Gottfried sometimes went to prostitutes and sometimes—on grand occasions, like the opening of Nobody's Gallery—Genevieve came from whatever city it was in the midwest—Cincinnati, or Boise, or Columbus: maybe Detroit. "Shredded swastikas, that's what," Genevieve announced. "Every single damn thing he does. All that terrible precision. Every last one a pot of shredded swastikas, you see that?"

He knew what she meant him to see: she scorned Germans, she thought him a Nazi sympathizer even now, an anti-Semite, an Eichmann. She was the sort who, twenty years after Hitler's war, would not buy a Volkswagen. She was full of detestable moral gestures, and against what? Who could be blamed for History? It did not take a philosopher (though he himself inclined toward Schopenhauer) to see that History was a Force-in-Itself, like Evolution. There he was, comfortable in America, only a little sugar rationed, and buying War Bonds like every other citizen, while his sister, an innocent woman, an intellectual, a loyal lover of Heine who could recite by heart *Der Apollogott* and *Zwei Ritter* and *König David* and ten or twelve others, lost her home and a daughter of eleven in an R.A.F. raid on Köln. Margaretchen had moved from Frankfurt to Köln after her marriage to a well-educated shampoo manufacturer. A horrible tragedy. Even the great Cathedral had not been spared.

"I was *sure* it was Freud Gottfried used for the quotation thing," Catherine demurred.

"Gottfried would never quote Freud, Kitty, it would only embarrass him. You know what Freud said? 'An abstinent artist is scarcely conceivable'—he meant sex, dear, not drink."

"Gottfried practically never drinks."

"That's because he's a mystic and a romantic, isn't he

stupid? Kitty, you really ought to do something to de-sober
Gottfried, it would do his work so much good. A little less
Apollo, a little more Dionysus."

Catherine tittered exactly as if she had seen the point of
some invisible joke: but then she noticed that the truckmen
had forgotten to set up the speaker's table, so she excused
herself very politely, gaping out at her father-in-law her
diligently attentive smile with such earnestness and breeding
that his intestines publicly croaked. The father of the artist
hated his daughter-in-law, and could not bear to share a roof
with her even for a single night; her conversation depressed
him and gave him evil sweated dreams: sometimes he dreamt
he was in his sister's city, and the bomb exploded out of
his own belly, and there rolled past him, as on a turntable
in the brutalized nave, his little niece laid out dead, covered
only by her yellow hair. Across the room Catherine was
supervising the placing of the lectern: he heard it scrape
through the increasing voices.

Meanwhile Genevieve still pursued. "Mr. Hencke, you
know perfectly well that Jung played footsie with the
Nazis. It's public knowledge. He let all the Jewish doctors
get thrown out of the psychological society after the Nazis
took it over, and he stayed president all that while, and he
never said a word against any of it. Then they were all
murdered."

"Gnädige Frau," he said—and dropped his suitcase to
the floor in a kind of fright. Since his wife died he had not
once spoken a syllable of German, and now to have such a
strangeness, such a familiarity, pimple out on his tongue with
a design of its own—and with what terrifying uselessness,
a phrase out of something sublimely old-fashioned, a stiff
staid long-ago play, Minna von Barnhelm perhaps, a phrase
he had never said in his whole life—"What do you want
from me?" he appealed. "I'm a man of sixty-eight. In sixty-
eight years what have I done? I have harmed no one. I have
built towers. Towers! No more. I have never destroyed."

He raised his suitcase—it was as heavy as some icon—
and walked through the chatter to the refreshment table
and set it down behind the chair thickened and duplicated
by the pattern of Genevieve's coat. The barman handed him
a glass. He received it and avoided the walls, no space of
which was unmarked by his son's Aztec emissions. He took
a seat in a middle row and waited for the speaker to come to
the lectern. At his feet lay a discarded leaflet. It was the
program. He saw that the topic of the lecture would be "In
His Eye's Mind: Hencke and the New Cubism." Then he
skipped a page backwards and under the title "Culled by
Hencke" he read a trio of excerpts:

"Schuppanzigh, do you think I write my quartets for you
and your puling fiddle?"—*Beethoven, to the violinist who
wailed that the A-minor quartet was unplayable.*

"It is better to ruin a work and make it useless for the world
than not to go the limit at every point."—*Thos. Mann.*

"For the people gay pictures, for the cognoscenti, the mystery
behind."—*Goethe.*

—All three items had the touch of Genevieve. He looked
for the quotation from Jung and found there was none. To
Catherine, Beethoven and Freud were just the same, burdens
indistinguishable and unextinguishable both. Undoubtedly
Genevieve had told her that Schuppanzigh was another Jewish psychiatrist persecuted by the Nazis and that Goethe
was a notorious Gauleiter. As for that idiot Gottfried, he read
the gallery notes in the *Times*, nothing more, and had a sub-
scription to *Art News*—he was two parts Catherine's money
to one part Genevieve's brain, and too cowardly altogether
to stir the mixture. Catherine, like all foolish heroines, believed that Genevieve (Smith '48, *summa cum laude*, Phi
Beta Kappa) was devoted to her (Miss Jewett's Classes '59,
graduated 32 in a class of 36) out of sentiment and en-
thusiasm. "Genevieve loves New York, she can't keep away

from it" was one of Catherine's sayings: alas, she uttered it like an epigram. They had met at Myra Jacobson's. Myra Jacobson (also Smith '48) was a dealer, one of the very best —she *made* reputations, it was said; last year (for instance) she made Julius Feldstein the actionist—and Catherine offered her a certain sum to take on Gottfried, but she refused. "You must wait till he's *ripe*," she told Catherine, who cried and cried until Genevieve appeared like Polonius from behind a Jackson Pollock and gave her an orange handkerchief to blow with. "Now, now," Genevieve said, "don't bawl about it, let me go look at him, you can't tell if he's ripe unless you squeeze." Genevieve was escorted to Gottfried's studio next door to Mrs. Siebzehnhauer, beheld the bed, beheld Gottfried, and squeezed. She pressed hard. He was not ripe. He was still a Nobody.

Hence Nobody's Gallery: Genevieve's invention. It was, of course, to mock Gottfried, who knew he was being mocked, and for spite agreed. Gottfried, like most cowards, had a dim cunning. But Catherine was infinitely grateful: a show was a show. Creighton MacDougal came terribly dear, but you would expect that of a man with a beard—he looked, Catherine said in another epigram, like God.

Applause.

God stood at the lectern, drew a glass of water from an aluminum spigot, sucked up the superfluous drops through the top part of his beard (the part that without the beard would have been a mustache), crackled an esophagus lined with phlegm, and began to talk about Melville's White Whale. For ten minutes Mr. Hencke was piously certain that the great critic was giving last week's lecture. Then he heard his son's name. "The art of Fulfillment," said the critic. "Here, at last, is no Yearning. No alabaster tail-fin wiggles beckoningly on the horizon. There is no horizon. Perspective is annihilated. The completion-complex of the schoolroom and/or the madhouse is master at last. Imagine a teacher with his back to the class, erasing the blackboard. He erases and erases. Finally all is clear black once again— except for a scrap of the foot of a single letter, the letter 'J'—'J,' ladies and gentlemen, standing for Justice, or for Jesus—one scrap of the foot, then, of this half-remaining letter 'J,' which the sweep of the eraser has passed by and left unobliterated. At this point it is the art of Gottfried Hencke I am illustrating precisely. The art of Gottfried Hencke rises from its seat, approaches the blackboard, and with a singular motion, a swift, small, and excruciatingly exact motion, wets its pinkie and smears away the foot of the 'J' forever. That, ladies and gentlemen, is the meaning of the art of Gottfried Hencke. It is an art not of hunger, not of frustration, but of satiation. An art, so to speak, for fat men."

Further applause: this time tentative, as by vulgarians who mistake the close of the first movement for the end of the symphony.

The aluminum spigot squeals. God thirsts. The audience observes the capillary action of facial hair.

"Ladies and gentlemen," continued the critic, "I too am a fat man. I cleverly mask not less than two chins, not more than three. Yet I was not always thus. Imagine me at seventeen, lean, bold, arrogant, aristocratic. Imagine snow. I run through the snow. Whiteness. The whiteness, ladies and gentlemen, of Melville's very Whale, with which I began my brief causerie. All men begin at the crest of purity and hope. Now consider me at twenty-four. I have just flunked out of medical school. Ladies and gentlemen, it was my wish to heal. To heal, my beauties. Consider my tears. I weep in my humiliation before the dean. I beg for another chance. 'No, my son,' says the dean—how kind he is! how good! and his wife is a cripple in a wheelchair—'you will have a long hard row to hoe. Give it up.' Now for thirty years I have tried to heal myself. Allegories, ladies, beauties; allegories, you darling gentlemen: trust me to serve you fables, parables, the best of their kind in season. The art of Gottfried Hencke is an intact art. Was there ever a wound in it? It is healed. It has healed itself, we all heal ourselves, thank you, thank you."

God waved fervently through the exalted shimmer of the final applause.

With inscrutable correctness, as though mediating a bargain in a bazaar, Catherine introduced her father-in-law to Creighton MacDougal. Mr. Hencke was moved. He felt stirred to hope for his son, and for his son's son, who had so far struck him as practically an imbecile. He undertook to explain to the critic about the old planes. "No, no," he said, leaning into a pair of jelly-red eyes, "the Fokker was the fighter as everyone knows, but the Hansa-und-Branden-burger did everything—strafed, bombed, a little aerial fight-ing, now and then a little reconnaissance over the water to look for your ships. Everything. Very versatile, very re-liable. At the end we used a lot of them. In the beginning we didn't even have the Fokker. All we had was the Rumpler-Taube, very beautiful. She was called that because she re-sembled a lovely great dove. Maybe you know her from the old movies. My daughter-in-law claims she saw one once in a movie at the Museum of Modern Art. I have a little fear of my daughter-in-law—spoils the stock, bad mental genes—a grandson two years old, very pretty boy, nothing mental. You won't mention this, yes? I say it in private. I have a liking for your face. You show a little of my father—the old school, as you say, very strict. Boys nowadays don't stand for that. We had also very strict teachers with the planes. All professors. They knew every-thing about an engine. The best teachers they gave us. I suppose in an emergency I could still fly something like a Piper Cub. We had the double wing in those days. The bi-plane, no closed cockpits. We had leather helmets. When it rained it was like needles on the eyeballs. We could go only a thousand feet—the height of the Empire State Building, yes? In the core of a cloud you are quite unaware it's a cloud, to you it's simply fog. Those helmets! In the rain they smelled like a slaughterhouse."

An intense young lady who had just written a book review took the critic away from him: he wiped his mouth. A long thread of detached mucus membrane lifted from its right corner. He snuffed up the odor of his own breath. It confessed that his stomach was not well. On the refreshment table there was a bowl of apples. He thought how one of these would clean the stink from his teeth. The bowl stood next to a platter of cheese sandwiches at the end of the table, near the chair with Genevieve's coat on it. But the coat was not on the chair. It was on Genevieve. She was whispering to Gottfried over the apples. He saw that she intended to leave before Gottfried, to fool Catherine. It was an assignation.

"Gottfried!" he called.

His son came.

"You're not going home?"

"Not for hours, papa. There's a little band coming in. Catherine thought we ought to have some dancing."

"I mean afterward. Afterward where are you going?"

"Home. Home, papa, where else at that hour? Catherine says you won't come with us. She says you're insisting on a hotel again."

"You're not going to the studio first?"

"Tonight, you mean?"

"After the band. After the band you're going to the studio with the bed in it?"

"I can't possibly do any work tonight, papa. Not after all this. Listen, what did you think of MacDougal?"

"The man misunderstands you entirely," Mr. Hencke said. " I talked to him privately, you observed that?"

"No," Gottfried said.

"I want you to take me to your studio," Mr. Hencke said.

"That's a change," Gottfried said. "You never want to see my things."

"You have something worth showing?"

"Oh, for God's sake," Gottfried said. "All ye who seek my monument, look around you. Don't you like a single thing on the wall?"

"I want to see what you keep in your studio."

"Well, I've got a new thing going over there," Gottfried said. "If you're interested."

"A new thing?"

"It's only one-quarter finished. The whole right bottom corner. Seems I've finally worked up the courage to try something in color. Cerulean blue compressed into a series of interlocked ovals and rectangles. Like sky enclosed in the nucleus of the atom. Actually I'm pretty hopeful about it."

"Tell me, Gottfried, who said that?" his father asked.

"Who said what?"

"The sky in the atom. Genevieve? Genevieve's words, hah? A brilliant lady. Very metaphorical. I want to see this sky. Explain to Genevieve that I am always glad to look at any evidence of my son's courage."

"All right, papa, don't get rough. I'll call for you in the morning if you want. It's so damn perverse of you not to come to the house."

"No, no, I have no interest in your house. I abominate high stoops—a barbarism. Tonight I want to see your studio."

"Tonight?"

"After the band."

"That's absurd, papa. We'll all be dead tired later on."

"Good, then we will take advantage of the convenience of the bed."

"Papa, don't get rough. I mean that. Don't get rough with me *now*, you hear?"

"When I myself was a very young man of thirty-seven I addressed my father with respect."

"God damn you, you want to break it up. You really want to break it up. Finally you want to. Why? You kept out of it long enough, a whole year, now all of a sudden it bothers you."

"A year and a half," his father said. "And still you like to call it a new thing. A new thing you call it."

"Do you *need* to break it up? You have to? What's it to you?"

"Poor, poor Catherine," his father murmured.

"Poor, poor Catherine," Genevieve said, coming up behind Gottfried. She was devouring a cheese sandwich, and bits of bread mottled her mouth and sprinkled down on the breast of her coat. Mr. Hencke confronted its design: a series of interlocked ovals and rectangles, dark and light. Looked at one way, they presented a deep tubular corridor, infinitely empty, like two mirrors facing one another. A shift of the mind swelled them into a solid, endlessly bulging, endlessly self-creating squarish sausage.

"He's trying to break it up," Gottfried told her.

"Foolish, foolish boy," said Genevieve, sticking out a cheesey tongue at the father of the artist.

"Are you listening?" said Gottfried.

"Yes, dear. I didn't know the dear knew anything."

"You liar. Big innocent wide-eyes. I told you I told him. I had to tell him because he guessed."

"I am Gottfried's confidant," Mr. Hencke said.

"Mine too," said Genevieve, and embraced the father of the artist. The very slight fragrance of the pumpernickel crumbs on the underpart of her chin—a chin just, just beginning to slacken: a frail lip-like turn of skin pouting beneath it—made a flowery gash in his vision. Some inward gate opened. He remembered still another field, this one furry with kümmel, a hairy yellow shoulder of a field shrugging at the wind. A smear of joy worsened his stomach:

at home one used to take caraway for a carminative. "Childe
Roland to the Dark Tower came," Genevieve recited, "and
broke it up. Gottfried, I vouch for your father. He has never
destroyed."

Mr. Hencke marveled.

"I am a deceiver," Genevieve cried, "I too need a confidant, I need one more than Gottfried. Gottfried's papa,
let me tell you about my extraordinary life in Indianapolis,
Indiana. My husband is an intelligent and prospering Certified
Public Accountant. His name will not surprise: Lewin. A
memorable name. Kagan would also be a memorable name,
so too Rabinowitz or Robbins, but *his* name is Lewin. A
model to youth. Contributor to many charities. Vice-presi-
dent of the temple. Now let me tell you about our four
daughters, all under twelve years. One is too young for
school. One is only in kindergarten. But the two older ones!
Nora. Bonnie. At the top of their grades and already reading
Tom Sawyer, *Little Women*, and the *Encyclopaedia Britan-
nica*. Every month they produce a family newspaper of one
page on an old Smith-Corona in the basement of our Dutch
Colonial house in Indianapolis, Indiana. They call it *The
Mezuzzah Bulletin*—the idea being that they tack it up on
the doorpost. They all four have the Jewish brain."

"Everyone's *looking* at you," Gottfried said angrily.

"That's because I'm wrapped in one of your satiated
paintings. Mr. Hencke, did you know that some of the most
avant-garde expressionism comes from the Seventh Avenue
silkscreen people? But I want to confide some more. Gottfried's papa, some more confidences. First let me describe
myself. Tall. Never wear low heels. Plump-armed. Soft-
thighed. Perfectly splendid young woman. Nose thin and
delicate, like a Communion wafer. Impression of being both
sleek and amiable. Large, healthy, indestructible teeth. Half
a dozen gold inlays, paid for by Lewin, the Certified Public
Accountant. Excellent husband. Now your turn, Mr. Hencke.
I've undressed myself for you. It's your turn, that's only

fair. Your brother-in-law the shampoo manufacturer that
Kitty once mentioned—the one who lives in Cologne, whose
house was bombed out?"
      Mr. Hencke begged, "What do you want from me?
Why do you talk about yourself that way?"
      "Tell about him. Confide in me the nature of the sham-
poo. What did he make it out of? Not now. I mean during
the war. Not the war you flew in, the war after that. He
was making shampoo in Cologne all the while you were an
American patriot architect, raising towers, never destroying.
Please discuss your brother-in-law's shampoo. What were its
secret ingredients? Whose human fat? What Jewish lard?"
      "Genevieve, shut up. Shut up, will you please? Leave
my father alone."
      "Poor, poor Catherine," Genevieve said. "I just fixed
everything up with her. I told her I was going to make the
midnight plane home and you had this inspiration and had
to stay up all night with it at the studio."
      "Just shut up, all right?"
      "All right, dear. I'll see you when Mrs. Siebzehnhauer's
cuckoo caws two."
      "Skip it. Not tonight."
      "Who says not? Gottfried's papa?"
      "I have nothing against you, believe me," Mr. Hencke
said. "I admire you very much, Genevieve. I have absolutely
no animus."
      "What a pity," said Genevieve, "every man should
have a nice little animus."
      "My God, Genevieve, leave him alone."
      "Goodbye. I'm going back to Nora Lewin, Bonnie
Lewin, Andrea Lewin, Celeste Lewin and Edward K.
Lewin, all of Indianapolis, Indiana. First I have to say goodbye to poor, poor Catherine. Goodbye, Mr. Hencke. Don't
worry about yourself. As for me, I am sleek and amiable.
My gold inlays click like castanets manufactured in Franco
Spain. My breasts are like twin pomegranates. Like twin

white doves coming down from Mount Gilead, O.K.?" She
kissed the father of the artist. The hairy kümmel valley was
photographed by flash bulb on the flank of his pancreas.
"Your cheek is like barbed wire. Your cheek has the ruts
left by General Rommel's tanks."

The artist and his father watched her go from them,
picking at crumbs.

"A superior woman," Mr. Hencke said. He felt a remarkable control. He felt as though he had received a command and disobeyed it. "A superior race, I've always thought
that. Imaginative. They say Corbusier is a secret Jew, descended from Marranos. A beautiful complexion, beautiful
eyelashes. These women have compulsions. When they
turn up a blonde type you can almost take them for our
own."

His son said nothing.

"Do you enjoy her, Gottfried?"

His son said nothing.

"I would guess you enjoy her, yes? Imaginative. I would
guess enjoyment. Superconsciousness."

Still his son held on. Mr. Hencke passionately awaited
the confessional tears. He conjured them. They did not
descend.

He said finally, "Does she boss you much?"

"Never," Gottfried said. "Never, never. I think you
broke it up, papa. God damn you to hell, papa."

His arms clutched across his back, the father of the
artist observed the diminishing spoor of visitors. In her bride's
dress Catherine glimmered at the top of the stairwell, speaking elegant goodbyes learned at Miss Jewett's. Creighton
MacDougal winked and saluted and snapped his heels like a
Junker officer. A wonderful mimicry spiraled out of his
head: the buzz of a biplane. Simultaneously a saxophone
opened fire.

"Dance with me, papa!" said Catherine. "—Oh, no,
you're just so out-of-date. Nowadays you're not supposed to

even *touch.*" She taught him how; he had never seen her so clever. "Mr. MacDougal had to leave, but you know what he said? He said you were a fine person. He said"—her laugh broke like a dish—"you were a natural hermit, and if you ever decided to put up a pillar to sit on top of, it would last a thousand years."

Mr. Hencke copied her but did not touch. "Have there been sales?"

"Not yet, but after all it's only the *opening*. And even if there aren't any that's not the point. It's just so Gottfried can feel encouraged. You have to be noticed in this world, you know that, papa? Otherwise you don't feel you really exist. You just don't understand about Gottfried. —No, papa, nobody *ever* dips at the end any more. It's so out-of-date to do that. I mean Gottfried works every minute he can. You make him feel awful when you talk the way you did before about Rockefeller. My goodness, papa, he's even going to work when we get through here, he's going over to the studio right afterward."

"I think not. I think he will be far too tired," said the father of the artist.

"But he *told* me he wanted to work tonight. He really meant it, papa. It's not as if I'm the only one he said it to, he's been saying it to everyone—" A scream leaped out of the bowl of apples. "Oh, look, what's the matter with Genevieve?" Catherine, inquisitive as a child, ran.

He delayed and envisioned wounds. In his heart she bled, she bled. He stepped away. He kept back. He listened to her voice—such a coarse voice. The voice or the bass fiddle? A Biblical yell, as by the waters of Babylon. Always horrible tragedy for the innocent. She was not innocent. He suspected what wounds. The saxophone machine-gunned him in the small intestine.

Catherine twitched back. "Someone's stolen Genevieve's pocketbook! She had it lying just like that on a chair, only it was all covered up with her coat, and there was this hun-

dred dollars in it, and her driver's license, and the plane
ticket, and a million other things like that. With all these
people, you wouldn't think there'd be a thief—"

He was bewildered. "Hurt? She's hurt?"

"Well no, she didn't even *leave* yet, she was just starting
to go. It's not as if somebody mugged her in the street or
held her up or anything. I mean they just *took* it. It was just
lying there, so they took it. Can you imagine anybody acting
like that?" A vividness disrupted but lit her; his daughter-in-
law exulted. She assumed the sheen her wealth deserved: he
descried in her at the moment of adventure those canny
cattle-buccaneers who had sired her temperament. Booty-
getting cannot be bred out: she was just then a true heiress,
and the father of the artist was for the first time nearly proud
his son had chosen her. What Gottfried had seen, he now
saw. Crime rejoiced her, crime loosened the puppet-strings
of her terrifying civility. Crime made her intelligent. He
himself knew what it was to be one whom crisis exalts. He
had once landed with half a wing shot off: his hero's wound
afterward seemed sweeter to him than any crisis of love-
making he was ever to endure.

"Gottfried thinks it must have been one of the truckmen," Catherine said. Ah, she hugged herself.

"Absolutely it was the truckmen," Mr. Hencke assented.
"There was no one else here like that."

"The barman?"

"The barman perhaps," Mr. Hencke once again agreed.

"But it couldn't be the barman, the barman's still *here*.
If it was the barman we could catch him red-handed. A thief
always disappears as fast as he can."

"Then the truckmen," Mr. Hencke said. "The truckmen without question."

"All right, but you know what *I* think, papa?"

"No."

Catherine sucked her lip until it gleamed. "Well, the
way that weird man *argued* about his fee when we hired

him—I guess you don't say hired for a critic, but I don't know what else we did if we *didn't* hire him—anyhow he didn't think he was getting enough, especially since that little FM station W-K-Something-Something sent over a couple of men to pick up his speech on a tape recorder, and he said he doesn't even get royalties from it, so what *I* think"—her beautiful shivery laugh broke and broke, if no longer like a plate then like surf—"is Mr. MacDougal decided to raise his own fee, hook or crook!"

"It was the truckmen," Mr. Hencke said with the delicacy of finality.

"I'm just *fooling*. You always agree with Gottfried, papa. I mean on fundamentals. I don't know why you argue about everything else."

"Genevieve must be given some money to go home with."

"She's terrifically upset, did you see her? You wouldn't think she could get so upset. She says her husband always tells her not to be highstrung and to carry checks—"

"Tell Gottfried to give her some money," Mr. Hencke said.

"Oh, papa, *you* tell him. If it's something important he never pays attention to any of my ideas."

He looked for Gottfried: there he was, quarreling with the barman, who said he had seen no one and knew nothing. Genevieve stood chewing on a glove.

"Don't fight with him, Gottfried, it's perfectly irretrievable. It's so silly, and really it's my own stupid fault. Ed'll kill me, not for the money but like they say for the principle. *You* know. He thinks I'm a terrible slob that way, he's a great one for believing in foreseeable actions. I lost the Buick last year, and the year before I lost the baby in the parking lot. God, how I hate people of principle. All the persecutors of the world have been people of principle."

"Genevieve invokes History always," Mr. Hencke said.

She unexpectedly ignored this; at once he regretted it.

She said hoarsely, "I'm simply resigned. I'll never get it back. O.K., O.K., so it's irretrievable."

"That is true of so much in life," Mr. Hencke said.

Gottfried darkly turned. "Papa, what do you want?" The barman escaped.

"I want you to give Genevieve money."

"Money?"

"Under the circumstances." The father of the artist tenderly uncovered his teeth.

Gottfried repeated: "Money?"

"For Genevieve. It's the least you can do, Gottfried."

"I don't give Genevieve money, papa."

He saw the damp creases under his son's nose. Even in America youth is not eternal.

"Ah, but you ought to, Gottfried. Nothing comes free in this life." He felt obscurely delighted by Gottfried's pale charged mouth. His son resembled a pretty little spotted horse spitting disappointing hay. "Airplane rides to Indianapolis, Indiana don't come free in this life," he finished in a brief mist of his own laughter.

"Well, look at that," Genevieve said. "Gottfried's papa wants to get rid of me. You were perfectly right about that, Gottfried, he wants to get rid of me."

"No, no," Mr. Hencke protested. "Only of the band. What ugly music. Saxophones frighten. Such a loud lonely forest sound. Why don't you dismiss them, Gottfried? There are no guests left, I think."

"Democracy," Genevieve divulged: Catherine was dancing violently with the barman.

"I see how it is done," Mr. Hencke said. "They move but don't touch. Touching is no longer the fashion. Catherine thinks she is dancing with the thief, yes? Gottfried, give Genevieve some money."

"Catherine can do it," Gottfried muttered; he swam toward his wife as through some thick preventing element.

"He is nearly inaudible when he feels he has been insulted," his father noted. "Did he say he would?"

"It was going to be over pretty soon anyway. How I hate a brouhaha," Genevieve said, staring after Gottfried.

"What an amusing word. After so many years I don't know all the words. Ah, a brilliant lady like yourself, you're bored with my plain-hearted son."

"I'm bored with Kitty. I'm bored with New York."

"And with art. With art too?" He paused desperately. "My son would not say whether it has been a success. He would not say whether there has been enjoyment."

"I wish," Genevieve said, "I just hadn't lost that damn pocketbook. The Certified Public Accountant gave me his last warning. It's the guillotine next."

"Please, please," Mr. Hencke said, "thieves and pickpockets occur everywhere."

"I don't *care* about the money," Genevieve said sourly.

"Dear lady, you care about dignity."

"Yes," Genevieve said, "that's it."

"Sit down," Mr. Hencke said, and scratched toward her the guilty chair. On this chair the stolen pocketbook had lain, and over it Genevieve's patterned coat. The chair was empty. Listlessly Genevieve gathered up the hem of her coat and sat down.

"My bag," Mr. Hencke said, picking it up and putting it at her feet.

"Well, I guess you're lucky they didn't take that too."

"Dignity," Mr. Hencke said. "Dignity before everything. I subscribe to that. Persons tend to assume things about other persons. For example, my son believes I came to New York entirely for this occasion—you understand—to see the gallery, to see the work. For the cognoscenti the mystery behind, yes? In reality tomorrow morning I will be early on a ship. I'm going for a beautiful trip, you know."

"To Germany?" But she seemed detached. She watched

the stairwell swallow the musicians. Catherine was using
Gottfried's back for a desk, writing something. Her pen
wobbled like a plunged and nervous dagger.

"Not Germany. Sweden. I admire Scandinavia. Exquisite
fogs. The green of the farmland there. Now only Scandinavia is the way I remember Germany from boyhood. Germany isn't the same. All factories, chimneys."

"Don't speak to me about German chimneys," Genevieve said. "I know what kind of smoke came out of those
damn German chimneys."

His eyes wept, his throat wept, she was not detached,
she was merciless. "I didn't have the heart to tell Gottfried
I'm traveling again. Don't tell him, hah? Let him think I
came especially. You understand, hah, Genevieve? To see his
things, let him think that, not just passing on the way to
travel somewhere else. I have the one bag only to mislead.
I confess it, purposely to mislead. In my hotel room already
there are four other bags."

"I bet you say Sweden to mislead. I bet you're going to
Germany, why shouldn't you? I don't say there's anything
wrong with it, why shouldn't you go to Germany?"

"Not Germany, Sweden. The Swedes were innocent in
the war, they saved so many Jews. I swear it, not Germany.
It was the truckmen, I swear it."

"I suppose it *was* one of the truckmen," Genevieve said
languidly.

"The most logical ones were the truckmen. I swear it.
Look, look, Genevieve, I'll show you," he said, "just look—"
He turned the little key and threw open his suitcase with so
much wild vigor that it quivered on its hinges. "Now just
look, look through everything, nothing here but my own,
here are my shirts, not all, I have so many more in my other
bags in the hotel, here I have mostly, forgive me, my new
underwear. Only socks, see? Socks, socks, shorts, shorts,
shorts, all new, I like to travel with everything new and
clean, undershirt, undershirt, shaving cream, razor, deodorant,

more underwear, toothpaste, you see this, Genevieve? I swear
it must have been one of the truckmen, that's only logical.
Please, I swear it. Genevieve," Mr. Hencke said, forcing his
fingers rigidly through the depth of his new undershorts,
"see for yourself—"

Catherine in her white dress (the wife of the artist was
seen in a white dress) jerked into view: she hung like a
marionette in the margins of his eye's theater. "Really, Genevieve, Gottfried's so funny sometimes, he has plenty of
money in his wallet, but he made me write you this check,
he absolutely insisted. Good grief, he's got checks of his
own. Can you still make the twelve o'clock plane, Gen?—
because look, if you can't, you can easily stay overnight with
us, why don't you, that nice room's all ready and papa isn't
staying—"

"Oh, no," Genevieve said, jumping up, "I'll never stay
overnight!"

She seized the check and ran down the long stairs. The
interlocked series of ovals and rectangles scorched into gray.
In his tenuously barbule soul, for which he had ancestral
certitude, the father of the artist burned in the foam of so
much kümmel, so many buttercups, so much lustrous yellow,
and the horse's mane so confusing in his eyes like a grid, and
why does the horse not go faster, faster?

"My goodness," Catherine said, "why've you got your
suitcase open and everything rumpled up like that? Papa, did
they steal from you too?" she gave out in her politest, most
cultivated, most ventriloquist tone. "Tonight what criminals
we've harbored unawares!"—it sounded exactly like a phrase
of Genevieve's.

The
Dock-Witch

THAT SPRING IT fell to me—as family pioneer, I suppose—to do a great deal of seeing-off. Which was a bit odd, considering how we are a clan of inlanders; for generations we have hugged those little southern Ohio hamlets that surprise the tourist who expects only another cornfield and is rewarded, appropriately, only by another cornfield—but this one marvelously shelters a fugitive post office and a perfectly recognizable dry goods store. We have long lived in these places contentedly enough, in summer calling across pleasantly through rusting screens from veranda to veranda, in winter warming our hands on hymnals in the overheated church. We have little dark lakes of our own, and we can travel, if we wish, to a green-sided river for a picnic, but otherwise water is not in our philosophies.

My own lodging is a seventeenth-floor apartment in a structure of thirty-one stories. I am a little low-down in that building, as you will calculate—perhaps there is still some adducent Ohioan matter in me that continues to seek the earth. The earth, however, is covered over with a stony veneer and is paced by a doorman costumed like the captain of a ship. There is something nautical about my house—from my windows I can see the East River, and I know that if I follow it downtown far enough I will find the mouth of the wide sea itself.

I am the only one of my family to turn Easterner. At first it was shrugged off as rebellion, then concentrated on

ferociously as betrayal, and finally they wrote me long letters
about the good old dry heat of home, and how I would
surely get rheumatism up so high at night in damp air, and
about how this or that farm was being taken over for "de-
velopment." There were progress and prosperity to be had at
home, they wrote, and girls of my own kind, and, above all,
the clear open purity of the land. I always answered by
telling my salary. In those early days I had what the partners
ritually called promise, and was paid in jagged leaps upward, like a graph of our national affluence—I was only two
or three years out of Yale Law, more dogged than preco-
cious, a mad perfectionist who chewed footnotes like me-
dicinal candy. The firm I worked for in turn worked for a
group of immense, mystically integrated shipping companies.
We younger men grinding away in the back offices were all
from landlocked interior towns; the cluster of our lawyerly
heads slogging over our crowded-together desks looked like
a breezeless patch of dun wheat. In the lunch-jokes we traded
(pressed hard, we mostly ate out of paper bags at our desks)
we snubbed landlubbers and talked about the wondrous
Queens, whose formidable documents passed through our
days like tender speckled sails. We all said we felt the sea
in those papers more intensely than any sailor below decks;
we toiled for the sea through the conscientious tips of our
ball-point pens. Of course we said much of this in self-
mockery, and some wag always found the opportunity to
hum "*po*lish up the *han*dle on the *big* front door" from
Pinafore, but there was a certain spirit in which we really
believed it. Those fabled white-thighed ships in the harbor
not many streets west of our offices meant commerce and
passengers, and *we* were the controlling godlets of commerce
and passengers. Our pens struck, and the ships would begin
the subtle, gigantic tremor of their inmost sinews; our pens
struck again, and the engines would die in the docks. Talk of
being lord of the waves! Curiously, I never had any desire
to journey anywhere at all in those days. On the one hand,

I didn't dare; to take a vacation and go blithely off to look at the world would have been to lose my place in line, and if I knew anything at all, I knew I was headed for the captain's table, so to speak, of that firm. And on the other hand, it was enough to smell the salt scent rising out of the mass of sheets on my blotter, each crowned with a printed QUEEN MARY, QUEEN ELIZABETH, QUEEN WILHELMINA, QUEEN FREDERICA, QUEEN EKENEWASA—it was the salt of my own loyal sweat. The ships themselves, of course, we never saw; they were brawny legends to us. Now and then, though, we would get to hear what we supposed was an actual captain. Whenever a captain showed up in our offices he was sure to be heard, and he was sure to be angry—usually at one of us. He would spend half an hour bawling at some tangled in- discretion of ours perpetrated in triplicate sheafs, and we could catch his vibrations through the partners' Olympian oak doors—shouts of wrath; but the shouts always disap- pointed. If you didn't understand to begin with that it was a captain in there, you might think it was the head of a button-manufacturers' union, or a furniture company, or a cotton farm. All that monsoon of rage was only about cargoes delayed on trains, or cargoes arrived three weeks too soon, or cargoes—mostly this—unpaid for. Or else it was a complaint about registry or tariffs, or a quarrel over tankers. It was no use visualizing commanders of triremes or galleons —almost all the captains we heard yelling through those oak doors were tanker-types, and when they came out, still vaguely snarling but mainly mollified (it was hardly coinci- dence that afterward one of us would feel the threat of get- ting fired), they all turned out to be rather short, flabby men wearing business suits and not very shiny brown shoes. My doorman had more of the salt about him than any of them.

Ah, well, the secret of it all was this: they were captains in our fancy only. What they really were, those furious or- dinary men, was executives of the shipping line come to un- ravel a mix-up in the charter contract. It was nothing but

contracts, after all—landlubber stuff. The farmers down near
Clarksburg used to growl just that way, no different, over
market-prices, subsidies, transport. And the captains—this
was the worst of it—the glorious captains, those princes and
masters whom we never saw and whose ships we only
imagined, were, like us, only employees. They had no sway
over the schemes of the sea, which belonged to our calm
partners behind their doors and to the plain farmer-tanker
sorts who ran the lines with their brown-shod feet set
squarely on a dry expensive rug.

But if you avoided the shipping executives and the freight
forwarders and stuck to the names of the Queens and kept
your pen charging through that stupendous geography of
paperwork—Porto Amélia, Androko, Funchal, Yokohama,
Messina, Kristiansand, Reykjavik, Tel Aviv, and whatnot—
you could preserve your sea-sense and all its luminous briny
tenets. There was a period one spring when, I remember, I
used to read Conrad far into the night and every night, novel
after novel, until I felt that, if I had not been a seaman in my
last incarnation, I was sure to be one in my next. And when,
in the morning, groping groggily at my desk, I confronted
a fresh envelope full of contradictory demands and excruciatingly detailed subclauses, it seemed like a plunge into the
wave of life itself: Aruba, Suez, Cristobal, and all the rest
crept up my nostrils like some unbearable siren's perfume,
all weedy, deep, and wild. Those days a hot liquid of imagination lived in the nerve of my joy.

Still, I never actually boarded a ship until my uncle Al, a
feed-man in Chillicothe, decided the time had come for Paris
and Rome to experience him. He was a thrifty person, but
not unprogressive; he had opted in favor of sea travel and
against flying because aunt Essie had always thought the
Wright brothers blasphemous. "If God had wanted people
to fly, you and I would be flapping this minute," Al quoted
her. She was dead three years, and my uncle's trip was a kind
of memorial to Essie's famous wanderlust. She had once

stayed overnight in Quebec, and it seemed to her it would be interesting to spend a week or so in a place where everyone acted insane; she meant the effect on her of a foreign language. Al said he himself wouldn't mind if he never set foot out of Chillicothe and environs, but it was for the sake of Essie he was going out to look at those places. "She would have wanted me to," he said, squinting through my windows at the river. There were no children to leave the money to; he was resolved to get rid of it himself. "Is that the ocean out there?" he asked. "It's the East River." "Pew, how can you live with the smell?" he wondered. The next day—it was a Saturday—we took a taxi to the piers. Al let me pay the fare. There was a longshoremen's strike on, so we had to carry the bags aboard ourselves. The ship was Greek, compact and confined. The patchy white paint on the walls of the tubular corridors was sweating. "Why, the downstairs powder room at home's bigger than this," Al said, turning around in the box of his room. He was sharing it with another passenger, who had not yet arrived; all we knew of him was his name, Mr. Lewis, and that he was from Chicago. "Big city guy," my uncle said in a worried voice. Mr. Lewis came so late that the visitors' leaving-signal, something between a gong and a whistle, had already been blown twice: he had only one little canvas bag, with a sort of tapestry design involving roses and a calligraphic letter L on the sides —he swung it between a pair of birch crutches. He told my uncle he was a retired cabinetmaker and had arthritis. His true name was Laokonos, and he was going to Patrai to meet his brother's family. Mr. Lewis had an objectionably strong accent, and I could see my uncle meant to patronize him all the way across. "Goodbye, have a good trip," I said. "Fine," my uncle said, "will do. You bet. Thanks for putting me up and all. I'll remember you in my will," he joked. The signal hooted a third time and I went down the gangplank and onto the covered pier—it was really a concrete roof with a solid concrete floor and open sides. It felt like the inside of

a queer sort of warehouse, not like a pier at all. You could
not even see the water—the bulk of the ship, pressed close
against the margins of the sidewalk, obscured it—but the
wind was tangible and shot through with an ecstatic gritty
taste. I thought I would wait to watch the ship move off into
the water. It was a small, pinched, stingy, disappointing
thing, apparently without a single sailor anywhere on board;
then it occurred to me that the owners might have been too
poor to afford proper sailors' dress, and passengers, visitors,
and mariners were all indistinguishably civilian. Anyhow
most were Greeks. On the pier all the people waiting for the
ship to shudder into action and farewell were talking Greek.
There we stood in a patient heaving jostling bunch, raggedly
crushed up against the barricade at the end of the sidewalk
under that warehouse canopy, staring at a long piece of peeling sunlit hull. The top part of the ship was hidden by the
roof of the pier, the middle part was cut off by the sidewalk,
and what we had framed for us was a quarter-mile of flank,
without even the distinction of a porthole. The Greeks went
on strangling themselves with their jabber, which seemed to
knock them in the teeth as they spoke; meanwhile the ship
did not stir. It was not what I had imagined a dock-scene to
be, and after half an hour of that mute vigil it struck me that
the intelligent thing to do would be to vanish. My uncle was
irretrievably encased somewhere in the marrow of this grimy
immobile crab, and in any event there was not even a deck
with a rail for him to lean over while we mutually waved
and mouthed—nothing of the sort. "You think something's
wrong? The engine?" one of the visitor-Greeks beside me
asked in perfectly acceptable New York English. "My
mother's on there, going to see relatives, you shoulda seen
her cry when I brought in the fruit. Who you got on?"
"My uncle," I said, reduced to a Greek with relatives. "Ever
been down here before?" the Greek asked—"how come they
take so long to get going?" "Bet they sprung a leak," someone volunteered. "The cook's got indigestion, by mistake he

ate what they serve the passengers." "There was a mutiny, they found out the captain ain't Greek." "A Turk, they threw him to the sharks." "Believe me, when you get back over there in a clean suit of clothes, they're worse than sharks, they think you're an American you're a millionaire." A local segment of the crowd gave a cheerful howl at this: there was a camaraderie of seers-off I had not suspected. "Excuse me," I said, attempting a passage through. "You leaving?" "What you want to leave for?" "She's gonna take off!" "You'll miss when she starts!" they cried at me from all around. And then, dropped with a startling clarity among the duller voices, a voice unlike the others: "Don't go. It's a mistake to go so soon. There's always a delay, even with the Queens, and if you go you won't see the milky part."

The cocky tone of this—and then the shimmering word "Queens," which secreted all my private visions—held me. I looked and looked. "Milk?" I called like a fool.

"The wake. It's like a rush of milk expressed from the pith of Mother Sea."

She was two yards from where I stood clamped by the laughing mob, a woman of forty or so, small, puffed out by an overstarched dress. It was gray but a little childish for her age and face. Her slivery eyes were darkly ringed like a night-bird's. "If you see someone off you should see it *through*," she chirped back at me.

I said helplessly, "I've waited—"

"So have we all. You're *supposed* to wait. It's part of the sacred rites of the pier. And when she heaves off you're supposed to give a great yell. I'll bet this is only your first time. I'll bet you're a dryfoot. Midwesterner?" she wondered from afar.

A growl was prepared under our feet. The concrete rumbled like a dentist's drill. "She's starting!" "She's going!" "I can see her move. She's moving!" The mangy rectangle of ship-side glared back at us without a sign of motion; as if to set it an example, the mob began to mill. Then, with a kind of gentle hiccup, the hull commenced to tingle visibly, almost to twitch, like the rump of a horse. A jungle-roar came out of her and struck our faces. "There!" "Can you see anybody?" "The deck's on the other side." "There ain't no deck." "Look for a porthole." "Porthole's too low down." "Oil, that's what it is. I told you oil."

A metal smell, the fragrance of some heavy untrustworthy machine, assaulted the wind. The water was all at once revealed, ·a vomit of snow. It piled itself on itself, whorl on whorl, before it melted into a toiling black, like an ominous round well or dark-blooded eye. The creamy wake ran swiftly after the stern. Without warning she was off and out, and we saw the whole of her, stacks, strakes, and all, grumbling outward. The farther she went the better she looked. She smoothed herself down into an unflecked unsoiled whiteness; she rode with her head up, like something royal, and the Greeks shrieked and waved. Then she made a wide turn, trailing out of the harbor into the shining platter of openness, and we could spy, on her other haunch, a tiny deck filled with tiny figures. My uncle and Mr. Lewis must have been among those wee dolls. But I had had enough, and walked the long dim concrete route out to Canal Street for a taxi, peculiarly saddened.

It was only a week after this that my young cousin's senior class came through, thirty fastidious crew-hatted girls from Consolidated High, headed for a tour of "Scotland, the Hebrides, England, and Wales": thus spake the tour pamphlet. "Not Ireland?" I said. "George, *no*body's interested in *Ire*land," my cousin said (she was really my first cousin once removed); "we're going to see an actual *stool* that Robert Burns sat on. It's in a museum in Edinburgh. Did you know there's a big castle, like an old king's castle, right in the middle of Edinburgh? It's in the catalogue, want to see its picture? I don't know how you can stand New York. Mama thinks you're crazy to live in such a place, full of killers with daggers." She made a pirate's face and handed me a goblet of champagne. They were giving themselves a party. All over the ship—it was a students' ship, and German —there were parties. A gang of boys had hauled the canvas off a lifeboat and were drinking from green bottles, their knees flattened under the seats. The ship smelled of some queer unfamiliar disinfectant, as though it were being scoured desperately into a state of sanitation. The students did not seem to mind the smell. Their bunks were piled with suitcases and stuffed knapsacks. "We're landing at Hamburg first, and then we have to go *back*wards to Southampton," my cousin explained. "It's cheaper to do it backwards. The champagne's all gone, you want some beer?" She went to get me some, but forgot to come back. The senior class of Consolidated High began to scream out a song. They screamed and screamed, and though I had promised my cousin's mother I would take care of Suzy as long as she was in New York, I felt suddenly superfluous and wandered off on my own. The disinfectant followed like a bad cloud. In a corner of a cabin two levels down, jammed into the angle of a bunk, I saw the starched woman. She was eating a piece of orange layer cake, and there were four shouting students squatting beside her. "Who're you seeing off now?" she addressed me out of the din. "Your sister?"

"Don't have a sister."

"Brother? Don't have a brother. Have some cake instead?"

I squeezed into the cabin and accepted a bit of icing on a paper plate. "Who're *you* seeing off?" I asked her.

"The sailors. What do you do?"

"Fine," I said.

"I didn't say how, I said what. I can see you're fine— you have very fine skin, you're not a sailor anyhow. My God, it's noisy on this one. I'm about ready for the dock. Will you wait till the end today?"

"The end of what?" I said; I thought her too friendly and too obscure.

"Of the dock part. You've got to see her go."

"I saw her go last time."

"You don't talk of time when you talk of Greek sailors. Greek sailors are timeless. Greek sailors are immortal. I bet you work in an office. Something dry, no leaks."

"A law office," I admitted.

"Makes sense, but I don't like lawyers. Wouldn't be one for anything. I'd be a sailor if I were a man. I suppose you're thinking I'm an old maid—well, I'm not. I've got a couple of married daughters, would you believe that?"

I politely muttered that the fact was hardly credible.

"I know," she agreed. "I've kept my youth." We struggled through the ship together, and finally out of it and down the gangplank, while I observed for myself that this last remark of hers was almost justified. "If you see someone off you should see it *through*," she said emphatically, in the same confident voice as last time. She had a long but all the same jolly face: long earlobes stuck through with long wooden earrings, a long square nose, a long hard chin. She wore her hair too long. The first quick look you gave her took off fifteen years, and turned her into a girl, not pretty, but rather of the "interesting" category, which I had always found boring; the second look, not so quick, put the years right back on, but assured you of something wise and pleasant. We waited for the ship's wake to form, and then waited for her to find a dairy metaphor that did for it. "Butter-churn," she said at last—"the ocean's butter-and-eggs route. I *don't* like adolescents. They can't concentrate. Sailors can concentrate—well, maybe it's because they *have* to," she conceded. "Do you have to go back now?"

"I'm past my lunch hour."

"Poor you. A little drudge. Do you see that drugstore down there—no, the one across, over there." She pointed along Canal Street. "That's my husband's. He's been a pharmacist around here for just about forever. A drudge worse than you, and been one longer. I doubt whether he's ever walked two blocks to the piers for the thrill of the thing. *I* do it practically every day. You like the water, don't you?" This startled me. "Yes," I said.

"Well, law leaves *me* all at sea too," she cracked, and fell into a tumble of laughter. She darted into the dark little store when we came to it. "In the afternoons I help out sometimes," she piped from the doorway.

After that it was a neighbor from home I put up, and then two members of the Clarksburg Post Office; and the Mayor actually. It seemed to me the whole timid town was emptying itself out, via my apartment and the docks, to throw itself on the breast of Europe. I could scarcely account for the miracle of all that fit of traveling that had fallen on the state of Ohio. As for the traffic that passed through my hands in particular (and my towels and my sheets), I soon began to understand how word had gotten back that I was, though crazy to live in such a place, cheaper than any hotel in the same place, and that I could "afford" it. This was the price I paid for having boasted so frequently of my grand salary, which now—after a weekend of restaurant dinners and taxi fares for a pair of honeymooners, children of the brother-in-law of a treasured friend of my great-aunt-by-marriage—hardly seemed so grand. The price my visitors paid was something else, and perhaps worse—word got back to *me*, ever so mildly, that in Ohio I was considered a dull unlively half-dead sort, a snob, preoccupied with my own vanity, a New York careerist. They wrote me off as a lifelong bachelor-to-be, without a heart.

On my side I thought them all wretchedly ungrateful, and if I kept my threshold open for them it was to study their ingratitude. They streamed in, earmarked by every cliché of inland dress, the men's trouser-legs ludicrously billowing, the women very large in their backward-brimmed hats and tunicked flowered rayon suits and chalky white shoes, all of them gloved and looking out cautiously from narrow-nosed, sun-fearful, flaky faces. I despised their slow voices

and I was certain they privately jeered at mine, with its
acquired pace hard-won at Yale. We made briskly poisonous
parties of it; I had the satisfaction of noting plainly how the
headwaiters shared my contempt for them. The truth was, I
suppose, that I courted and fed on my contempt, glad to see
what I was well out of. The women asked pityingly whether
I had never been abroad, and when I admitted I hadn't, the
men laughed through cigar mist and said, "Now then, y'see,
I've always maintained there's no one more provincial than a
New Yorker. Never seen the Eiffel Tower? Never seen
Rome? Well I tell you, George, go ahead and have a look at
Rome. One thing about Rome, it's worth a whole roll of
film."

That spring I saw the inside of all sizes and varieties of
ships and ship-cabins, the greasy and the glittering, wherein I
nuzzled elbow-to-elbow with my recent guests, all of us
gripping our modest drinks in an unconfident little group and
sick to death of one another's shafts. By then they had
stopped asking when I was going to get some sense into my
head and come back home to live in the real America; but
by then the relief that always followed the self-indulgence
of my scorn for them had begun to take hold. Standing,
secretly frightened, in their narrow traveling-closets, they
stood for everything I had escaped. They went on their
foolish ritual tours and thought themselves worldly, and by
Christmas would have forgotten it all if it had not been for
the ritual color slides they showed as ritual proofs of the
journey. And I, meanwhile, took *them* as ritual proofs of
my own journey—of how perilously near I had been to becoming a boarder of ships, instead of a seer-off. The passenger inexorably returns to his town in the stupid marrow of
the land; the man on the dock quivers always at the edge of
possibility. What I had attained, in my short stride from
midland to brink, was width, endlessness. Waving vainly on
the pier, I waved goodbye to all my dead ends. When at last

the ship ground vibrating out through its scribble of spume, headed not really for its destination but more essentially for the way back, something like prayerfulness ascended in me. I thought at first it was only pleasure that the burdensome visitors were gone; but then I knew it was the peace of clinging to the rim of infinity, without the obligation of resuming the limits of my old land-sewn self.

Through it all I never missed glimpsing the starched woman, with her long head and her deceptive long-haired girlishness; it was like being startled by a constantly yielding keyhole; sometimes I caught a curious view of her in someone's cabin, noiselessly clinking her earrings in an abyss of noise, and now and then I saw her leaning, always in a festive mob, holding on to a cookie, over a deck-rail, or threading in rope sandals through a slender corridor with a slender searching eye. Then the leaving-gong would clamor, and often enough I would find her beside me in the dock crowd, thirsting downward into the white whirl excreted by the outgoing ship. She was always dressed with a noticeable cleanness and stiffness—her sleeves and skirts were as rigid as a dark linen sail. "Whipped cream," she said of the wake, and then as usual we walked out with self-gratified wise sadness into the noon glister of Canal Street, until the black doorway of the drugstore sucked her suddenly in.

Or she would not be there. And then—the day after I had seen someone off and she was not there—I would leave my office at lunchtime and take my sandwich in my paper bag with me and walk west to the docks, along Canal Street, past the hardware marts spread outward on all the sidewalks, and choose a pier alongside which lay a white liner, and look for her. And there she would be, laughing seriously among strangers, eating cake, stamping her feet with their visible clean toes on the concrete, all for farewell to the departing voyagers. Or else would not.

She would not be there more often than she would be

there, and on those days I was always disappointed. I circled
the cement dock-floor awhile, chewing my sandwich at the
side of an idle Cunarder, and tramped back, inflamed by
regret and belching mustard, to my desk and its spotted documents. The Queens did not satisfy me then; I had the itch of
curiosity. She was never there to see anyone in particular off,
I had learned; no one she knew ever went abroad; she was
there for the sake of the thing itself—but I never could
fathom what that thing was: was it the ships? the sailors?
the polyglot foreignness? Was it only an afternoon walk she
took to the nearest bustling place? Was she a madwoman?
I began to hope, for the colorfulness of it, that she might
really be cracked; but whenever we conversed, she was
always decently and cheerfully sound—though, it must be
said, not like others. She was a little odd.

She asked me one day whether I was good at cross-
examination.

"We don't do much of that in our office. Mostly it's
desk work. We don't go to court hardly at all—the idea is we
try to keep the clients *out* of court," I explained.

"Haven't you ever been to a trial?"

"Oh, I've *been* to 'em."

"But never broke a witness down?"

I smiled at this brutality of hers. "No. Really, I'm not a
trial lawyer. I just sit at a desk."

"You're a passive intellectual."

"No, I'm not. Not really."

"Well, I'm glad you're not the sort who tries to get
things out of people—admissions."

"You don't have to admit anything to me," I promised.

"I wouldn't anyhow," she said. "I'm the sort who doesn't
tell things. If you tell things you don't get to keep them."

"*I* don't like to keep things," I said.

"Do you like to keep people?"

"I guess not. If I did I wouldn't always be sending them
off."

"You're not sending anyone off today," she observed. "And you were here day before yesterday, and you didn't send anyone off then either."

"True," I said.

"Are you keeping someone back?"

I had to laugh, though not pleasantly. "I guarantee you my apartment's empty right now."

"I want to see it. Your apartment. You said you can see the water from it?"

"Not this water—just the river."

"All water is one," she announced. "I want to see. No one's there at all?"

"I don't keep anyone. Really. Not even a mistress."

She looked offended at this. "I have married daughters, I told you. And a husband. They're my wake. You understand? When you live you leave a wake behind you, and it always follows you, whatever you do. What you've been and where you've been are like a milk that streams out past you all the time, you can't get free of them. Mortality issues its spoor."

I was suddenly angry; she was lecturing me with platitudes, as though I were a boy. "Well, don't worry," I said. "I haven't invited you to be kept!"

"You haven't," she agreed. "But you will. Oh, you will, you will."

I said, exasperated, "Are you a clairvoyant?"

"Don't sneer. Everyone is who goes along with Nature. You're not made of wood."

I touched the side of her dress, which extended as crisply as the hide of a tree. "No," I said, "but *you* are. Why do you dress like this? Why don't you ever wear anything soft?"

"To armor myself. If I were soft you'd want to keep me."

"Oh, go to the devil."

"And the deep blue sea," she said, turning her hard back on me.

I stayed away, after that, for almost a whole week. I did not even know her name (though she knew mine), and still I disliked her. She was a triviality, a druggist's wife, a crank who hung around the docks, and I thought myself absurd for having given so many lunch-hours to her queer company. I kept my sandwich on my desk and rattled papers while I ate it; my colleagues did the same; I had already, as a consequence of having sacrificed all those bright noons to the docks, fallen a little behind them. We were in an unacknowledged race. The more documents one digested, the more one was digested by the firm: I had to remind myself that my whole ambition was assimilation into that mystical body. But I felt vaguely enervated. The race seemed not quite to the purpose; yet I hardly knew what was more to the purpose. My colleagues struck me as silly now when they whistled *Pinafore* or snickered out their little jokes about tanker-types. I withdrew from them—I don't think they noticed at first—and immersed my unexpectedly bored brain in the Queens' sheets. But now they seemed not so much like sails as—well, sheets. They fluttered under my hands with the limpness of unruly bedclothes. Their salt emanation I knew to be no more and no less than human sweat. I gave up reading at night; I gave up sticking at home nights. I put on my oldest pair of shoes and scuffed along the riverside—to reach it I had to dare the Drive that swarmed on its ledge. The car lights smacked my eyes and I ran for my life across that wild road with its wild shining herds. Up from the stinking water came the noises of melted garbage sloshing against the artificial bank. Rarely I saw a barge creep by. The river was not enough.

On Friday night—the end of that same week of abstinence—I walked crosstown and took a bus that sliced inexorably toward the lowest part of the city, where the harbor lay pining. A pungent mist crowded the air. It was dark down there, a dark patrolled by the scowls of guards. They would not let me out onto the piers, so I prowled the cobbled sidewalks, looking down alleys; once I saw a pair of rats the size of crouched penguins, one hurrying after the other in a swift but self-aware procession, like a couple of priests late for divine service. The docks were curiously uninhabited, except by a row of the smaller sort of ship, bleak cut-outs with irregular edges as if chewed out by bad teeth—the mammoth prideful ones were all out at sea, or else dispersed among the world's more fortunate ports. I longed sorely for one of these: one of the radiant Queens—it was for these I had made this nighttime pilgrimage, hoping for the smell and signal of deep deep ocean. The loneliness of that place was excruciating; now and then a derelict lurched by, or a hushed criminal sliding forth on an errand of rape. For the first time I had an unmistakable desire to go on a voyage—I was aware of it as surely as of a taste: I had to have the marrow of a fleck of salt. I had to search into the inmost corridor of my urgency. I scurried eastward, then south (imitating the pace and gait of those sacerdotal rats), to the death-lit Battery. The terminal was as brilliantly electric as some hell. A ferry stood panting in its slip, and I boarded it on the run, just as the gate began to close. The dock and the stern split apart and the tame water dandled and puddled between them, nearly under my feet. A froth spit up all the way, stronger and stronger. The wind on the deck was harshly warm. I sank my gaze into that harbor-pool, and pulled a rope of sea-smell into a gluttonous lung; it was not enough. It was not the Thule of depths, it was not ocean enough, it was not savage enough. It was not salt enough.

Returning from Staten Island I slept on one of the side-deck benches; a drunk and I tenderly shared shoulders. The ferry was as bright as a wedding-palace or carousel. It was full of music borne by lovers embracing transistor radios. Once when the drunk's head fell from my shoulder, I awoke and saw in the blackness beyond the ferry's aureole a fantastic parade, majestically decorous—I thought it was a galaxy of rats riding the top of the water; I glimpsed pointed alert ears. But it was sails. I saw the sails of galleons, schooners,

Viking vessels, floating full and black; dark kites.

On Saturday morning I kept away; it seemed to me I had a fever, though my thermometer registered normal. All the same I wallowed and rooted in my hot bed all day, rising out of it only to drink ice water. I drew the blinds so as to shut out the river; I was frighteningly parched. In the evening I poured whiskey into the cold water, and then a little water into much whiskey. On Sunday, though feeling no better, in an atavistic fit I went to church. The text was Jonah: "For thou hadst cast me into the deep, in the midst of the seas; and the floods compassed me about: all thy billows and thy waves passed over me." Afterward I vomited in the vestry.

The next day, at noon (but I had brought no lunch), I was too impatient to walk, so I hailed a taxi for the piers, but leaped out of it in the middle of Canal Street, within a block's sighting of the wharf buildings. We had been halted by thickening traffic; I could not endure it. The rest of the way I ran. I ran up the stairs and into the long concrete hall. Everything was as usual—the mob, the noise, the familiar screeches of goodbye. Dimly from the bowels of a dim-gray ship I heard the leaving-gong. It was a Jewish ship heading for the Holy Land—it had an unhealed gash in its prow and along part of its visible side. All around were Orthodox sectarians wearing black hats and long black coats and antic beards, some of them clownishly red. They were weeping as though the broken wall of the ship were some ancient holy ravaged mortar. I flagged my arms like a fleeing ostrich through their cries and forced myself into the stream descending the gangway. A huge-breasted woman in a robust white uniform, robustly striped at the wrists, called to me to desist, but I pushed harder against the breasts pressing downward against my climb. Still-struggling I was freed into the ship, heard a wired voice command departure, and began to comb the passageways for my stiff prey. Almost instantly I found her: she was leaning against the door of a public lavatory, gleaming with splendid tears: her long face looked varnished. The gong struck again, the voice in the loudspeakers hoarsened and coarsened. "Why are you crying, for God's sake?" I said. "Everyone else is," she said, "everyone all over the place." "Quick, let's hop off or we'll end up in Jerusalem." I pulled her by the sleeve—the starch of it scratched my palm—and we flew downward. In a moment the hastening ship began to moan itself loose from the dock. The onlookers sent out a tremor of ecstasy. They joined themselves neck to neck and kicked out, kicked in, spun: they were dancing the ship toward the sacred soil. "Let's dance too," I said; I was overjoyed at the miracle of having seized her in the pinch of my will. "No, no," she said, "I don't dance, dancing makes me simply creak, I'm an antique for goodness' sake, I'm not young." I lifted her in the air—but she was as heavy as a beam—and flung her down again, out of breath. "See?" she said. "I told you." "What's your name?" I demanded; "all weekend I remembered that I don't know your name." "Undine." "Undine?" "Call me Undine," she insisted. "I will if you want me to. What does the druggist call you?" "Sylvia," she replied, "a name for a stick. A stick-in-the-mud name." "Undine," I said.

That afternoon we became lovers. She peered down from the windows of my apartment. "I like it up so high," she squealed—"you said you could see the river, though."

"There it is."

"That little dirty string?"

"All water is one," I said, mimicking her.

She looked at me meditatively. "*I* taught you that." And then, rattling the sash: "Oh, I like it up so high! I miss being up high. Where I live now it's low."

"That window's not made to open," I explained, "we're air-conditioned, can't you tell?"

"Sure I can tell. Air out of a machine. That's abnormal. It isn't natural, I'm against it."

"Come back to the bed," I begged, "it's all right here."

"They'll miss you at your office."

"They're all drudges at my office."

"I taught you that."

"Teach me, teach me," I said.

"I'll teach you fashion first. You don't like my clothes."

"I'm against clothes, they're not natural. You're not fashionable anyhow—your clothes are like bark. I peel bark, that's what I do."

"I know you do. I knew you would."

"You're a clairvoyant."

She laughed with an eery autumnal clarity, like a flutter of leaves. "No I'm not. I just go along with the tide. If I see a tidal wave I just mount it, that's all."

"I'm the tide," I said.

"I'm a wave."

"I'm the crest of the wave."

"I'm the trough."

"We coruscate."

"Like a fish's back."

"We rock, we tumble, we turn."

"I can see all the world's water from here, it's so high."

"You stay down," I ordered her.

She stayed all that night, and all the next day and all the next night. Early on the third day I put on a business suit— how strange it felt on my liberated, my sharpened, skin!— and came into my office as in a trance. My colleagues looked oddly nonhuman, like some unfamiliar species of sea-animal; the papers languishing on my desk seemed to have rotted. "You didn't answer the telephone," they accused, "were you away? An emergency?"

"I think I was sick," I said, and at once believed it.

"You look thin," they said, "how thin you've gotten."

In the mirror in the washroom I examined my thinness. It was true, I had grown very thin.

"Are you staying in for lunch?" they asked me. "Or are you going out like week before last?"

"Sure," I said, unsure of either.

"We had a man over from one of the Queens the other day. You missed some real roars, boy. A tycoon."

"A typhoon?" I said.

"Are you sick? You look sick," they said, giggling.

"I'd better go home again," I agreed, and went. The apartment smelled of decay. She was gone; she had turned off the air-conditioner and the refrigerator. My pillow smelled of rot. The milk had soured; so had the wine and the cream; two or three peaches were black. A bowl of blueberries had been transformed into an incredibly beautiful flower, all gilded over with mold.

I lay in my bed, exhausted by desire for desire; spiraled in reverie, I dreamed our three-days' love-making. I thought how she had slid from her parchment sheath and how all my pulse had mingled with hers. "Undine," I pronounced to myself, depleted. The belt of her dress was coiled on a chair; I reached out a languid hand and unfurled it. It was stiff, like frozen linen, like the side of a fossil-tree. But her waist had been flesh, and as pliant as a tongue. I hid the belt under my pillow; she had returned to her husband—this made me spring up. In half an hour I was beating Canal Street with truculent shoe-soles. I stamped and scudded, afraid to go over to the other side. Across the street, between two hardware vendors, the drugstore squatted like a dark fly. No one went in and no one came out. I wondered what sort of a living they could make in a place like that. A truck blinded the road and I ran in front of it; horns sang at me, for no reason I was still alive; I bought the first object my hand seized—a washboard. Clutching it like a lyre, I entered the drugstore. Behind a fly-flecked cardboard-crowded counter she stood holding (I thought) a real lyre, laughing her confident laugh. "We're working on a lipstick display. Isn't it nice? Look—" Her instrument turned into a thin tray fluted with golden tubes, each bloody at the tip. I read the names of all the lipsticks: Purple Fire, Crimson Ice, Silver Gash, Heart's Wound.

"The pharmacist is out," she said; "I mean he's in the cellar. He's bringing up cartons. Cosmetics. Woman's weakness since Cleopatra. Nothing touches *my* face, let me tell you— only water. If you wait you can meet him."

"Please," I said, "come back to the apartment."

"Suppose your cousins are there? Or your brother? Or your uncle?"

"You know I don't have a brother. No one's there," I swore. "No one. No one's expected. The place is empty."

"I shut off all the fake cold, did you notice?"

"Come back with me, Undine."

"Sylvia. *He* calls me Sylvia. He used to be all right but now he's all dried up, he's practically not there. I don't love him. I don't know why I stay here. Where else would I stay? It isn't as though we had any children."

"Your daughters? Your married daugh—"

Out of a hole in the flooring in the back part of the store a big tan box floated upward; behind it (seeming to paddle up, as out of a whirlpool) Undine's husband emerged. "My husband's name is George too, did I tell you that?"

He was clearly disappointed that I was not a bona fide customer; we shook hands, and then he lifted the very hand he had given me and parted the fingers to make horns behind his head. "She met you down there?" he asked. "At the docks? She always hangs around there. Eventually I get to see 'em all. Don't think I mind, it's all the same to me, buddy." He glared at my washboard. "Did you pay for that thing?"

"It's his, honey, he bought it next door. We don't sell that item," Undine said.

"Well, then put it on the order book, I don't mind the competition. One hundred thousand items in stock. Hairpins to Sal Hepatica. Paregoric to pair-of-garters. We don't do much prescription business, though. They all go uptown to those cut-rate places. Robbers, they cheat on the Fair Trade Law, cut off their nose to spite their face."

"I hate my nose," Undine said. "It's too long. I look like Pinocchio with it, don't I?"

"Quit fooling around," George said. "You want to go out with him, go out with him. I got plenty to do here, I don't need help either."

"Let's see if there's a ship going off," she assented, "one with real sails," and I followed her out of the store.

"Why do you treat him like that?" I asked.

"Oh, I don't know. Because I want to. Because he looks just like the Devil. Doesn't he look just *exactly* like the Devil, I mean really and truly?"

I considered it; she was perfectly correct. He was all points, like the ears of a rat—he was the driest, thinnest man I had ever seen. For some reason I felt cooled toward her. Her toes in her rope sandals looked too straight, too rigid. The tops of her sleeves jutted straight up from her shoulders. Her hem was like a rod.

"All the sails have come in by now. Did you read about it in the papers? From all over the world. They train sailors on those old sailing ships. Replicas. That's how they teach them about ropes and things. There's a Viking one from a movie they made. Did you see about it in the papers? Every single country's sent a sailing ship into New York harbor. It's a show, didn't you read about it?"

I said hoarsely, "I haven't seen a newspaper in three days."

"Well, they came before that. They started to come in last week. It's thrilling, don't you think it's thrilling?"

"I don't want to go to the docks. I want you to come home with me," I said, but I hardly knew now whether I meant it. Guilt over her husband ground in my throat. "Why did you say you had daughters?"

She stopped. "Oh, you're a liar."

"*I* haven't told any lies."

"You said you never cross-examine. You said you never

pry. You said you don't try to *get* things out of people."

"What's that got to do with daughters or no daughters?"

"Of *course* I've got daughters," she said sullenly. "I have a husband, don't I?—They're married, I told you, and gone away."

"All right," I said. "I misunderstood."

"I don't want you any more."

"I don't want you either."

"You're a drudge. You look exactly like the Devil yourself."

"I've lost weight," I said, defending my body.

"You might have a cancer. Cancers always begin that way.—Look at the sails!"

We had come to the end of an alley opening on the water: a thousand dazzlements cluttered the sky. Sails, sails —it was as if some suddenly domesticated goddess had reached down to hang an aeon's worth of laundry. Or it was as if a flight of enormous gulls had paused in silence to expose their perfect bellies to the equal perfection of the daylight's brilliance. The harbor seemed very still. "If it's a show," I said, "where's everybody? If it's a flotation museum, where are the visitors?" "Shush," said Undine, "it's just maritime business, who said the public was invited?" "Where are the sailors?" "*I* don't know. Ashore maybe. Asleep. Don't ask me, maybe we're having a hallucination. Look at this one!" Almost from the utmost stretch of our fingertips a great enameled bow rose, as curved and naked as a scimitar, shining wetly in the sun-gaze, like a nude breast: above the bare cutwater stood thirty-seven white-clad sentries, stiff at attention in the clear air—it was a full-rigged ship under plain sail. "Look at the masts!" Undine cried—"they're like a forest. Big heavy trunks, then branches and twigs." "I don't like the hull," I said, "it looks too fragile. Potential sawdust. Give me steel every time." "Oh, that's wicked!" she said— "steel comes out of a furnace, and then out of a machine, it isn't natural—" "Sawdust," I insisted, squinting upward at the empty prow. It seemed to me there should have been a figurehead there.

She stomped after me reluctantly, scowling, kicking heavily, banging at things with my washboard. All the way uptown she would not speak to me; she spat at the doorman when he turned his glorious captain's coattails; she scratched her nails savagely on the elevator's gray metal walls. She would not come into the bed. "I'm hungry," she said. "You switched off everything and spoiled all the food," I complained. She sidled out of the kitchen frowning with contempt, grasping a tiny silver coffee spoon—then she went to the bedroom window and stabbed the handle through the glass. It did not shatter; it only gulped out a little hole, like a mouth, with creases and cracks and wrinkles radiating outward. "Air," she said in triumph, and at last, at last, we made love.

But she was as weighty as a log. The mattress descended under her, groaning. She raised her legs and thrust them on my shoulders, and it was as though I had dived undersea, with all the ocean pressing on my arched and agonized spine. I felt like a man with a yoke, carrying on its ends a pair of buckets under a spell—the left one held the Atlantic, the right one the Pacific. When I slid my hand under her nape to lift her mouth to my gasping mouth, it seemed to me her very neck was a cord of wood. Her hair oppressed the pillow, each strand a freight, a weight, a planet's burden of gravity. How heavy she had become! Her tongue lying on my tongue exhausted me. I toiled over her unrefreshed, unspeakably wearied, condemned to a slavery of sledging logs.

"What's the matter?" she whispered. "Don't you love me? Are you tired?"

With convulsed breath I told her I loved her.

"You satisfy me," she said.

She stayed the night. We ate nothing, drank nothing; we never left the bed. In the morning I said I would go out. "No, no," she commanded. She snatched her belt from under the pillow, where she had discovered it, and buckled her wrist to the bedpost. "I'm attached," she said. "I can't leave, and neither can you. I've got to stay forever, and so do you."

"My job," I said.

"No."

"Your husband," I appealed.

"I don't have a husband."

"Undine, Undine—"

"Come on me again," she said. "Come aboard, I want you."

"We'll starve. We'll perish. They'll find our bodies—"

"I don't have a body. Don't you want me?"

"I want you," I wept, and heaved myself into the obscuring billows of my bed. She made me sweat, she made me a galley slave, my oar was a log flung into the sea of her.

"No more!" I howled; it was already dawn.

"But you satisfy me," she said reasonably. "Don't I satisfy you?"

I kissed her palms, her mouth, her ears, her neck, for gratitude, for torment, for terror. "Let's go for a walk," I begged.

"Where? I'm welded here, I told you."

"Anywhere. I'll take you home. We'll walk all the way."

"It's miles and miles. Will you carry me?"

"I've carried you miles and miles already."

"I don't want to go home."

"Then wherever you want."

"I have no home. I'm homeless. I'm adrift."

"Wherever you want, Undine! Only to leave here awhile. Air."

"But I broke the window for you, didn't I?" she said innocently.

"We'll go look at the sailing ships," I proposed.

She had hold of my hair. She licked my eyelids. "No. No, no, no."

"Never mind," I said, practical and purposeful. "Put on your clothes."

"I have no clothes."

"Where did you drop them?" I looked all around the room; they were not there, except for her starched belt, which still waggled stiffly from the bedpost. But on the chair I saw the washboard—she had brought it all the way from Canal Street.

"Here," she said, grabbing it. "I'll play you a tune. Can you sing?"

"No." For the moment I forgot that I had been in the Clarksburg church choir.

She drubbed her nails back and forth across the washboard.

"That sounds terrible. Stop it. Put on your clothes."

"I have no husband, I have no daughters, I have no house, I have no body, I have no clothes," she sang. "Your love is all I have."

I said in a fury, "Then I'll go out alone."

"All right," she said mildly. "Where?"

"To work. You know what I want?" I said. "I want to go to my office and put in a good day's work, that's what."

It was true; all at once I had a rapturous craving for work. In the street I passed a crew of diggers, sunk to their waists in a ditch, wearing yellow helmets. I envied them violently. Their backs were glazed, their vertebrae protruded like buried nuggets, under the lips of their helmets they lifted sweated wine-dyed lips. They grunted, quarreled, cursed, barked (a few yards away it all turned into a liturgy), and all the while their spines dipped downward, straining for the bottom of the ditch. They had nothing to do but devote themselves to the ditch. They were like a band of monks, ascetic, dedicated, their shining torsos self-flagellated.

The sight of them deflected my feet. I hated my office. I hated its swarming susurrant documents—they were all abstract, they were no more than buying and selling, they were only cadaverous contracts. The rest was myth and fantasy—the captains, the salt spray, the Queens. All mist, all nothingness. What I wanted then was work—shovels, pitchforks. I thought then of those inland towns and farms I had left behind, where the work was real and not a figment, where the work could be felt in the spine; work was earth and earth was work. I thought, for want of earth, I would go down to the docks and hire myself out for a longshoreman or, better yet, a sailor. I felt I had given myself out too long to fancies, and, just as I was meditating on this very notion—how passion is no more palpable than the spume's lace and lasts no longer—I came to the drugstore, and went in, and had the horrified sense of looking into a mirror.

"We got 'em now," said my double, "a whole new shipment. Arrived today."

"Shipment of what?" But I was shrill as a parrot.

"Them." The druggist pointed to a pile of cheap washboards. "I maintain if they got something next door, we got to take it in too, otherwise the competition smothers you."

"But you look like me," I said.

He was indifferent to this.

"Like *me*," I insisted, stretching my eyelids, exposing my face. I could scarcely believe I had grown so spare, for he was as dry as a length of hay, and his skin was blotched and fulvous, and his jaw was sharp as a pin. His eyes were at the same time shrewd and hopeless, like those of a man resigned to his evil, though he might covertly despise himself for it.

"Look at me!" I said.

"Don't shout," he warned in a voice of dignity. "This is a professional pharmacy, ethical. Where's she at now?"

"In my bed."

"Don't be too sure of that, buddy."

"It's where I left her."

"You left her there don't mean she's still there."

"I don't like your looks," I said.

"Then how come you zoomed all the way downtown to check on 'em? Listen," he offered, "I got a glass in the back, Sylvia uses it sometimes." He led me past the prescription counter—it was scabbed with dust and antique droplets—and then down two steps to a small rear cubicle. A long piece of stained mirror clung to the wall. We stood side by side in front of it. "See?" he sneered. "Peas in a pod."

I was staring at two straw-like creatures with pointed chins and ears and flickering eyes. "A pair of Satans," I cried.

"Well, we got different occupations," he said soothingly. "What kind of work you do?"

"A sailor," I said. "I'm going to ship out as soon as I get my papers." But at the word "papers" I suffered a chill.

"I used to be a sailor. Pharmacist's mate, S.S. *Wilkinson*. I been everywhere."

"I haven't been anywhere."

"With me it came out the opposite. She made me stick in one place. She got me rooted to this hole and I can't get out. I never get out. See that?" He waved a dry arm at a bundle in a corner. It was a narrow campbed tangled up in dirty blankets. "I even sleep here. It's like the hold of a ship back here."

"Where does your wife sleep?"

He gave a scornful smirk. "You can answer that one better than me, buddy."

"Look here," I said, all business. "I want to get rid of her. Get her out of my hair, will you?"

"Had enough? Too bad. That means she's only just getting started on you."

"Quit grinning," I yelled.

"I got to grin, why not? She runs her course."

"How long?"

"How should I know? Depends how long she gets something out of it. With me it was only a year or so—"

"A year? One year? But you've got children, daughters, grown children—"

"*She's* the one with the daughters, not me. *She's* got daughters all over."

"She said two. A couple, she said."

"A couple of thousand, for all I know about it."

"She said married!"

"Listen, she'll call anything a marriage. A blink, and it's a wedding."

"Isn't she your wife?"

"Why not?"

I fled.

It was late when I arrived, even though I had not stopped for breakfast. My colleagues were already immersed at their desks; their papers shimmered and shuddered. From the partners' office came whip-sounds of bleating winds: a quarrel. "It's over you," they told me. "They want to fire you. Old Hallet's holding out for you, though. Says your stuff's been very good up till now. Advocates mercy.'"

"The reason I'm here," I said bravely, "is to resign."

They tittered. "Now you won't have to."

"I have my pride," I said.

"You leaving? Where've you been? You look like the devil, my God, you look like hell," they said.

"If a woman comes here, don't let on you've seen me," I pleaded.

"Little odd stout woman?" one of them said. "Youngish and oldish both? Nice firm breasts? Nice hard belly? Nipples like carvings? She's already been."

Terrified, I crept back from the door. "*Been* here?"

"Turned up an hour ago asking for you. Dishabille, so to speak."

"Please!" I said out of a burning lung.

"Naked. Nude. In her birthday suit, George. Fine figure, straight as a pole."

"Asking for me?"

"Asking for George."

"Where is she?" I whispered.

"Lord knows. We sent for an ambulance, y'know. Had to. Not that a law firm's no place for loons, mind you—" The shouts from the partners' office swelled; I heard my name. "She was carrying a lyre. She was covering her modesty with it."

"A washboard you mean," I said.

"*There's* a loon for you. Poor poor George—it's *pos*sible to tell the difference, y'know."

"It was only a washboard," I persisted.

"A lyre," they said. "It looked like the real thing, that's the nuttiest part of the whole show. Made out of a turtle-shell, green all over. Phosphorescent sort of. Could've been dragged up out of the bottom of the sea, from its looks. Think she swiped it from a museum? If they don't get her on disorderly conduct they'll get her for that. Poor George. A friend of yours?"

I ran from them, choking.

She was waiting for me in my apartment: I was scarcely surprised. "That was mean," she said; in a shower of her long hair she squatted on my bed. "They took me into a sort of truck. You let them do that! I had an awful time running away from them. They would've thrown me into prison!"

"You're out of your mind," I said, "going up there like that. You've lost me my job."

"What do you care? You didn't want it anyhow."

This was incontrovertible, though I wondered how she had guessed.

"Come here," she commanded.

"You can't just go up into offices stark naked."

"Who said I did? Oh, for goodness' sake, don't lecture, I only went up there to look for you. It's your fault, you shouldn't have gone away."

"You can't *do* a thing like that in a civilized country. You'll probably get us into the papers. For all I know the police'll be up here in a minute."

"I wasn't stark naked."

"They said you were."

"You believe everyone but me! I bet you'd even believe George, and George is about as steady as a leaf on a stem."

"They said you didn't have anything *on*," I said.

"I was in a hurry. Didn't I *tell* you I wanted you? You had no business running off. I couldn't find my clothes, that's all."

"A stupid stunt."

"Now you're in a rage again. Always in a rage."

"I'm not—"

"Besides, I was covered up anyhow."

"With what?"

"You're cross-examining again," she accused. "It's none of your affair. I covered up what's supposed to be covered up in a civilized country, that's all."

"Where's that lyre thing?"

"Don't be stupid. How should I know? Come here, I want you."

She tossed up a smooth leg. Against my will I went to her. "They said you stole it."

"Where on earth would I get a lyre? A funny thing like that? You're insulting." She reached under my pillow, laughing crossly. There it was: the ancient little hand-harp. "On my way up to your office I passed a pawnshop and saw it in the window and bought it."

"Went into the pawnshop without any clothes on?"

"Oh, don't *dig* like that. Mind your own business. Look, I'll sing some more, all right? Do you know Greek? I'll sing you a Greek song."

"*You* don't know Greek," I said.

"Oh, don't I? I know all the languages. I know Greek, I know Walloon, I know Orangutan—"

But when she began to sing it was in German:

Meine Töchter sollen dich warten schön;
meine Töchter führen den nächtlichen Reihn
und wiegen und tanzen und singen dich ein.

Her voice was coarse; it recalled a plank of fresh-cut wood thumped against the grain, and it was somehow blurred, like a horn heard from afar, or as if her lung had been afflicted by a fog. "You don't sound like yourself," I complained.

"A cold," she assented. "Don't interrupt."

"Stop," I said, "I don't like it."

"Are you one of those people who think every unfamiliar language makes a bad noise? You ought to have more sense than that," she said, "a man like you."

This shamed me, so I listened mutely. But now she was continuing in new syllables I could not recognize, very short and rough. "What language is that?"

"Phoenician," she answered.

"Oh come on, is it Arabic?"

"I just told you, it's Phoenician. It's about the sea when the waves are especially high and the rowers can't see over their tops."

I was annoyed. The dark queer burr in her throat had begun to arouse me, and I could not bear to be teased just then. I wanted to get rid of her. "All right," I said, "you found an old song-sheet wrapped in an old scroll in an old jar in an old cave, is that it? Fine. Now go home, will you?"

"It wasn't like that at all. I just happened to pick up the words one time."

"On the docks, I know. From the current crop of Phoenician sailors. Go home, Undine."

"I have no home."

"Then just go away."

"You'll be sorry if I do."

"Damn it, I want to get some sleep."

"I won't bother you. Come into the bed."

"No."

"Come here," she insisted.

"Go away. It's *my* apartment. I didn't invite you here."

"Yes you did."

"Ages ago. It doesn't count."

"Last week."

'It feels like an aeon."

"Come here," she said again. She dipped two fingers into the strings of the lyre and provoked a vicious ripple. "Because if you don't, do you know what I'm liable to do? I'm just liable to throw this thing right through that window."

"I want to be let alone," I said.

She threw the lyre through the window. It penetrated sideways and cleanly, like the cut of a knife, with a soft clear click of struck sound—a thin pale note came out as it hit, and the pane and the lyre went gyrating downward to the street together; I was in time to glimpse the two objects still gleaming and braiding in air. They fell not far apart, between two cars in the road.

"You could've killed someone down there!"

"I warned you, didn't I?"

I went to her docilely enough then; it was as though she had broken something in me—some inner crystal, through which up to the moment of its shattering I had been able to see rationality, responsibility; light. I saw nothing now; her mouth became a wide-open window, and I hurled myself through it, whirling my tongue like a lyre. I stretched the strings of her hair and webbed them and plucked at them; they seemed in my teeth as tough as rope. I was blind and faint, but her body took me ravenous for it; no sooner did I slip into consolation than a gong of lust pealed me alert. All the same the dreaded faintness returned, it kept returning, I awoke to her and it returned, I could not endure it, I was

drained, behind my heated eyeballs it grew ladder-like and
dark.

It was night.

"I want to sleep," I moaned.

"Tired already? Ah, little man-darling." And would not
release me; and I had to tense again for the plunge. All that
night it was a dream of plunging and diving; the undersea of
her was never satiated, the dive was bottomless, plummeting,
vast and vast. "Soon, soon," she promised me, "soon you'll
sleep, you'll see, trust me, always rely on me, I keep faith
with everyone, don't I?" She crooned; and the warp of her
voice lifted me alive like a tree. "Aren't you happy now?
Aren't you glad I stayed?" she asked me. "Yes, yes," I always
replied, swimming in the wake of gratefulness.

At three o'clock—a blessed little nap had momentarily
reposed her, and she lay in my arms while my open scared
eyelids flickered like flies—the telephone rang. "It's nobody,"
she reprimanded with a yawn, but she passed the receiver to
me, wreathing my member with the cord to hold it captive.

"That you, George?"

It was my uncle Al.

"Listen, George," he said, "I made it back sooner'n I
thought I was ever going to—didn't like it over there.
Neither did Nick. You wouldn't remember him, little gimpy
foreign guy, this Greek I went over with, same cabin and
all? This fella Lewis? Fact is he's with me now. I don't like
to call you in the middle of the night, George boy, that's the
truth—"

"Where are you, Al?"

"Down at the docks. My God, George, you ought to
see what they got going down here—spooky enough to give
you the creeps, about a hundred of them old wooden tubs
all over the place, out of a goddamn storybook, sheets out
like a pack of Hallowe'eners. Back home we got bathtubs
better-looking than some of that. Say listen, George, the

truth is I'd like to know if you could put up the two of us for the night? Me and this Greek fella, he's not a bad little guy—"

"You mean you want to come up here right *now?*" I said.

"Well, yeah. Just stepped off the boat. Managed to get a spot back on this little Eye-tie job, accommodations a little on the spaghetti side, but you don't waste a cent—"

"Look, Al," I said, "maybe you could get yourself a hotel room around about there, it's pretty late—"

"That's the *point*, kid, Nick here with his arthritis and all, it's kind of late to go looking around, couple of strangers in town—"

"I don't know, Al," I said, "this place is sort of a wreck at the moment. I mean it's sort of a wreck."

Undine pulled on the telephone wire. "Don't talk any more. I want you. Come back," she called.

"Oh, come on, it's all in the family. We don't mind a little mess. Unless you got a lady-friend up there?" he hooted.

"No, look, all right," I said. "That's fine. Sure, Al, you come on over," I said.

Her nostrils had turned rigid. Her neck twisted up like a root. "What did you do that for? *We* don't want anybody."

"I owe it to my uncle. He's bringing along that Greek too. You'll have to leave now," I told her.

"But you said I made you happy!" she wailed.

"I *tried* to put him off, didn't I? You heard me."

"All I heard was you said the place was a wreck. It's not, it's perfectly nice. I like it."

"It was a way of telling him not to come, that's all. *You* heard. I couldn't help it, he insisted."

She leaned her breasts against the bedpost, meditating; but her arms strove backward. "You don't want me really?"

"Enough is enough," I said.

"Enough," she said—and with an easy slap broke off the knob of the bedpost—"is enough"—and with a stray sliver of window-glass shredded the bedclothes. Bits of rubber foam twinkled upward.

"Undine—"

"A wreck, you're right, a wreck," she cried—she was solemn and slow. She cradled the shade of a lamp, tender as a nursemaid, then crushed it under her naked toes, and used the brass lamp-pole to smash the frame of the bed. Her blows were cautious, regular, and accurate. She hewed the arm off a chair and the arm demolished the bureau. Drawer-knobs in flight mobbed the air. In all the rooms the floor-boards sprang up groaning. Vases went rolling, limbs of little tables disported. Piece by piece the air-conditioner released its diverse organs; in the kitchen the ice-trays poured and clattered, the stove-grates ground the refrigerator door to a yellowish porcelain dust, the ceiling was pocked with faucet-handles embedded like silvery pustules. She slashed the sofa pillows, and crowing and gurgling with fury and bliss felled the toilet-tank. Mound by mound she heaped it all behind her—barrows rose suddenly up at her heels like the rapid wake of disappearing civilizations. A cemetery grew at her thrust. She destroyed with a marvelous promiscuity—nothing mattered to her, nothing was too obvious to miss or too minuscule to ignore. She was thorough, she was strong. I waited for the end, and there was no end. What had been left large she reduced; what had been left small she pulverized. The telephone (I thought of calling the police, but reserved this for the neighbors) was a ragged hillock of black confetti.

Finally she went away.

I lay down in the wreckage and slept moderately until my uncle and the Greek arrived. There was no door for them to come through: they simply came in, trampling sawdust.

"Good Lord," Al said. "Sweet Jesus. Was it burglars?"

"A bitch," I said.

"A witch?" said the Greek, hobbling from waste to waste on polished crutches.

"We always say back home that this here's one dangerous city to live in," Al said. "If you had half a brain, George boy, you'd come on home. Practically all of Europe's just the same. No good. I saw that Mediterranean, and I didn't like the smell. You got to go deep inside a country, away from the shore line, if you want decency."

"There is no witches," Mr. Lewis said boldly.

"The boy knows that," my uncle said. "Here come the police."

The neighbors came too; there was a confusion, in which the Greek forgot his English, all but the odd word "witch"; they took him off to the station house, and my uncle loyally followed to post bail. "Superstitious little runt," he explained, enjoying the crowd.

Morning was not yet; I ran through crepuscular streets, liberated. Now and again I stopped before a display window to pose and observe my reflection; it seemed to me I had none. How thin I must have become! I ran and ran, into the seeping dye of dawn. I felt an insupportable vigor. My feet scooped up miles—the miles themselves appeared to have been exorcised by my vigor and my glee, and grew improbably briefer. In an instant I was on Canal Street, half an instant afterward I was scudding past the drugstore—it looked intact, and fleeing it I wondered whether the druggist's mirror might deliver up my lost reflection. But I could no longer halt, I ran on, I ran to the gray piers, I ran to the morning-tipped sails wind-full in the harbor. All the way I jogged her name in my teeth.

I knew where to look for her.

"Undine!" I shrieked into that deserted alley I remembered.

"Sylvia!" howled the druggist. His bits of hair stood aloft in peaked tufts, his jagged ears bristled, his triangular chin poked the bone of his chest. He was so wafer-like that I feared for him to show me his profile; I was certain he would vanish into a line. "You too?" he said when he recognized me.

"She's left me," I croaked.

"And me," he informed me.

We hugged one another; we danced on the edge of the pier; we babbled at our luck.

"Will she come back?" I asked him.

"Who knows? But I bet not. Not after this time, I bet. She's all worn out, it looked like."

"Did she tell you where she's going?"

"To visit her daughters, she said."

"Where are they?"

"India, she said. Also Africa."

Triumphantly I took this in. "Did you ever see her off before?"

"One time I did. But after that she came back. She went on a Queen, that was the trouble—they caught her, scraped her right off. And anyhow she said she hated the thing, all cold metal, like riding a spoon, she said. Don't shoot me so many questions, buddy. I ain't your teacher."

"I only want to know if you can see her."

He squinted into the yolk-colored sky. "Not yet. Look for yourself."

"But there are so many ships, I can't tell—"

"She might not be aboard yet."

We skimmed up and down the alley, sniffing at the water. It brightened under the dawn; it spun out slavering columns of red.

"See that two-master? She ain't on that one."

"I can't—no, that's right, not on that one."

Down to the horizon, into the very bottom of the sun, the flotilla stood, bark after bark after bark, the galleys and galleons, the schooners and sloops, the single high Norsemen's vessel, the junks and the dhows and the xebecs and the feluccas, with their painted whimsical hulls and their multi-

tudinous sails in rows and banks and phantasmal tiers, paper-
white geometries clambering like petals out of the masts, and
the water galloping and spitting beneath their tall arched
bows.

The druggist's glance hopped from ship to ship.

Then I—too shy of what I sought to look so far—spied
her: she hung nearly over our heads, she was an eave shadow-
ing our heads, her hair streamed backward over her loins,
her left hand clasped a lyre, her right hand made as if to
pluck it but did not, her spine was clamped high upon the
nearest prow. Although her eyes were wide, they were
woodenly in trance: I had never known her in so pure a
sleep.

"Undine!"

"Sylvia!" mocked the druggist.

"She doesn't answer."

"She won't," he responded with satisfaction. "You can
go on home now, buddy."

"She won't answer?"

"Use your eyes, buddy. Does she look like she will?"

I saw the long and delicate grain in her thighs, the
nodules in her straight wrists, the knots that circled and
circled about her erect and exact nipples, the splintered
panel that cleft her flank. (I recalled a mole in that place.)
"Look at that," said the druggist, pointing to the notch,
"she's getting old. More'n a century, I'd say. Want to bet she
doesn't make it back? Falls right plump into the Atlantic?
Her rigging's weak, she looks glued on, water'll wash her
right off."

I pleaded with him: "She won't answer?"

"Try her."

I flung back my neck and shouted up: "Undine—"

A figurehead does not breathe.

"Go on back, boy," said the druggist.

"And you?" I asked him; but did not leave off gaping
into the flock of sails that seemed to spring from her im-

mutable shoulders like a huge headdress of starched fans. They gasped and vaguely hissed, and she beneath them strained her back to meet the prow's grand arch, and threw into their lucidities her stiff gaze.

"I got my business to take care of," he told me. "Build it up a bit now maybe. Hire somebody with better customer-visibility. *She* never let me hire anybody."

"She wrecked my apartment," I confided. "She lost me my job."

"That's the least of it. Believe me, buddy, the least. That's the stuff you can fix up."

"I guess I can fix up my apartment," I said dejectedly.

"You going for a sailor, like you said?"

"No." And spotted panic in me.

"Going back to wherever you come from?"

I considered this; I thought of the fields of home. "No," I said after a moment.

"Well, so long, buddy, I wish you luck with things when you find out."

I said in the voice of a victim, "Find out what?"

But he had turned his side to me, and, though I stared with all my strength, I could no longer see him.

The
Doctor's
Wife

THE DOCTOR's three sisters had gathered to make salads in the house of the sister who had the biggest kitchen. They were preparing for the doctor's fiftieth birthday. Quite logically, the sister who had the biggest kitchen also had the biggest house; but she was not the richest sister. Alas, none of them was rich, not a single one, though Sophie —the sister who had the biggest house—perhaps should have been. Her husband was a puffy-necked, mostly bald dentist with intact teeth of his own, which he was always lifting up to the light in perpetual melancholy glinting laughter. He had the sort of fat-lidded marble eyes that make anyone look prosperous, but he liked to gamble at the harness races, and, worse yet, he liked to dance. In the winter he shut up his practice for half a month at a time to take part in dance contests, dance marathons, dance exhibitions. In the summer he went alone to resort hotels with celebrated orchestras. He was short, still blond at the back of the head, and he had a lewd tongue, but was as scholarly as any adolescent about the newest steps. Except for the doctor, the dentist was the poorest of them all—two of his boys were in expensive colleges, and sometimes he had to ask his assistant to wait a week or two until he could find the money to catch up with the salary he owed her.

The other brothers-in-law were a teacher and a photographer. The teacher, a bleak stern man who hated his job, was

married to Frieda. They lived with five bickering children
in a cramped apartment at the bottom of a two-family house.
Olga was the youngest of the sisters and had only one little
girl, who was either sickly or dull, and was never seen to
blink at her father's flash-bulbs. The photographer, a big,
hairy, muscular fellow, actually had the temperament of a
child, but his noisy football-coach mannerisms belied this.
He was constantly daydreaming. His business was mostly
baby portraits, yet he hoped for fame and harangued the
doctor with his theories of photographic satire.

The doctor was really very poor, but he was the sisters'
saint.

Frieda loved her husband. Sophie and Olga did not love
theirs.

Sophie and Olga were extraordinarily alike. Everyone
swore that Sophie, with her mirror-like gray eyes, was the
family beauty, whereas Olga's hair would not curl and her
bosom was monstrous. But otherwise they were very nearly
psychological twins. Both were bored by babies, both were
artistic, both were discontent, both loathed housekeeping.
They had both decided long ago that they were superior to
Frieda, who was humdrum and without talent. Before her
marriage Frieda had been a nurse, and even now her face
was always steamy, as though she had just emerged from
sterilizing bedpans. Frieda's tedious motto was to make the
best of things, and this to Sophie and Olga smacked of
slavishness. Sophie and Olga considered themselves rebels,
but while Sophie escaped to her piano and her water-color
box, Olga read religious philosophy. She was attracted to all
manner of arcane cults, and, though Sophie laughed at her,
she was almost as tolerant as Frieda: Olga was their baby.

The doctor was the oldest. He was unmarried, and did
not differentiate among the sisters or their husbands. He
accepted it that the dentist was a rough sort who gambled
and danced and was unfaithful to Sophie every summer, that

the photographer fell into terrifying fits of vanity and humiliation and raged over Olga's superstitiousness, and that the teacher was so stingy that Frieda was made to buy the cheapest cuts of meat and walked right through the soles of her shoes. Sometimes he confused the husbands, called them by the wrong names, and mixed up their occupations and their vices.

The doctor, it seemed, was not very attentive to his sisters. This was because they were women, and women have no categories. He did not notice his sisters as individuals, but he noticed what they were. They were free. They were free because they were unfree; they were exempt from choices. They did not have to *be* anything; it was enough that they were women. Their bodies were their life's blueprints: they married, became pregnant, nursed their infants, fussed over the children's homework. The doctor marveled that the three little persons in this one room had borne, all together, nine new souls. One day they would attend the children's weddings and then they would have nothing to do but grow comfortably old. What lives! He sat in the chair that caught the best light from the fluorescent rod over the sink and watched Frieda chop celery in a wooden bowl that had belonged to their grandmother half a century ago. Everything they did struck him as play. Here was Sophie licking mayonnaise from a big stirring-spoon, and there was Olga peeping over her chest and counting dishes.

"Tuna, tuna, salmon, tuna, salmon. It's monotonous. It's fishy," Olga said.

"Egg salad next," Frieda promised, chopping so hard that the loose fat on her arms quivered. She had a roly-poly but spry and tidy little figure, and the ends of her blouse were always tucked in exactly. Her complexion was open-pored and very red. "What's wrong with fishy? Caviar is fishy. King and queens and movie people eat caviar, don't they? Fish is brain food anyhow."

"Then Pug doesn't need any. Pug's the Smartest Man in the World," Sophie said.

The doctor folded up his newspaper and looked at the clock.

"Pug, aren't you the Smartest Man in the World?"

"No, he's not," Olga said. "He's the Third Smartest."

"So who's the First and Second Smartest?" Sophie demanded.

"A man named Sidney Morgenbesser is Second and a man named Shemayim is First."

"Good God, Sidney *who?*"

"They're philosophers," Olga said. "One's at Cambridge, Massachusetts and one's at Columbia University in New York. I read about them. They're antispiritual."

"Is she right, Pug?" Sophie asked.

The doctor smiled. He had a very little air of self-regard, but he kept it hidden, even from himself. He had never heard of Sidney Morgenbesser or Shemayim. "Well, in that case maybe it's only Fourth for me," he said. "Olga's ahead of me. Olga knows all the philosophers."

"Not personally," Olga said.

"Carnally," Sophie explained. "Pug, where are you *going?*"

"I have house calls tonight."

"On Thursday? I thought you did house calls on Wednesday," Olga said.

"This is a different house call, puss, ask him what *kind* of house. Probably the kind all you bachelors go to now and then, right, Pug?"

"Leave the boy be," Frieda said. "Where's that mayonnaise spoon, I just *had* it—"

"Don't you dare have house calls tomorrow night," Sophie warned. "Miss your birthday and we'll see you never have another."

"Soph, you've *licked* it, wash it off first."

"I don't believe in germs," Sophie said. "I believe in what I can see."

"Do you believe in radio waves?" Olga said. "You can't see them and they're there."

"Now don't start with your spooks. Thank God it's broken anyhow—the radio. I've had two whole nights without WPAP and Art Kane's Swinging Doodlers Direct from Miami Beach. Speaking of radios."

"Stop that, Soph, you like to dance yourself," Frieda said, sponging the spoon with detergent.

Olga suddenly giggled. "Where's Saint Vitus gone tonight?"

"To the movies."

"Because *I'm* here," Olga said. "He's afraid to meet Dan in case Dan comes to call for me. Which he will."

"You should put a mask on Dan," Sophie suggested, "and introduce him as somebody else. Then they might start speaking again."

"It wouldn't work," Olga said. "If they haven't spoken for two years—*is* it two years?—they'll never speak. Anyhow Dan won't."

"With a mask," Sophie said, "you could introduce Dan as Sidney Morgenfresser."

"Besser."

"Besser late than never," the doctor said, and put on his jacket. "I've got to be off. What time do you want me tomorrow night?"

"Oh, wait, don't you want to see the cake?" Olga cried.

"I'll see it tomorrow, won't I?"

"Oh, but *look*. Look what it says. Frieda did it with a tube thing that you squeeze. It's going to have five candles—"

"One for each decade," Sophie intervened.

"Pug can do arithmetic, stupid. Look what it says!"

He read, among pink sugar-roses, LOVE TO OUR DEAR

DOCTOR PUG FOR PUGNACITY.

"Isn't it smart! Sophie thought of it but Frieda didn't like it."

Frieda said, "If there's one word that *doesn't* describe—"

"My God, Frieda, that's the point, it's teasing, it's a joke. Good God, the way you fight jokes, *you're* the pugnacious one."

"Wonderful," the doctor said, but he was embarrassed by the "Doctor." After so many years they never let him rest with it. They savored his degree, they munched on his title. If someone asked after him, they never said simply "my brother"—it was always Doctor Pug. His name was Pincus but they were ashamed of it. His father said Doctor Pug too; he howled at his son but boasted to the laundryman. They esteemed him the way peasants esteem the only lettered person in a village. The ignorance, the pitiful ignorance!

He went back to his office and found the waiting room full, though he had made no appointments. He was still belching from the fat-soaked dinner Sophie had given him. It was forced on him because the sisters thought it would be a treat to have him there the one night they were all working together. At Frieda's house, despite the inconvenience and squeezing-in at table, he ate well. But Sophie's dishes were only yearnings: she tried to imitate those colored family scenes of splendid dining in the life-insurance advertisements, and approximated only the order of the forks. It was like chewing paint. She had fed him beef tonight that was all muscle. He had lied about the house calls, otherwise they would have kept him longer—house calls started early.

As usual, his patients had divided the room between them. The Negroes all sat on one side, near the door, and the Italians angrily on the other, monopolizing the magazine bench. The magazines were tattered, which was odd, since he never noticed that anyone read them. His practice embraced only the poorest. The neighborhood had been decaying since Adam left Eden. For a long while it had been inhabited mainly by old immigrants, but now it was sulkily mixed; the crouching Italians peered over their tomato plants in the lots on the corners and saw the moving vans bringing the Negroes' sticks and shreds. Some of the Italians told him they would not come back if he took the Negroes for patients. But most stayed, because if they said they had no money to pay he charged them only fifty cents for the visit and promised he would collect it next time. But next time he always forgot.

Among these people there were surprisingly few physical diseases. An old Sicilian had a cataract. An adolescent girl with skin luminous as dyed silk who came in clinging to her aunt had a tiny cyst at the margins of the breast tissue. But the most ordinary complaints were headache, backache, sleeplessness, fatigue, obscure traveling pains. It was the old recurrent groan of life. It was the sound of nature turning on its hinge. Everyone had a story to tell him. What resentments, what hatreds, what bitterness, how little good will! Wives and husbands despised one another, grandchildren were spiteful, the money went on liquor, the children were marrying haughty strangers, the daughter-in-law was a cold-hearted wretch, the fathers left home in the middle of the night. Bedlam, waste, misery—it was humanity seething in its old pot.

The doctor was writing a prescription for phenobarbital for a woman who believed she had a hole in her lung (but the truth was her son had been married for twelve years and still had no bambini) when there was a knock on the window. He thought it was a branch of the elm and told the woman to take the medicine three times a day and the feeling of the hole would go away. "Maybe they should stitch it up, the hole?" she asked. Her face was like a hound's: the ears were pulled down into abnormal lengths by pendent glass cylinders. "Your lungs are perfectly sound, Mrs. Filletti," he said, and heard the window crack.

The dentist was weeping under the elm, holding a fistful of stones.

"Irwin!" the doctor called down.

"Pug, I'm lonely. Pug, I'm terribly lonely."

"Irwin, I can't hear you. Come up, will you?"

"You've got people?"

"A few left."

"I can't come up, I might be recognized. I'm a professional in this town same as you," the dentist sobbed.

"Do you want money?" he said through the window.

"Please, don't shame me. Listen, what's money to me? I want happiness, happiness."

"All right, go over to the house and I'll see you in a little while."

"Don't try to send me where Dan is, Pug. That's all over. A finished relationship. You can't reconcile oil and water, Pug."

"I mean my house, not yours."

"Your old man puts his nose in everything."

"Irwin, I have patients."

"So do I, so do I! They act as if you're the only professional in the family. Look, hurry up, I've got the car, we'll ride around."

The doctor took his time, bandaged a boy who had been beaten in a lot fight, listened to half a dozen more tragedies, inscribed *t.i.d.* on his pad with such pressure that his forefinger began to ache, shut off the lights, locked up, and went down to the dentist's enormous globular car, which he had bought twenty per cent down and could not afford.

They rode through streets smelling of lilac. It was a May night. The car was crackly with candy wrappers, and somehow this, and the lilacs which every spring struck him as some new marvel of the senses he had never before passed through, reassured and caressed the doctor: for a moment he thought that perhaps everything was really temporary, his life now was only a temporary accommodation, he was young, he was preparing for the future, he would beget progeny, he would discover a useful medical instrument, he would succor the oppressed, he would follow a Gandhi-like figure in a snow-white loincloth, he would be saved; the childlike fragrance radiated a conviction that his most intense capacities, his deepest consummations, lay ahead. His brother-in-law, wiping dirty moist furrows across his scorched and unshaven chin, turned off into a neighborhood once rich and glorious, with huge houses set on huge hilly lawns, and trees thick as a forest. The houses were now all converted to apartments and bleated television noise. The lawns were striped and spotted with wagons and trucks, and children's wagons and trucks filled the spaces between them. Voices of nighttime quarrelers sprang from house to house like terrible peregrinating angels. "Life is transient," the doctor said. "Everything changes, what difference does it make to you?"

"But they did it out of malice," his brother-in-law said. "They did it out of spite. When I came in the house there he was. They know he's my enemy, and there he was."

"Irwin, you have no enemies. You're your own enemy, like everybody else."

"Am I? I'm my own enemy? *I* didn't ask him to come to my house. *They* did. *I* went to a movie."

The doctor said with a smile, "You should have gone to a double feature. You went to a single feature and it wasn't long enough, you see? Otherwise he would have been gone by the time you got back. He only came to call for Olga."

"Olga's a fool. She's a vicious fool too. Don't get the wool pulled over you by that damn malicious laugh she puts on, it's poison. And Sophie's worse. Sophie actually let him into the house. I can't stand the sight of him, I do everything I can to avoid him, isn't it enough I have to look at him tomorrow night? I'm a man of peace. Peace, peace, peace—"

"So is Dan," the doctor said. He concentrated; he meditated; he speculated; he could no longer remember the cause of the estrangement. Was it money? Jealousy? Surrender? Failure? A promise subverted?

"What *he* is, he's a hunter, a primitive hunter. He still stalks the jungles. Me, I'm sick and tired of being his prey. Listen, Pug, all I want is one very simple thing, all I want is to be happy, is that too much for a human being to ask?"

"You've got the boys, you've got Sophie."

"The boys think they're smarter than me. Even the little fellows. All right, I admit it, they're smarter, it's true, I don't deny it. When the other two were home Christmas I said something and they laughed in my face and started talking biochemistry like I didn't exist. And Sophie, Sophie used to be a gorgeous woman, before we were married we used to go on in a certain way for hours. Right after your grandmother's funeral we did it, even then. It was a fantastic attraction, I'm telling you. Between me and Sophie it was something special, fantastic. Not that she ever let me go the limit, as they say, but she let me feel under her bra and sometimes down under, you know Then, afterward, we got married, nothing. I says let's go to Pug and get his advice, she says no, it's my brother, I'd die. Last summer in the mountains, place called Shady Green, very bad toilets, up there they throw down anything and everything, they don't care, even Kotex, they wouldn't hesitate to throw down a dead body if you ask me, anyhow there was this girl, not old, not young, maybe thirty-two-three, with her it was like it was with Sophie at the beginning. Same physical type, short waist, big hips, a lot of silly talk, you know what I mean—"

He stopped the car in a cave of blossoming trees. The din from the houses and the lawns crowded with vehicles prodded them like a horn. Under the leaves sound and shape seemed in heat; then demonically mated.

"I'm telling you the truth, Pug, sometimes I don't think I can live with it any more. I want something, I have

this hollow feeling in me all the time, no, I mean it's more
like a full feeling, there's something I want to get rid of
inside me and I don't know what. Like if I could suddenly
vomit it up I'd feel better, you know?"

The doctor said, "You should pay more attention to
your practice, Irwin. Not because you owe a lot, that's not
the issue. Work helps a person, Irwin."

"For a distraction it helps. That's my trouble, I'm not
like you, I don't *want* distraction. I want to pull the rotten
core out of me and look at it. I want to be happy, that's
all. How do you get to be happy?"

"I don't know," the doctor said.

"Listen, you know why I go to the track, say? I don't
go for distraction, whatever you want to call it. Just the
opposite, I go because it scares me there. I'm scared stiff
of losing, I get these dunning letters from the kids' bursars.
I get so damn scared. But when I'm scared it's like I *feel*
myself, you know what I mean? I start believing in my own
existence, you know what I mean? It's like dancing. God,
I'm forty-six, I start doing some of those bits I'm so out of
breath I think I'm getting a heart attack. But I start feeling
my heart *beat*, I know it's there, and I figure well, if I have
a heart I have a body, if I have a body I'm alive. I figure
if I'm alive there's something to be alive for."

"There *is* something to be alive for," the doctor said.

"Well, what? Go ahead, what? You tell me."

"I don't know," the doctor said.

"And to Sophie, I mean this as true as I'm sitting here,
to Sophie you're God! Go on, if you're God tell me what
I'm alive for."

"Nobody can answer that question."

"You mean nobody can *ask* it. Who asks such a thing?
Go on, tell me, you know somebody else who asks a question like that, what he's alive for? There's this power in me,
Pug, it's eating me up. I think it's sex. Maybe I need more
sex, or maybe different sex. You think I need more sex, Pug?

Look, I'm not asking anything personal, but what happens
when a nice guy like you wants a woman? Except for the
toilets you ought to try Shady Green, Pug, honest to God."

The doctor's father was awake and waiting for him. He
was a stringy tottering old man, in an incessant fury, run
down, paralyzed in random places—a patch on the throat, a
piece of the lip, his left shin, two fingers of his left hand, a
single toe on the right foot. His fury rose with him in the
morning and went to bed with him at night; fury was his
wife. "Where you've been? Where you've been?" he yelled
at his son, and his gums—he had already put his teeth in a
glass of water mixed with a powder—looked clean, ruddy,
healthy and shining.

"I took a ride with Irwin."

"Took a ride, took a ride! His father can rot in the
house. You know what I ran out of today? You didn't bring?
You never bring! Citrus! I got no grapefruits, I got no
lemons, I got no Sunkist. Go, go, take a ride!"

"I'll buy some oranges tomorrow," the doctor said.

"Tomorrow isn't today, tomorrow I could be dead. Go
take a ride with a professional bum! You know you missed
somebody, you weren't here? Three somebodies you missed.
Olga, Dan, and the little stupid. What a stupid! God forbid,
four years old, eyes like a sheep. You think it's right Dan
should take the child out this time of night? He went to
drive Olga, why? She couldn't come later on with Frieda?
Frieda's got no looks, I'll admit it, but a *mensch*, she drives
a car. He went to drive Olga, he took the child. I tell you
that's why she's got no brain—abuse! Day and night they
abuse her. Olga feeds her something? Nose in the book,
that's all she knows. Religion religion. She thinks if she'll
read a book she'll find out why God puts wax in the ears.
A pox on religion and a pox on God! What good did God
ever do me? How many strokes I got with or without God?"

"What did they want?"

"Who?"

"Olga and Dan."

"You they want. You should be a middleman, a magician, the foot on the button so the button shouldn't break off. You'll call them up."

"Not tonight."

"So they'll call you. Good night, good night, my angel, my darling! A doctor and he leaves me to die without Vitamin C."

"I'll get oranges, don't worry. Go to bed, pop, don't worry."

"First look in my eye."

The doctor looked.

"Idiot, stupid, the other eye, darling. You see bloodshot? You see swollen?"

"Nothing wrong with it."

"I took a bath, I got soap in it! And he says nothing wrong. An angel! A darling! A doctor!"

The doctor went into his room and, still wearing his jacket, lay down on the bed. Then he realized the window was shut, so he got up with a whistle of disgust, opened it, and fitted an old screen into the sash. The air had altered. It felt clotted, sluggish, hot, partisan and impassioned, like the breathing of a vindictive judge. He hung his jacket on the doorknob and returned to the bed and blew into the pillow. Then, turning on his back to face the ceiling with its crafty stains, he began, quite consciously, to grieve: he thought how imperceptibly, how inexorably, temporary accommodation becomes permanence, and one by one he counted his omissions, his cowardices, each of which had fixed him like an invisible cement, or like a nail. What he had not done accumulated in his mouth from moment to moment —the pity of so many absences worked in him the way a gland works, emitting, filling, discharging, and his mouth overflowed with saliva, it ran down his chin and along his neck, the quilt under his neck became wet. At twenty he had endured the stunned emotion of one who senses that he has

been singled out for aspiration, for beauty, for awe, for
some particularity not yet disclosed. At thirty he believed
all that had been a contrivance of his boy's imagination
(exasperation over growing old is at no time more acute or
melancholy than at thirty), but he was still delighted by his
energies, he knew he had a vulgar talent for compassion
just as, say, Sophie had a talent, equally vulgar, for copying
landscapes; he saw himself, in fact, as an open plaza, already
well-trod, waiting to be overcome by a conquest, by an in-
vasion of particularities, by those purposeful scrapings that
would mark the tiles as a place where plainly something has
happened. At forty he was still without a history—his sisters
were having their last babies, his father his first strokes—
and he became guilty and cynical about his own nature, and
began to despise himself because he had put his faith in the
possibility of significant, of miraculous, event. Too late he
made up his mind to marry, but fell in love, as men of that
age will, with a picture. He recognized the person in a
biography of Chekhov (aha, who was also a doctor, a bachelor up to the last minute): a photograph, captioned Family
and Friends, date 1890, location Sadovaya-Kudrinskaya
Street, under a grape-trellis—the young Chekhov, his sister,
his sister's friend, his three brothers, his white-bearded father,
his mother in a ribboned cap but with her ears showing, a
schoolboy called Seryozha in a uniform with an over-
sized hat, holding a looped twig—and there, there, second
row, far left, with smooth hair, spacious forehead, a perfect pointed chin, smiling merely with half her mouth,
thereby causing a vale, a dimple (oh, remarkable!), in her
left cheek—his beloved. Her name in the caption was Unknown Friend. Today, if alive (since in the photograph she
looked no more than nineteen or twenty), she was ninety-
three or -four; but then, when the doctor was forty, and she,
in her tormenting anonymity, sitting nameless, Unknown,
next to Lika Mizinova (Chekhov's sister's friend), drew the
side of her lip in at him and took his soul, *then* she was—if

alive—only eighty-three or -four. With this Unknown Friend, this eternally dimpling girl (a withered old woman, a great-grandmother by now, somewhere in the Soviet Union; an embittered spinster emigré living in a basement apartment in Queens, New York; or, more likely, dead; dead!), the doctor was in love. He sought, he said (but only to himself —this was his wretched secret), the style of that face, sharp chin, narrow Slavic eyes vaporously Tatar yet clamoring impudence, and that neck slightly straining, anticipatory, the shoulders under their white scarf nervously hunched. If she spoke he would not understand. There was no other like her. The original was a crone or buried, and at fifty, sweating on his back in his own stark bed, the doctor resolved to throw away the biography with its deeply perilous photograph. (Actually he could not throw it away because he did not own it to begin with—it was a library book, he had kept it overdue, he paid his fine, now and then he passed it on the T-shelf—perversely catalogued under "Tchekhov"—and visited surreptitiously with Unknown Friend's sly shy eyes.) What he meant by this was that he must throw illusion away. All the photographs of the mind—out! All the photographs of hope and self-deception—out! Everything imprinted, laminated, sealed, without fruit, without progress or process—out! Immobility, error, regret, grief—out!

For the second time that night he heard a bang on the window. To himself, released, joyful, he confessed all that was necessary: that his life was a bone, that he had nobody and nobody had him, that he was unmarried because he had neglected to look for a wife, that the human race—husbands, wives, children—was a sink, a drainpipe, a sewer, that reconciliation was impossible, that his waiting room would remain divided, that his brothers-in-law would remain divided, that his sisters were no more than ovum-bearing animals born to enact the cosmic will, that he himself was sterile by default, and would remain sterile; and that all the same it was possible to be happy. At which, another whack on the pane—whack, clump; the dentist summoning him once more for philosophy, for solace, for justice. Jumping up from his bed, he wondered how he would explain his stupendous discovery—that the worthlessness of everything was just what gave everything its worth. Divine overwhelming exquisite beautiful irrationality! Nonsense holy and pellucid!—for an instant he wrested a comely logic from the character of this nonsense, then it eluded him, then (meanwhile his brain roared like a sunflower) he seized it again, for one noble static sliver of a second he grasped all things—why we are here, the meaning of the alimentary canal, who Zeus was—then wisdom shook itself like a drop off a dog and he lost it.

A bag of knuckles hit the window. Lightning without thunder, bewildered blinks of a golden eyelid, and great lucent dice hammering.

In the course of this marvel the telephone rang.

"We've got another sign, Pug. *Another* sign."

"Dan? I heard you stopped by," the doctor said.

"Yeah, yeah, you remember the time with the radio waves?"

"That's all over, Dan, take it easy," the doctor said.

"I'm crippled, I'm wounded, I'm bled, I'm dead. *Who's* it over for? For me? She read somewhere they interfere with the radioactive emanations of the human spirit? Hey Pug, I wake you, you sleeping yet?"

"It's finished, no harm done, why bring it up all over again?" the doctor said.

"Yeah, ask me why. Six months with the shades pulled down and crawling under the windows so's not to get hit by the radio waves coming in? You think I forgot? Sneaking under the windows? I'm dead, she's killed me, she's my murderer.—Hey, tell the truth, you weren't asleep, Pug?"

"No. No, I'm still up."

"I mean I wouldn't like to wake you, but it's not *one* sign tonight, Pug, it's two. First when Filth-Face Irwin

showed before he was supposed to. Ancient gypsy evil
omen: the Unexpected Guest. Then she brings up for Sign
Number Two the Egyptian plagues. Murrain I don't see, I
says, frogs and locusts I don't see. Hail! she says. It's hailing,
I swear to God it's hailing, Pug. Ack-ack. In May."
        "Yes. This part of town too. I hear it."
        "It takes two omens to start the action off. An old
Chaldean saying, pal. Listen, old socko, so you know what
now?"
        "All right, Dan. Don't blow up. She needs consolation.
You see yourself she needs consolation. Whatever it is, she'll
get over it same as always."
        "Sure she will, same as always, then starts the next
thing. Come on, boy, *count*—Rosicrucian, Galilee Scientist,
Old Believer, Theosophical Analyst, Chapel Roller, Judas
Praiser, Speaker in Tongues, and on top of it keeps strict
kosher—you name it, she's been there. You people don't
realize what I have to put up with, that featherbrain Sophie,
what's *she* see? And Frieda tells me to my face I make it
all up. You people try to sweep it under the Bible, the old
man worst of all. Tells me I damaged the kid tonight, because I wanted to get Olga in early! Goddamn fool, your
old man, what does he know about it? She says she has to
be in by ten o'clock to sing her goddamn night office, and
I go along with her on it, what'm I supposed to do? I'm the
one that's stuck with her—if not for the kid I'd make tracks,
I swear. All I need's the contacts, I could sell my photosatire
idea to *Life*, I know that, believe me. Believe me I know
how good I am. What kind of contacts d'you get with a nut
wife? Astral bodies? You people don't realize, if I wasn't
ten years dead I'd make Stieglitz look like Johnny One-
Note."
        "What do you mean, 'night office'?"
        "It's a correspondence course on how to be a nun right
in your own home, guaranteed no convent necessary. God-

damn her to hell, she takes four-hundred-and-fifty out of the joint account to pay these fakers and doesn't say a word. All night I'm trying to tell her the Unexpected Guest doesn't count, Ice-Eyes Irwin's the host in that house allegedly. Some host—he threw me out, Pug, he threw me out. God, I'd like to crack up that blue-jaw mug of his. Then it starts to hail, and that's the camel's back, Pug. Omen Number Two, she's starting her vows as of immediately. She was undecided, now she's positively decided, the heavens have spoken. As of immediately she's a nun, only bite your tongue, I'm not supposed to let on to anybody except Pug. Doctor Pug does not revile. So from now on she's a celibate and I'm supposed to be a celibate too. Like whaddayacallem, Abelard and Heloise, who if I took their picture I'd show 'em hanging on to Krafft-Ebing by the goddamn fly-leaves—"

"Let me speak to Olga," the doctor begged. "Calm down, Dan, what's the good of shouting at her? Let me speak to—oh. Olga? Hi, puss, pop mentioned you were here—"

"Frieda said to stop about the fruit, he was complaining he's out of fruit," Olga said, patient, reasonable. "Frieda's going to bring him oranges I think, she told me to tell him not to worry about the fruit, but you know Dan, the way Dan was carrying on after Irwin showed up, it was upsetting and I forgot."

Olga gave her frail mocking giggle.

The doctor did not wait to hear it out. "What's this about being a nun?"

"Oh, that's Dan's talk," she said with scorn. "He's against the Constitution, he doesn't believe in freedom of religion. He's too literal-minded for mysticism, he takes every metaphor seriously. My goodness, Pug, I was *born* somebody's sister. You can *call* me Sister if you want to, I don't mind."

"It's not true, Olga?" he said.

"Did you ever read *The Kreutzer Sonata*, it's by Tolstoy? I just want to be chaste, Pug, that's all."

"Olga, a married woman *is* chaste."

"I mean *really* chaste. I just want one thing, purity, is that a sin? Dan acts like it's a terrible sin. He never reads *any*thing, he can't understand. 'Purity of heart is to will one thing,' that's Kierkegaard who said it, but all Dan can do is scream at me all day. You *know* what I mean, don't you, Pug? I mean chaste like you're chaste. It isn't true what Sophie says, is it? About you? I *know* it isn't true."

"What?"

"About going to houses—"

There was a scramble. The doctor's mouth gorged saliva. "Olga? Olga? Dan, why did you—Dan?"

"You see? You see? Am I lying, am I making it up? You people don't realize, this is what's dragging me down in the world, it's sucking my blood, I'm the dregs, I'm a failure, ten years I'm stone dead—"

They kept it up for an hour, and he stood victimized, his ear clammy, inwardly spinning, rattling like a gong, burning against the instrument, his throat a cornucopia of garbage, his chest a vessel under sail beaten and beaten, taking it in and taking it in. What they spewed he chewed. His brother-in-law shot grievances like beads across an abacus and went on adding them up in a pitch of torment which tomorrow would deliver him to the doctor whimpering for an electrocardiogram, his hand over his broad left nipple. And Olga, a mouse of persistence, a beam of inflexibility, tapping her small, laughing, modest voice, through it all tittered Universal Love. Egotism, egotism! She was a secretive girl who aspired beyond her probabilities. She was unintelligent, hiddenly arrogant yet ordinary, plain, fat-legged, sycophantic, but her eyes were round and brown; she had the power of permanent spite. The world supposed her to be only another one of these domestic bundles rolling between

stove and mattress—never mind: her vision declared her Joan
the Maid. Hence the smile, the laugh, the slow fawning of
her patience: if only they knew!

The hail left off, the clouds wheezed on, a bold tongue
of a moon licked the top of the sky.

At noon the next day the doctor remembered his father's
oranges.

He admired the carts, how one fitted into another, and
how the plastic handles were blue, green, and red, each from
a different supermarket, but long since strayed from home,
so that he saw "Finast" and "A & P" and "Bohack" nested
together like ingenious silver cages, peaceful, twinkling. He
pulled one out of its system of stubborn interlockings and
tested it, drawing it this way and that, trying little turns: it
rolled without resistance on its fat rubber wheels, and he was
pleased that the handle was blue, and that it had a special
compartment formed by a grid that could fold away flat.
He took his cart and trundled it into an indoor garden.
Everything delighted and awed him: cucumbers banked two
feet high, their waxy skins glinting droplets, a blazing pyramid of apples, the lettuces like garlands of faint green roses,
the sober maroon shining eggplants, the celery with their
flowery heads, the mushrooms heaped in oval crates of the
thinnest and most pungent wood, the attendant in his carrot-
stained apron with its string tied in front and his crayon
over his ear, the bits of onion-peel skittering on the linoleum
floor, the three sizes of tan paper bags each in its proper
bin, the women wandering, plucking, weighing, pinching,
filling their carts. It seemed to the doctor he had come upon
a diligent and orderly little farm, where everyone reaped
serenely, and ladies wearing trousers had faces full of thanks-
giving for such plenitude, for such roundness, for such births
of color and depths of brightness. The oranges in their
slatted pine buckets were redolent of some spectacular sul-
tanate. How thick, ardent, and multitudinous they were!
And what a wonder their mysterious navels, through which

protruded sometimes the little plump shoulders of the sections inside, pouting with juice!

"Pug," said Frieda, "you skeleton, not even a sandwich today? Look at you. What are you doing here? I caught you just in time, you would've bought everything I bought!"

The doctor hated to be scolded for not eating lunch.

In Frieda's cart there were six splendid oranges.

"Didn't Olga tell you I was coming down to do the shopping today? Suppose I didn't bump into you, pop would be drowning in double of everything."

"Frieda, you don't buy him enough and he runs out of things."

"You, you never notice prices," she said indulgently. "The radishes are orchids and as far as their oranges go it's Tiffany's here today. They think their potatoes are diamond chips! Honeydew seventy-nine cents each! Cantaloupe forty-nine! Oh, oh, look at *this* beautiful one—"

Maternally she picked up a grizzled melon, squeezed the stem-depression, sniffed it, shut her eyes at the hummingbird sweetness, and restored it to the rack like a baby prince.

"Too much, too much. Marvin wouldn't like it. Marvin says he wishes we all took after you and never ate anything, we could save a lot that way. Why're you skipping lunch again? Why?" she demanded.

"I'm not hungry. I didn't sleep much," he admitted.

"The hail," Frieda said. "Wasn't that something? It woke us too. All the kids yowled, wasn't it something? Come home with me, I'll feed you right now, Marvin's at a meeting."

"I have to get back to the office," he said.

"At least take a nap!"

"I'll be all right."

"It'll be like last year, I know it, we all know it. You'll fall asleep at your own party and we'll have our hands full with Sophie crying again."

"No, no, I'll be all right," he said.

"At least come on time—"

"I'll try. It depends." He counted out half a dozen more oranges and five grapefruits brilliant as planets. "I'll do my best," he said.

"You let them eat you alive, those people. Low-class people, deadbeats. Prescribe soap. (They're eleven cents each, that fruit, too early in the season.) Listen, you're a G.P. in the sticks, not a Madison Avenue psychoanalyst. You want to act like their analyst, charge 'em, charge 'em through the nose. (Get the cherry tomatoes, they're down to thirty-nine cents a box.) You let them *eat* you enough, don't you?"

"Don't worry, Frieda, I'll be there by eight. By nine at the latest."

"We'll be lucky if you'll come ten. We'll congratulate ourselves. Only one thing, Pug, don't get mad—"

"Looks like we're in the way here," the doctor said. Carts butted and crashed. They retired under the eave of a shelf of soda bottles. The ladies in trousers glowered.

"—but stop off home first and change your tie, all right? Put on a nice dark one, maybe a gray, you know the one, the gray with the thin stripe?"

He protested, "If you want me *early*—"

"There's this girl," Frieda said vaguely. "Now don't get mad, she was transferred to Marvin's school only last month, she's not just a teacher, she's the guidance counselor for the whole school. Pug, just once don't say no. She's only thirty-three or so, Marvin says she's very sweet-looking."

"Frieda, Frieda," the doctor said, "what do I want with a girl? I thought it was just the family tonight."

"Marvin asked her, she accepted, she's coming. It's done. —Nobody says you have to *marry* her," Frieda retorted, and he saw in the snap of her rough nostril-caps the superior conjectures of a matchmaker.

But he said dimly again, "What do I want with a girl?" The executioners' eyes of the ladies in trousers startled him.

The garden grew corrupt and vicious: he was surrounded by organic matter destined to rot, and just then, seizing his cart to join the queue in the cashier's aisle, he discovered a cyst of fresh peanut butter on the underpart of its fair blue handle. He cleaned his fingers with the edge of a paper bag, then with the hide of an eleven-cent peach, and knew that his birthday was pretext, that deceit ruled him, pretense sapped him, egotism devoured him, hope and dignity were fugitive. They meant, even now, to marry him off.

All the rest of that day an imagined chin inhabited the private side of his eyelids: the daring chin of Unknown Friend, which he dutifully glued to the unimaginable face of the guidance counselor.

In his office he attempted unions. He made everyone stand up, said it was an urgency of ventilation, dragged the magazine bench into the center of the room, redistributed the chairs, shuffled the lamps, announced that it was imperative for them all to sit as near the open window as possible, and waited for the mingling to begin. Piously they obeyed him, but the Italians chose the far side of the window and the blacks the opposite. He had shifted the dividing-line from diagonal to vertical: he felt like a trickster, a fascist. A wind flapped over the magazines and plucked up the pages leaf after leaf, an unseen reader, uncovering four-color refrigerators, washing machines, television sets, toasters. The Italians, some of them negroid, looked at their shoes; the Negroes, some of them olive, looked at their fingernails. There was a flurry, not yet an epidemic, of rubella, and the doctor rejoiced at the simplicity of a rash. A rash is a friend, a brother, it erupts, mildly pruritic, in the epidermises of all nations and races, it declares human-ness. He wrote the same prescription for everyone—a lotion, a unifying lotion, sending diverse men to diverse drugstores with a single purpose, alleviation, reconciliation, unexceptionable evidence for the equality of skins.

Mr. Gino Angeloro told him confidentially that the

niggers with their dirty habits were spreading the disease from yard to yard.

Mrs. Nascentia Carpenter told him confidentially that the wops with their wormy tomato plants were spreading the disease from block to block.

He went home and changed his tie.

His father was already gone from the house—they had arranged it that Frieda and Marvin would drive him to Sophie's, a chancy trip in Marvin's second-hand little English car: the five children and Marvin's guitar vying in the back seat, his father thin and barking, lunging against the strings.

In the empty corridor outside his bedroom the doctor knotted his tie, from a distance, in his dresser mirror, surveying himself: his already distinct hunch, his hair beginning to cloud over everywhere (as though his scalp were sweating a creeping white mist), the flat bony beak of his angled forehead: this glimpse of what he had become—while he was not even noticing; behind his own back—filled his mouth again, and as he was going out he stopped at the kitchen sink and abundantly spat into it.

When he arrived they called (Sophie's joke) "No surprise!" and "Happy birthday!" and he saw all of yesterday's salads, undermined, burrowed into, in a row on a fresh tablecloth, and DOCTOR PUG gleaming greasily on the cake. He was late, they had all eaten, paper plates tumbled with pumpernickel crusts littered the coffee table; but they applauded him, the children shrieked, the guitar slammed a chord, a turmoil of laughter, kisses, cries of "Speech!" churned and crimped the air. The doctor, unmoved, hiding his coldness, thanked them: "I've come this far and I'm still an honest man, at least I've got an honest body, it always tells the truth—after half a century my hair is grayer than pop's, I've got a fine hump coming up like a tree between my shoulders, I guess I'm too tough to please any cannibal," and the children shouted at the comedy of it. The photographer posed him, aimed elaborately, displayed finesse, temperament, commanded him immobile under lights that bloodied his eyes without mercy, then he was presented with the cake to blow at, cut up, give out—he held the knife like a dagger in the act of murder, icing tinged his cuffs and smeared his eyebrows, he felt at last a little dirty, whitened and wizened, a tired waiter gone to seed. The dentist and the photographer passed within inches (elbows lifted so as not to touch), ostentatious in a common silence, each invisible to the other; meanwhile Olga fed a slice of cake—the top said TORPUGF —into the automatic jaws of her little girl: the dullness of the child's eyes deepened and deepened, like a voluptuous ember. Finally the dentist took him aside and showed him a new letter, received that morning, from his oldest boy—"See, what'd I tell you, Pug? Smart! Look at those grades! I tell him follow in your uncle's footsteps, make Phi Beta Kappa, get the key! You want to get into med school like Pug? Get your key! I tell them both that, not just Richy, I tell Petey the same thing." Frieda brought him a plate of herring salad. Against the farthest wall, under a watercolor of Sophie's called Moonlight and Pines, serious, mild, his glasses blinking, Marvin was talking to a strange young woman, but the big guitar obscured her. His father was asleep in a pocket of the sofa, his head stiff and to the side, like the bust of a minor Roman official, his mouth a stone yawn, his gums glabrous, glistening, vibrant—his teeth were in his hand. The photographer began to try out his latest ideas for political satire— catch, with camera on the *qui vive*, the Russian ambassador in the urinal, the President smacking the First Lady, the Defense Secretary working out in boxing gloves. He was bullied, cornered, inextricable; then Sophie flew up—"Pug! I nearly forgot to introduce you, come on!"—she wore cheap Chinese slippers strewing flakes of cardboard gold, and her heated smile was chipped, hazy.

But Marvin was already playing in earnest. He played

like a warlock, his guitar was his life, he had the knack of a
demon piper. The children went mad, the dentist went mad,
even Olga's flawed little girl was snatched by spasms of bliss
—she circled and circled, raised her dress, stared at her knees
shuddering, screeched like a nighttime cat. The teacher threw
his white pick on the floor and dipped his naked fingers into
the strings, as into a harp, or a pool crisscrossed by contend-
ing wakes, or a barred cell; and jounced, bounced, trounced
his classes, the living he had to ply from πr^2, the head of the
department, the principal, the wild boys who smoked at the
back of the room: jounced them, bounced them, trounced
them, until he was worn with the flogging, until he was
cleansed for the sake of this shiver, this shimmer—then, in
a splatter, like the steely water that shoots from a diver pene-
trating, the true and absolute music stuttered: a stick on
spokes. The teacher tweezed it, struck it, beat it out, and the
children rolled in panting heaps on the carpet, spent, belly-
hurting with glee. Sophie shut her piano. Envy made her
shut it with the plain grace of someone just back from a
failed foreign tour—if not for the sting of this guitar (it
nosed out into the room, a rapid loud gigantic subtle insect,
billion-legged, nylon-winged, no-waisted, with quick insinu-
ating antennae), she would even now be flourishing the long,
Continental gigolo-thrills of Massenet's Elegy: it was her
best piece.

So Frieda took him instead. "Pug? Come and meet Gerda."

He followed her. The seat of his pants was cruelly
plucked; his buttock was pinched hard. "My angel, this time
don't be so foolish, darling. A nice female, I seen her myself,
I keep my eyes open, bloodshot don't prevent!" said the doctor's father, wide awake. With the gesture of a gloved cava-
lier he opened his fist and thrust his teeth back into his face;
all alone they smirked. "You'll like her you'll marry her, if
not not, only why not like? To like is easy. Someone the
same as your sisters, only nice, educated—good girls, good

enough! If she'll read too much you'll tell her to cut it out.
Enough is enough, fifty years old is enough, get married!
Tomorrow we'll make a wedding, sonny, darling, doctor,
fool, idiot, maniac—"

Frieda persuaded him into the kitchen for orange juice.
Then "Pug," said Frieda, "this is Miss Steinweh. Gerda,
please meet my brother, Doctor Pincus Silver."

"Steinway?" the doctor inquired.

"A very distant relative of the instrument people, col-
lateral branch entirely, but about me I'm afraid there's nothing piano, not even my legs," said the guidance counselor:
a humorist.

They sat together on the sofa, watching the Virginia
reel.

"You have a big practice?"

"Fairly large," the doctor said, concealing poverty.

"My cousin Morris is a pharmacist. He says all doctors
could use handwriting analysis."

"Do you find," the doctor asked desperately, "that more
students are college-motivated nowadays?"

"Come see come saw. Who's that?"—Miss Steinweh
pointed. "The bald one doh-see-dohing with the kids? The
clown. I know him."

"My brother-in-law. Irwin Sherman."

"A professional also?"

"A dentist—"

"I thought so. Talk about small worlds. He's the one
that gave my girlfriend the runaround last year in the mountains. Said he wasn't married, then she looks in his pocket
where he keeps his keys and finds a wedding ring. He's
married to *that* one?"—Miss Steinweh pointed.

"No, that's my sister Olga. Sophie is Irwin's wife."

"She's very attract-ive. Believe it or not, I never knew
Marv was musical. In school he's a hundred per cent geometry,
very quiet. Did his wife know?"

The doctor was confused.

"About the mountains? His *wife*. That he was going around saying he wasn't?"

"Wasn't—"

"Married. Look at him. A clown, thinks he's still a kid." —Miss Steinweh pointed. "Which reminds me, many happy returns of the day."

"Thank you," said the doctor, feeling choked.

"I hear you're still a bachelor. At your age. Well, look, never mind, I have the same attitude. Either it's Mister Right or it's nobody."

The doctor exerted himself. He ignored the nervous cramp in his calf. He did what his sisters expected: his voice turned effortful, high. Life! he cried. Life, life, where are you, where did you go, why didn't you wait for me? Let me live! he cried. "Oh you," he said in a voice that was new, light, aggressive yet dim, hopeful, "you're scarcely in *my* boat, Miss Steinweh—"

"Gerda. You don't think thirty-six is old? Believe me it's not young. Everyone says my trouble is I have an M.A., it's in clinical psychology. I tell them it was a slip I made. Believe me I treat it like a slip, I don't let it show." Miss Steinweh laughed and pointed at her thighs, over which lay, presumably, her underwear. "Actually, I'm reconciled, I really am. Are you?"

"Reconciled?" he said. He was aware of a collapse. His voice was heavy, heavy.

"To being a bachelor."

"Oh, but I'm not," the doctor said.

"You aren't?"

"No, no, I'm not."

"I figure by age fifty a person would be reconciled."

"No," the doctor said urgently, "I don't mean that. I mean I'm not what you think. I'm not—" how heavy, heavy his voice was, his breath!—"I'm not a bachelor."

"You're not? But Frieda—" Miss Steinweh pointed at

Frieda. Far off, in the kitchen, she was washing the cake knife. "Frieda *told* me you were."

"Frieda doesn't know. Neither does Marvin. Nobody does."

"I don't get it," said Miss Steinweh, and for the first time the doctor took her in. Already the misery of having yielded whipped her mouth. She was like his sisters, lost: his father with the acumen of chronic insult had already recognized the daughter of his spirit, the failed daughter of the failed peddler; his father with his tradesman's cleverness had already descried the yielding and the loss. Miss Steinweh was dark like dark Olga, but her eyes were gray like Sophie's, and under them the doctor observed a certain ruffling, a certain gathering-up, a suggestion of the drawstring; under her chin the same, a weariness of the mold, a pucker, a yielding, a loss of earliness. And in spite of this she had long girlish hair, and girlish glasses, and an abrupt girlish nod, and a girlish forefinger pointing: she was a sunset, it was the last hour before her night, the warmth of her last youth was ebbing, she was at the excruciating fulcrum of transition. The doctor pitied her. What had happened to him would happen to her. He saw her fifty and alone, less than his sisters, sculptured in cosmetics, her birth canal desolate, her red tides shrinking, vanishing; her powerful cheeks malevolent. "Is it a joke?" she said. "I can take a practical joke, believe me."

"I have a wife," the doctor said.

"You're married?"

"Yes," he said.

"And they don't know about it? Your sisters? Your father? I don't get it." She flung him a crafty look. "Then why tell *me*?"

But he was craftier still. "The compulsion of contrast. You don't remind me of my wife. My wife is different from you. She's different from Sophie, she's different from Olga. God knows she's not like Frieda."

"A secret marriage?" said Miss Steinweh, leaning near. "How long has it been?"

He picked (he put it to himself) a number. He was cunning enough, he was the scion of cunning, cunning was his sister, cunning was the primaeval gene. "A dozen years. It had to be, it has to be. Who could take my father? Every one of us is poorer than the next—"

"Poor?" she intervened, and pointed at his breast pocket. "You said you have this big practice."

"This big, big, poor, poor practice," he said.

"You could have waited till it grew," she said practically. "Grew financially, I mean."

"There are things in this world that don't grow. They're born a certain way and they stay the way they were when they came." He stopped to notice Olga's little girl in her glowing dance, weaving through the weavers of the reel, solitary, on the trail of something private: a gem always just ahead of her, radiant, summoning. "You can't have remorse over something that never was. You measure life by what's happened to you, not by what didn't happen. You think my sisters can grow? You think my father can grow? Can a stone grow? Who waits for a stone to grow?" He considered her. "You don't believe me?"

"I don't get it. Just on account of your father it was? Couldn't he come to live with you?"

The doctor covered his face. A live violence entered his throat. "I—cannot—live with my father," he said.

This made her strange; she whispered. "What you're telling me," she said, "is it—it's not just—*you* know, just an arrangement—"

"A marriage," he said solemnly, and peered at her. "We have a bona fide marriage certificate. We have children."

"Children!" said Miss Steinweh, and did not point.

"Three," he said. "Eleven, nine, and four. Two girls and a boy."

"And she *takes* it—she stands for it? Your wife? What kind of a marriage is that? What kind of a father are you?" He said, "Normal. Everything normal. No secret husband, no secret father. It's easy. One night a week I take the train to New York. Twenty-minute trip. My sisters think I do house calls. Every weekend I take the train. The families of traveling salesmen have it worse."

"And they don't know? You've never told them? Your sisters, your father? Why don't you tell them?"

"It's too late," he said. "Too hazardous. My father's been having this series of vascular constrictions, I'm not confident he could survive a bad surprise—a shock."

"You could tell your sisters," Miss Steinweh persisted, "and tell them not to tell your father."

"It would get to him. Things always get to him."

"But why didn't you tell everybody to begin with!"

—By default, by default! he cried. He said humbly, "I wanted a different life."

"It's different all right!" said Miss Steinweh, in the tone of one who laughs: but did not laugh, did not nod; she looked at the doctor. "What is she like?"

"My wife?"

"Yes. A person like that."

"Very young. Years younger than myself. Far younger than you." It did not pass him how this hurt her. "An émigré. A fugitive. Suffered horrible privations getting through. Very shy. Never learned English well. Speaks Russian like a bird."

"Russian?"

"The children are completely bilingual. Except for that, and whatever is deposited in my wife's brain—she never mentions her memories, only the snow and the Moscow skating—we have nothing Russian in the apartment. Oh, a samovar, but we bought it in New York. We bought it on Delancey Street," the doctor said. "She's older than she was

when I first saw her, but she's still a beautiful girl. A soul in
her." The teacher loosed a sudden coruscation out of his
guitar and the doctor trembled in its resonance.

"*Now* I see," said Miss Steinweh. "She doesn't know
what she's mixed up with. She doesn't know the ways of the
country. She's absolutely in your hands, she's at your
mercy."

"She belongs to me," the doctor admitted.

"It's not nice," Miss Steinweh said. "It's awful. You
should bring her into your own town. You should introduce
her to your sisters."

"Oh—my sisters!" the doctor said.

She stood up and went on greedily looking at him. "Are
you happy that way?"

"We are both very happy." Then a resplendent word
discharged itself like a ghost: beatific; but he did not use it.
"Both of us are happy. The children are well."

"As long as the children are well," she said, "that's the
main thing, the children are well." He was amazed. She was
jeering at him. "What pigs you all are—pigs, fakers, otherwise why would I be here, I don't have days to waste out of
my life! Pigs! I don't have nights!"

When the dentist spotted her coming his way on her
shaky high heels, immediately his neck puffed red and he im-
portuned his brother-in-law to play a rhumba.

The doctor watched the dentist and the guidance counselor dance. Miss Steinweh danced well—she was not so
expert as the dentist, but she was not afraid of him. Her arms
were thick but sinuous. Across the width of Sophie's living
room, layered with Sophie's brutish copies of Van Gogh and
Degas, she looked kind. She danced with the dentist and
was kind to him.

Then the photographer captured the doctor again and
began to outline another idea he had to make him famous.

The
Butterfly
and the
Traffic
Light

JERUSALEM, that phoenix city, is not known by its
street-names. Neither is Baghdad, Copenhagen, Rio de
Janeiro, Camelot, or Athens; nor Peking, Florence, Babylon,
St. Petersburg. These fabled capitals rise up ready-spired,
story-domed and filigreed; they come to us at the end of a
plain, behind hill or cloud, walled and moated by myths and
antique rumors. They are built of copper, silver, and gold;
they are founded on milkwhite stone; the bright thrones of
ideal kings jewel them. Balconies, parks, little gates, columns
and statuary, carriage-houses and stables, attics, kitchens,
gables, tiles, yards, rubied steeples, brilliant roofs, peacocks,
lapdogs, grand ladies, beggars, towers, bowers, harbors,
barbers, wigs, judges, courts, and wines of all sorts fill them.
Yet, though we see the shimmer of the smallest pebble beneath
the humblest foot in all the great seats of legend, still not a
single street is celebrated. The thoroughfares of beautiful
cities are somehow obscure, unless, of course, we count
Venice: but a canal is not really the same as a street. The
ways, avenues, plazas, and squares of old cities are lost to us,
we do not like to think of them, they move like wicked
scratches upon the smooth enamel of our golden towns; we
have forgotten most of them. There is no beauty in cross-
section—we take our cities, like our wishes, whole.

It is different with places of small repute or where time has
not yet deigned to be an inhabitant. It is different especially

in America. They tell us that Boston is our Jerusalem; but, as anyone who has ever lived there knows, Boston owns only half a history. Honor, pomp, hallowed scenes, proud families, the Athenaeum and the Symphony are Boston's; but Boston has no tragic tradition. Boston has never wept. No Bostonian has ever sung, mourning for his city, "If I do not remember thee, let my tongue cleave to the roof of my mouth"—for, to manage his accent, the Bostonian's tongue is already in that position. We hear of Beacon Hill and Back Bay, of Faneuil market and State Street: it is all cross-section, all map. And the State House with its gilt dome (it counts for nothing that Paul Revere supplied the bottommost layer of gold leaf: he was businessman, not horseman, then) throws back furious sunsets garishly, boastfully, as no power-rich Carthage, for shame, would dare. There is no fairy mist in Boston. True, its street-names are notable: Boylston, Washington, Commonwealth, Marlborough, Tremont, Beacon; and then the Squares, Kenmore, Copley, Louisburg, and Scollay—evidence enough that the whole, unlike Jerusalem, has not transcended its material parts. Boston has a history of neighborhoods. Jerusalem has a history of histories.

The other American towns are even less fortunate. It is not merely that they lack rudimentary legends, that their names are homely and unimaginative, half ending in -burg and half in -ville, or that nothing has ever happened in them. Unlike the ancient capitals, they are not infixed in our vision, we are not born knowing them, as though, in some earlier migration, we had been dwellers there: for no one is a stranger to Jerusalem. And unlike even Boston, most cities in America have no landmarks, no age-enshrined graveyards (although death is famous everywhere), no green park to show a massacre, poet's murder, or high marriage. The American town, alas, has no identity hinting at immortality; we recognize it only by its ubiquitous street-names: sometimes Main Street, sometimes High Street, and frequently Central Avenue. Grandeur shuns such streets. It is all ambition and aspiration there, and nothing to look back at. Cicero said that men who know nothing of what has gone before them are like children. But Main, High, and Central have no past; rather, their past is now. It is not the fault of the inhabitants that nothing has gone before them. Nor are they to be condemned if they make their spinal streets conspicuous, and confer egregious luster and false acclaim on Central, High, or Main, and erect minarets and marquees indeed as though their city were already in dream and fable. But it is where one street in particular is regarded as the central life, the high spot, the main drag, that we know the city to be a prenatal trace only. The kiln of history bakes out these prides and these divisions. When the streets have been forgotten a thousand years, the divine city is born.

In the farm-village where the brewer Buldenquist had chosen to establish his Mighty College, the primitive commercial artery was called, not surprisingly, "downtown," and then, more respectably, Main Street, and then, rather covetously looking to civic improvement, Buldenquist Road. But the Sacred Bull had dedicated himself to the foundation and perpetuation of scientific farming, and had a prejudice against putting money into pavements and other citifications. So the town fathers (for by that time the place *was* a town, swollen by the boarding houses and saloons frequented by crowds of young farm students)—the town fathers scratched their heads for historical allusions embedded in local folklore, but found nothing except two or three old family scandals, until one day a traveling salesman named Rogers sold the mayor an "archive"—a wrinkled, torn, doused, singed, and otherwise quite ancient-looking holographic volume purporting to to hold the records and diaries of one Colonel Elihu Bigghe. This rather obscure officer had by gratifying coincidence passed through the neighborhood during the war with a force of two hundred, the document claimed, encountering a skirmish with the enemy on the very spot of the present firehouse—the "war" being, according to some, the Civil War, and in the positive authority of others, one of the lesser Indian Wars—in his private diary Bigghe was not, after all, expected to drop hints. At any rate, the skirmish was there in detail—one hundred or more of the enemy dead; not one of ours; ninety-seven of theirs wounded; our survivors all hale but three; the bravery of our side; the cowardice and brutality of the foe; and further pious and patriotic remarks on Country, Creator, and Christian Charity. A decade or so after this remarkable discovery the mayor heard of Rogers' arrest, somewhere in the East, for forgery, and in his secret heart began to wonder whether he might not have been taken in: but by then the Bigghe diaries were under glass in the antiseptic-smelling lobby of the town hall, school children were being herded regularly by their teachers to view it, boring Fourth of July speeches had been droned before the firehouse in annual commemoration, and most people had forgotten that Bigghe Road had ever been called after the grudging brewer. And who could blame the inhabitants if, after half a hundred years, they began to spell it Big Road? For by then the town had grown into a city, wide and clamorous.

For Fishbein it was an imitation of a city. He claimed (not altogether correctly) that he had seen all the capitals of Europe, and yet had never come upon anything to match Big Road in name or character. He liked to tell how the streets of Europe were "employed," as he put it: he would people them with beggars and derelicts—"they keep their cash and their beds in the streets"; and with crowds assembled for riot or amusement or politics—"in Moscow they filled, the revolutionaries I mean, three troikas with White Russians and shot them, the White Russians I mean, and let them run wild in the street, the horses I mean, to spill all the corpses" (but he had never been to Moscow); and with travelers determined on objective and destination—"they use the streets there to go from one place to another, the original design of streets, *n'est-ce pas?*" Fishbein considered that, while a city exists for its own sake, a street is utilitarian. The uses of Big Road, on the contrary, were plainly secondary. In Fishbein's view Big Road had come into being only that the city might have a conscious center—much as the nucleus of a cell demonstrates the cell's character and maintains its well-being ("although," Fishbein argued, "in the cell it is a moot question whether the nucleus exists for the sake of the cell or the cell for the sake of the nucleus: whereas it is clear that a formless city such as this requires a centrality from which to learn the idea of form"). But if the city were to have modeled itself after Big Road, it would have grown long, like a serpent, and unreliable in its sudden coilings. This had not happened. Big Road crept, toiled, and ran, but the city nibbled at this farmhouse and that, and spread and spread with no pattern other than exuberance and greed. And if Fishbein had to go to biology or botany or history for his analogies, the city was proud that it had Big Road to stimulate such comparisons.

Big Road was different by day and by night, weekday and weekend. Daylight, sunlight, and even rainlight gave everything its shadow, winter and summer, so that every person and every object had its Doppelgänger, persistent and hopeless. There was a kind of doubleness that clung to the street, as though one remembered having seen this and this and this before. The stores, hung with signs, had it, the lazy-walking old women had it (all of them uniformly rouged in the geometric centers of their cheeks like victims of some senile fever already dangerously epidemic), the traffic lights suspended from their wires had it, the air dense with the local accent had it.

This insistent sense of recognition was the subject of one of Fishbein's favorite lectures to his walking companion.

"It's America repeating itself! Imitating its own worst habits! Haven't I seen the same thing everywhere? It's a simultaneous urbanization all over, you can almost hear the coxswain crow 'Now all together, boys!'—This lamppost, I saw it years ago in Birmingham, that same scalloped bowl teetering on a wrought-iron stick. At least in Europe the lampposts look different in each place, they have individual characters. And this traffic light! There's no cross-street there, so what do they want it for in such a desert? I'll tell you: they put it up to pretend they're a real city—to tease the transients who might be naïve enough to stop for it. And that click and buzz, that flash and blink, why do they all do that in just the same way? Repeat and repeat, nothing meaningful by itself. . . ."

"I don't mind them, they're like abstract statues," Isabel once replied to this. "As though we were strangers from another part of the world and thought them some kind of religious icon with a red and a green eye. The ones on poles especially."

He recognized his own fancifulness, coarsened, labored, and made literal. He had taught her to think like this. But she had a distressing disinclination to shake off logic; she did not know how to ride her intuition.

"No, no," he objected, "then you don't know what an icon is! A traffic light could never be anything but a traffic light. —What kind of religion would it be which had only one version of its deity—a whole row of identical icons in every city?"

She considered rapidly. "An advanced religion. I mean a monotheistic one."

"And what makes you certain that monotheism is 'advanced'? On the contrary, little dear! It's as foolish to be fixed on one God as it is to be fixed on one idea, isn't that plain? The index of advancement is flexibility. Human temperaments are so variable, how could one God satisfy them all? The Greeks and Romans had a god for every personality, the way the Church has a saint for every mood. Savages,

Hindus, and Roman Catholics understand all that. It's only the Jews and their imitators who insist on a rigid unitarian God—I can't think of anything more unfortunate for history: it's the narrow way, like God imposing his will on Job. The disgrace of the fable is that Job didn't turn to another god, one more germane to his illusions. It's what any sensible man would have done. And then wouldn't the boils have gone away of their own accord?—the Bible states clearly that they were simply a psychogenic nervous disorder—isn't that what's meant by 'Satan'? There's no disaster that doesn't come of missing an imagination: I've told you that before, little dear. Now the Maccabean War for instance, for an altogether unintelligible occasion! All Antiochus the Fourth intended—he was Emperor of Syria at the time—was to set up a statue of Zeus on the altar of the Temple of Jerusalem, a harmless affair—who would be hurt by it? It wasn't that Antiochus cared anything for Zeus himself—he was nothing if not an agnostic: a philosopher, anyway—the whole movement was only to symbolize the Syrian hegemony. It wasn't worth a war to get rid of the thing! A little breadth of vision, you see, a little imagination, a little *flexibility*, I mean—there ought to be room for Zeus *and* God under one roof. . . . That's why traffic lights won't do for icons! They haven't been conceived in a pluralistic spirit, they're all exactly alike. Icons ought to differ from one another, don't you see? An icon's only a mask, that's the point, a representational mask which stands for an idea."

"In that case," Isabel tried it, "if a traffic light were an icon it would stand for two ideas, stop and go—"

"Stop and go, virtue and vice, logic and law!—Why are you always on the verge of moralizing, little dear, when it's a fever, not morals, that keeps the world spinning! Are masks only for showing the truth? But no, they're for hiding, they're for misleading, too. . . . It's a maxim, you see: one mask reveals, another conceals."

"Which kind is better?"

"Whichever you happen to be wearing at the moment," he told her.

Often he spoke to her in this manner among night crowds on Big Road. Sometimes, too argumentative to be touched, she kept her hands in her pockets and, unexpectedly choosing a corner to turn, he would wind a rope of hair around his finger and draw her leashed after him. She always went easily; she scarcely needed to be led. Among all those night walkers the two of them seemed obscure, dimmed-out, and under a heat-screened autumn moon, one of those shimmering country-moons indigenous to midwestern America, he came to a kind of truce with the street. It was no reconcilement, nothing so friendly as that, not even a cessation of warfare, only of present aggression. To come to terms with Big Road would have been to come to terms with America. And since this was impossible, he dallied instead with masks, and icons, and Isabel's long brown hair.

After twilight on the advent of the weekend the clutter of banners, the parades, the caravans of curiously outfitted convertibles vanished, and the students came out to roam. They sought each other with antics and capers, brilliantly tantalizing in the beginning darkness. Voices hung in the air, shot upward all along the street, and celebrated the Friday madness. It was a grand posture of relief: the stores already closed but the display-windows still lit, and the mannequins leaning forward from their glass cages with leers of painted horror and malignant eyeballs; and then the pirate movie letting out (this is 1949, my hearties), and the clusters of students flowing in gleaming rows, like pearls on a string, past posters raging with crimson seas and tall-masted ships and black-haired beauties shrieking, out of the scented palace into drugstores and ice cream parlors. Sweet, sweet, it was all sweet there before the shops and among the crawling automobiles and under the repetitious street lamps and below the singular moon. On the sidewalks the girls sprouted like tapestry blossoms, their heads rising from slender necks like woven petals swaying on the stems. They wore thin dresses, and short capelike coats over them; they wore no stockings, and their round bare legs moved boldly through an eddy of rainbow skirts; the swift white bone of ankle cut into the breath of the wind. A kind of greed drove Fishbein among them. "See that one," he would say, consumed with yearning, turning back in the wake of the young lasses to observe their gait, and how the filaments of their dresses seemed to float below their arms caught in a gesture, and how the dry sparks of their eyes flickered with the sheen of spiders.

And he would halt until Isabel too had looked. "Are you envious?" he asked, "because you are not one of them? Then console yourself." But he saw that she studied his greed and read his admiration. "Take comfort," he said again. "They are not free to become themselves. They are different from you." "Yes," Isabel answered, "they are prettier." "They will grow corrupt. Time will overwhelm them. They have only their one moment, like the butterflies." "Looking at butterflies gives pleasure." "Yes, it is a kind of joy, little dear, but full of poison. It belongs to the knowledge of rapid death. The butterfly lures us not only because he is beautiful, but because he is transitory. The caterpillar is uglier, but in him we can regard the better joy of becoming. The caterpillar's fate is bloom. The butterfly's is waste."

They stopped, and around them milled and murmured the girls in their wispy dresses and their little cut-off capes, and their yellow hair, whitish hair, tan hair, hair of brown-and-pink. The lithe, O the ladies young! It was all sweet there among the tousled bevies wormy with ribbon streamers and sashes, mock-tricked with make-believe gems, gems pinned over the breast, on the bar of a barrette, aflash even in the rims of their glasses. The alien gaiety took Fishbein in; he rocked in their strong sea-wave. From a record shop came a wild shiver of jazz, eyes unwound like coils of silk and groped for other eyes: the street churned with the laughter of girls. And Fishbein, arrested in the heart of the whirlpool, was all at once plunged again into war with the street and with America, where everything was illusion and all illusion led to disillusion. What use was it then for him to call O lyric ladies, what use to chant O languorous lovely November ladies, O lilting, lolling, lissome ladies—while corrosion sat waiting in their ears, he saw the maggots breeding in their dissolving jewels?

Meanwhile Isabel frowned with logic. "But it's only that the caterpillar's future is longer and his fate farther off. In the end he will die too." "Never, never, never," said Fishbein; "it is only the butterfly who dies, and then he has long since ceased to be a caterpillar. The caterpillar never dies.—Neither to die nor to be immortal, it is the enviable state, little dear, to live always at the point of beautiful change! That is what it means to be extraordinary—when did I tell you that?—" He bethought himself. "The first day, of course. It's always best to begin with the end—with the image of what is desired. If I had begun with the beginning I would have bored you, you would have gone away. . . . In my ideal kingdom, little dear, everyone, even the very old, will be passionately in the process of guessing at and preparing for his essential self. Boredom will be unnatural, like a curse, or unhealthy, like a plague. Everyone will be extraordinary."

"But if the whole population were extraordinary," Isabel objected, "then nobody would be extraordinary."

"Ssh, little dear, why must you insist on dialectics? Nothing true is ever found by that road. There are millions of caterpillars, and not one of them is intended to die, and they are all of them extraordinary. *Your* aim," he admonished, as they came into the darkened neighborhood beyond Big Road, "is to avoid growing into a butterfly. Come," he said, and took her hand, "let us live for that."

Virility

YOU ARE too young to remember Edmund Gate, but I knew him when he was Elia Gatoff in knickers, just off the boat from Liverpool. Now to remember Edmund Gate at all, one must be a compatriot of mine, which is to say a centagenerian. A man of one hundred and six is always sequestered on a metaphysical Elba, but on an Elba without even the metaphor of a Napoleon—where, in fact, it has been so long forgotten that Napoleon ever lived that it is impossible to credit his influence, let alone his fame. It is harsh and lonely in this country of exile—the inhabitants (or, as we in our eleventh decade ought more accurately to be called, the survivors) are so sparse, and so maimed, and so unreliable as to recent chronology, and so at odds with your ideas of greatness, that we do indeed veer toward a separate mentality, and ought in logic to have a flag of our own. It is not that we seclude ourselves from you, but rather that you have seceded from us—you with your moon pilots, and mohole fishermen, and algae cookies, and anti-etymological reformed spelling—in the face of all of which I can scarcely expect you to believe in a time when a plain and rather ignorant man could attain the sort of celebrity you people accord only to vile geniuses who export baby-germs in plastic envelopes. That, I suppose, is the worst of it for me and my countrymen in the land of the very old—your isolation from our great. Our great and especially our merely famous have slipped from

your encyclopaedias, and will vanish finally and absolutely
when we are at length powdered into reconstituted genetic
ore—mixed with fish flour, and to be taken as an antidote immediately after radiation-saturation: a detail and a tangent,
but I am subject to these broodings at my heavy age, and
occasionally catch myself in egotistical yearning for an ordinary headstone engraved with my name. As if, in a
population of a billion and a quarter, there could be space
for that entirely obsolete indulgence!—and yet, only last
week, in the old Preserved Cemetery, I visited Edmund Gate's
grave, and viewed his monument, and came away persuaded
of the beauty of that ancient, though wasteful, decorum.
We have no room for physical memorials nowadays; and nobody pays any attention to the pitiful poets.

Just *here* is my huge difficulty. How am I to convince
you that, during an interval in my own vast lifetime, there
was a moment when a poet—a plain, as I have said, and
rather ignorant man—was noticed, and noticed abundantly,
and noticed magnificently and even stupendously? You will
of course not have heard of Byron, and no one is more
eclipsed than dear Dylan; nor will I claim that Edmund Gate
ever rose to *that* standard. But he was recited, admired, wor-
shiped, translated, pursued, even paid; and the press would
not let him go for an instant. I have spoken of influence and
of fame; Edmund Gate, it is true, had little influence, even
on his own generation—I mean by this that he was not much
imitated—but as for fame! Fame was what we gave him
plenty of. We could give him fame—in those days fame was
ours to give. Whereas you measure meanly by the cosmos.
The first man to the moon is now a shriveling little sta-
tistician in a Bureau somewhere, superseded by the first to
Venus, who, we are told, lies all day in a sour room drinking
vodka and spitting envy on the first to try for Pluto. Now it
is the stars which dictate fame, but with us it was *we* who
made fame, and we who dictated our stars.

He died (like Keats, of whom you will also not have heard) at twenty-six. I have this note not from Microwafer Tabulation, but from the invincible headstone itself. I had forgotten it and was touched. I almost thought he lived to be middle-aged: I base this on my last sight of him, or perhaps my last memory, in which I observe him in his underwear, with a big hairy paunch, cracked and browning teeth, and a scabby scalp laid over with a bunch of thin light-colored weeds. He looked something like a failed pugilist. I see him standing in the middle of a floor without a carpet, puzzled, drunk, a newspaper in one hand and the other tenderly reaching through the slot in his shorts to enclose his testicles. The last words he spoke to me were the words I chose (it fell to me) for his monument: "I am a man."

He was, however, a boy in corduroys when he first came to me. He smelled of salami and his knickers were raveled at the pockets and gave off a saltiness. He explained that he had walked all the way from England, back and forth on the deck. I later gathered that he was a stowaway. He had been sent ahead to Liverpool on a forged passport (these were Czarist times), from a place full of wooden shacks and no sidewalks called Glusk, with instructions to search out an old aunt of his mother's on Mersey Street and stay with her until his parents and sisters could scrape up the papers for their own border-crossing. He miraculously found the Liverpudlian aunt, was received with joy, fed bread and butter, and shown a letter from Glusk in which his father stated that the precious sheets were finally all in order and properly stamped with seals almost identical to real government seals: they would all soon be reunited in the beckoning poverty of Golden Liverpool. He settled in with the aunt, who lived tidily in a gray slum and worked all day in the back of a millinery shop sewing on veils. She had all the habits of a cool and intellectual spinster. She had come to England six years before—she was herself an emigrant from

Glusk, and had left it legally and respectably under a pile
of straw in the last of three carts in a gypsy caravan headed
westward for Poland. Once inside Poland (humanely governed by Franz Josef), she took a train to Warsaw, and liked
the book stores there so much she nearly stayed forever, but
instead thoughtfully lifted her skirts onto another train—how
she hated the soot!—to Hamburg, where she boarded a neat
little boat pointed right at Liverpool. It never occurred to her
to go a little further, to America: she had fixed on English as
the best tongue for a foreigner to adopt, and she was sus-
picious of the kind of English Americans imagined they
spoke. With superior diligence she began to teach her great-
nephew the beautiful and clever new language; she even
wanted him to go to school, but he was too much absorbed
in the notion of waiting, and instead ran errands for the
greengrocer at three shillings a week. He put pennies into
a little tin box to buy a red scarf for his mother when she
came. He waited and waited, and looked dull when his aunt
talked to him in English at night, and waited immensely, with
his whole body. But his mother and father and his sister
Feige and his sister Gittel never arrived. On a rainy day in
the very month he burst into manhood (in the course of
which black rods of hairs appeared in the trench of his
upper lip), his aunt told him, not in English, that it was no
use waiting any longer: a pogrom had murdered them all.
She put the letter, from a cousin in Glusk, on exhibit before
him—his mother, raped and slaughtered; Feige, raped and
slaughtered; Gittel, escaped but caught in the forest and
raped twelve times before a passing friendly soldier saved
her from the thirteenth by shooting her through the left
eye; his father, tied to the tail of a Cossack horse and sent to
have his head broken on cobblestones.

All this he gave me quickly, briefly, without excitement,
and with a shocking economy. What he had come to America
for, he said, was a job. I asked him what his experience was.

He reiterated the fact of the greengrocer in Liverpool. He had the queerest accent; a regular salad of an accent.

"That's hardly the type of preparation we can use on a newspaper," I said.

"Well, it's the only kind I've got."

"What does your aunt think of your leaving her all alone like that?"

"She's an independent sort. She'll be all right. She says she'll send me money when she can."

"Look here, don't you think the money ought to be going in the opposite direction?"

"Oh, I'll never have any money," he said.

I was irritated by his pronunciation—"mawney"—and I had theories about would-be Americans, none of them complimentary, one of which he was unwittingly confirming. "There's ambition for you!"

But he startled me with a contradictory smile both iron and earnest. "I'm very ambitious. You wait and see," as though we were already colleagues, confidants, and deep comrades. "Only what *I* want to be," he said, "they don't ever make much money."

"What's that?"

"A poet. I've always wanted to be a poet."

I could not help laughing at him. "In English? You want to do English poetry?"

"English, righto. I don't *have* any other language. Not any more."

"Are you positive you have English?" I asked him. "You've only been taught by your aunt, and no one ever taught *her*."

But he was listening to only half, and would not bother with any talk about his relative. "That's why I want to work on a paper. For contact with written material."

I said strictly, "You could read books, you know."

"I've read *some*." He looked down in shame. "I'm too

lazy. My mind is lazy but my legs are good. If I could get to be a reporter or something like that I could use my legs a lot. I'm a good runner."

"And when," I put it to him in the voice of a sardonic archangel, "will you compose your poems?"

"While I'm running," he said.

I took him on as office boy and teased him considerably. Whenever I handed him a bit of copy to carry from one cubbyhole to another I reminded him that he was at last in contact with written material, and hoped he was finding it useful for his verse. He had no humor but his legs were as fleet as he had promised. He was always ready, always at attention, always on the alert to run. He was always *there*, waiting. He stood like a hare at rest watching the typewriters beat, his hands and his feet nervous for the snatch of the sheet from the platen, as impatient as though the production of a column of feature items were a wholly automatic act governed by the width of the paper and the speed of the machine. He would rip the page from the grasp of its author and streak for the copy desk, where he would lean belligerently over the poor editor in question to study the strokes of this cringing chap's blue pencil. "Is that what cutting is?" he asked. "Is that what you call proofreading? Doesn't 'judgment' have an 'e' in it? Why not? There's an 'e' in 'judge,' isn't there? How come you don't take the 'e' out of 'knowledgeable' too? How do you count the type for a headline?" He was insufferably efficient and a killing nuisance. In less than a month he switched from those ribbed and reeky knickers to a pair of grimy trousers out of a pawnshop, and from the ample back pocket of these there protruded an equally ample dictionary with its boards missing, purchased from the identical source: but this was an affectation, since I never saw him consult it. All the same we promoted him to proofreader. This buried him. We set him down at a dark desk in a dungeon and entombed him under mile-long strips of galleys and left him there to dig himself out. The print-shop helped by providing innumerable shrdlus and inventing further typographical curiosities of such a nature that a psychologist would have been severely interested. The city editor was abetted by the whole reporting staff in the revelation of news stories rivaling the Bible in luridness, sexuality, and imaginative abomination. Meanwhile he never blinked, but went on devotedly taking the "e" out of "judgment" and putting it back for "knowledgeable," and making little loops for "omit" wherever someone's syntactical fancy had gone too rapturously far.

When I looked up and spotted him apparently about to mount my typewriter I was certain he had risen from his cellar to beg to be fired. Instead he offered me a double information: he was going to call himself Gate, and what did I think of that?—and in the second place he had just written his first poem.

"First?" I said. "I thought you've been at it all the while."

"Oh no," he assured me. "I wasn't ready. I didn't have a name."

"Gatoff's a name, isn't it?"

He ignored my tone, almost like a gentleman. "I mean a name suitable for the language. It has to match somehow, doesn't it? Or people would get the idea I'm an impostor." I recognized this word from a recent fabrication he had encountered on a proof—my own, in fact: a two-paragraph item about a man who had successfully posed as a firewarden through pretending to have a sound acquaintance with the problems of water-pressure systems, but who let the firehouse burn down because he could not get the tap open. It was admittedly a very inferior story, but the best I could do; the others had soared beyond my meager gleam, though I made up for my barrenness by a generosity of double negatives. Still, I marveled at his quickness at self-enrichment—the aunt in Liverpool, I was certain, had never talked to him, in English, of impostors.

"Listen," he said thickly, "I really feel you're the one who started me off. I'm very grateful to you. You understood my weakness in the language and you allowed me every opportunity."

"Then you like your job down there?"

"I just wish I could have a light on my desk. A small bulb maybe, that's all. Otherwise it's great down there, sure, it gives me a chance to think about poems."

"Don't you pay any attention to what you're reading?" I asked admiringly.

"Sure I do. I always do. That's where I get my ideas. Poems deal with Truth, right? One thing I've learned lately from contact with written material is that Truth is Stranger than Fiction." He uttered this as if fresh from the mouths of the gods. It gave him a particular advantage over the rest of us: admonish him that some phrase was as old as the hills, and he would pull up his head like a delighted turtle and exclaim, "Now that's perfect. What a perfect way to express antiquity. That's true, the hills have been there since the earth was just new. Very good! I congratulate you"—showing extensive emotional reverberation, which I acknowledged after a time as his most serious literary symptom.

The terrible symptom was just now vividly tremulous. "What I want to ask you," he said, "is what you would think of Edmund for a poet's name. In front of Gate, for instance."

"*My* name is Edmund," I said.

"I know, I know. Where would I get the idea if not from you? A marvelous name. Could I borrow it? Just for use on poems. Otherwise it's all right, don't be embarrassed, call me Elia like always."

He reached for his behind, produced the dictionary, and cautiously shook it open to the Fs. Then he tore out a single page with meticulous orderliness and passed it to me. It covered Fenugreek to Fylfot, and the margins were foxed with an astonishing calligraphy, very tiny and very

ornate, like miniature crystal cubes containing little bells.
"You want me to read this?" I said.
"Please," he commanded.
"Why don't you use regular paper?"
"I like words," he said. "Fenugreek, an herb of the pea
family. Felo-de-se, a suicide. I wouldn't get that just from
a blank sheet. If I see a good word in the vicinity I put it
right in."
"You're a great borrower," I observed.
"Be brutal," he begged. "Tell me if I have talent."
It was a poem about dawn. It had four rhymed stanzas
and coupled "lingered" with "rosy-fingered." The word
Fuzee was strangely prominent.
"In concept it's a little on the hackneyed side," I told
him.
"I'll work on it," he said fervently. "You think I have
a chance? Be brutal."
"I don't suppose you'll ever be an original, you know,"
I said.
"You wait and see," he threatened me. "I can be brutal
too."
He headed back for his cellar and I happened to notice
his walk. His thick round calves described forceful rings in
his trousers, but he had a curiously modest gait, like a pre-
occupied steer. His dictionary jogged on his buttock, and his
shoulders suggested the spectral flutes of a spectral cloak, with
a spectral retinue following murmurously after.
"Elia," I called to him.
He kept going.
I was willing to experiment. "Edmund!" I yelled.
He turned, very elegantly.
"Edmund," I said. "Now listen. I mean this. Don't
show me any more of your stuff. The whole thing is hope-
less. Waste your own time but don't waste mine."
He took this in with a pleasant lift of his large thumbs.
"I never waste anything. I'm very provident."

"Provident, are you?" I made myself a fool for him:
"Aha, evidently you've been inditing something in and around
the Ps—"

"Puce, red. Prothorax, the front part of an insect. Plec-
trum, an ivory pick."

"You're an opportunist," I said. "A hoarder. A rag-
dealer. Don't fancy yourself anything better than that. Keep
out of my way, Edmund," I told him.

After that I got rid of him. I exerted—if that is not too
gross a word for the politic and the canny—a quiet urgency
here and there, until finally we tendered him the title of
reporter and sent him out to the police station to call in
burglaries off the blotter. His hours were midnight to morning. In two weeks he turned up at my desk at ten o'clock,
squinting through an early sunbeam.

"Don't you go home to sleep now?" I asked.

"Criticism before slumber. I've got more work to show
you. Beautiful new work."

I swallowed a groan. "How do you like it down at head-
quarters?"

"It's fine. A lovely place. The cops are fine people. It's
a wonderful atmosphere to think up poems in. I've been
extremely fecund. I've been pullulating down there. This
is the best of the lot."

He ripped out Mimir to Minion. Along the white
perimeter of the page his incredible handwriting peregrinated:
it was a poem about a rose. The poet's beloved was compared
to the flower. They blushed alike. The rose minced in the
breeze; so did the lady.

"I've given up rhyme," he announced, and hooked his
eyes in mine. "I've improved. You admit I've improved, don't
you?"

"No," I said. "You've retrogressed. You're nothing but
hash. You haven't advanced an inch. You'll never advance.
You haven't got the equipment."

"I have all these new words," he protested. "Menhir. Eximious. Suffruticose. Congee. Anastrophe. Dandiprat. Trichiasis. Nidificate."

"Words aren't the only equipment. You're hopeless. You haven't got the brain for it."

"All my lines scan perfectly."

"You're not a poet."

He refused to be disappointed; he could not be undermined. "You don't see any difference?"

"Not in the least.—Hold on. A difference indeed. You've bought yourself a suit," I said.

"Matching coat and pants. Thanks to you. You raised me up from an errand boy."

"That's America for you," I said. "And what about Liverpool? I suppose you send your aunt something out of your salary?"

"Not particularly."

"Poor old lady."

"She's all right as she is."

"Aren't you all she's got? Only joy, apple of the eye and so forth?"

"She gets along. She writes me now and then."

"I suppose you don't answer much."

"I've got my own life to live," he objected, with all the ardor of a man in the press of inventing not just a maxim but a principle. "I've got a career to make. Pretty soon I have to start getting my things into print. I bet you know some magazine editors who publish poems."

It struck me that he had somehow discovered a means to check my acquaintance. "That's just the point. They publish *poems*. You wouldn't do for them."

"You could start me off in print if you wanted to."

"I don't want to. You're no good."

"I'll get better. I'm still on my way. Wait and see," he said.

"All right," I agreed, "I'm willing to wait but I don't want to see. Don't show me any more. Keep your stuff to yourself. Please don't come back."

"Sure," he said: this was his chief American acquisition. "You come to me instead."

During the next month there was a run of robberies and other nonmatutinal felonies, and pleasurably and with relief I imagined him bunched up in a telephone booth in the basement of the station house, reciting clot after clot of criminal boredoms into the talking-piece. I hoped he would be hoarse enough and weary enough to seek his bed instead of his fortune, especially if he conceived of his fortune as conspicuously involving me. The mornings passed, and, after a time, so did my dread—he never appeared. I speculated that he had given me up. I even ventured a little remorse at the relentlessness of my dealings with him, and then a courier from the mail room loped in and left me an enormous envelope from an eminent literary journal. It was filled with dozens and dozens of fastidiously torn-out dictionary pages, accompanied by a letter to me from the editor-in-chief, whom —after a fashion—I knew (he had been a friend of my late and distinguished father): "Dear Edmund, I put it to you that your tastes in gall are not mine. I will not say that you presumed on my indulgence when you sent this fellow up here with his sheaf of horrors, but I will ask you in the future to restrict your recommendations to *simple* fools— who, presumably, turn to ordinary foolscap in their hour of folly. P.S. In any case I never have, and never hope to, print anything containing the word 'ogdoad.' "

One of the sheets was headed Ogam to Oliphant.

It seemed too savage a hardship to rage all day without release: nevertheless I thought I would wait it out until midnight and pursue him where I could find him, at his duties with the underworld, and then, for direct gratification, knock him down. But it occurred to me that a police station is an inconvenient situation for an assault upon a citizen

(though it did not escape me that he was still unnaturalized),
so I looked up his address and went to his room.
He opened the door in his underwear. "Edmund!" he
cried. "Excuse me, after all I'm a night worker—but it's all
right, come in, come in! I don't need a lot of sleep anyhow.
If I slept I'd never get any poems written, so don't feel bad."
Conscientiously I elevated my fists and conscientiously
I knocked him down.
"What's the idea?" he asked from the floor.
"What's the idea is right," I said. "Who told you you
could go around visiting important people and saying I
sicked you on them?"
He rubbed his sore chin in a rapture. "You heard! I bet
you heard straight from the editor-in-chief himself. You
would. You've got the connections, I knew it. I told him
to report right to you. I knew you'd be anxious."
"I'm anxious and embarrassed and ashamed," I said.
"You've made me look like an idiot. My father's oldest
friend. He thinks I'm a sap."
He got up, poking at himself for bruises. "Don't feel
bad for me. He didn't accept any at all? Is that a fact? Not
a single one?" I threw the envelope at him and he caught
it with a surprisingly expert arc of the wrist. Then he spilled
out the contents and read the letter. "Well, that's too bad,"
he said. "It's amazing how certain persons can be so un-
sympathetic. It's in their nature, they can't help it. But I
don't mind. I mean it's all compensated for. Here *you* are.
I thought it would be too nervy to invite you—it's a very
cheap place I live in, you can see that—but I knew you'd
come on your own. An aristocrat like yourself."
"Elia," I said, "I came to knock you down. I *have*
knocked you down."
"Don't feel bad about it," he repeated, consoling me. He
reached for my ear and gave it a friendly pull. "It's only
natural. You had a shock. In your place I would have done
exactly the same thing. I'm very strong. I'm probably much

stronger than you are. You're pretty strong too, if you could knock me down. But to tell the truth, I sort of *let* you. I like to show manners when I'm a host."

He scraped forward an old wooden chair, the only one in the room, for me to sit down on. I refused, so he sat down himself, with his thighs apart and his arms laced, ready for a civilized conversation. "You've read my new work yourself, I presume."

"No," I said. "When are you going to stop this? Why don't you concentrate on something sensible? You want to be a petty police reporter for the rest of your life?"

"I hope not," he said, and rasped his voice to show his sincerity. "I'd like to be able to leave this place. I'd like to have enough money to live in a nice American atmosphere. Like you, the way you live all alone in that whole big house."

He almost made me think I had to apologize. "My father left it to me. Anyway, didn't you tell me you never expected to get rich on poetry?"

"I've looked around since then, I've noticed things. Of America expect everything. America has room for any-thing, even poets. Edmund," he said warmly, "I know how you feel. R.I.P. I don't have a father either. You would have admired my father—a strapping man. It's amazing that they could kill him. Strong. Big. No offense, but he restrained himself, he never knocked anyone down. Here," he pleaded, "you just take my new things and look them over and see if that editor-in-chief was right. You tell me if in his shoes you wouldn't publish me, that's all I want."

He handed me Gharri to Gila Monster: another vapid excrescence in the margins. Schuit to Scolecite: the same. But it was plain that he was appealing to me out of the pathos of his orphaned condition, and from pity and guilt (I had the sense that he would regard it as a pogrom if I did not comply) I examined the rest, and discovered, among his daisies and sunsets, a fresh theme. He had begun to write about girls: not the abstract Beloved, but real girls, with names like Shirley, Ethel, and Bella.

"Love poems," he said conceitedly. "I find them very moving."

"About as moving as the lovelorn column," I said, "if less gripping. When do you get the time for girls?"

"Leonardo da Vinci also had only twenty-four hours in his day. Ditto Michelangelo. Besides, I don't go looking for them. I attract them."

This drew my stare. "You attract them?"

"Sure. I attract them right here. I hardly ever have to go out. Of course that sort of arrangement's not too good with some of the better types. They don't go for a poet's room."

"There's not a book in the place," I said in disgust.

"Books don't make a poet's room," he contradicted. "It depends on the poet—the build of man he is." And, with the full power of his odious resiliency, he winked at me.

The effect on me of this conversation was unprecedented: I suddenly began to see him as he saw himself, through the lens of his own self-esteem. He almost looked handsome. He had changed; he seemed larger and bolder. The truth was merely that he was not yet twenty and that he had very recently grown physically. He remained unkempt, and his belly had a habit of swelling under his shirt; but there was something huge starting in him.

About that time I was asked to cover a minor war in the Caribbean—it was no more than a series of swamp skirmishes —and when I returned after eight weeks I found him living in my house. I had, as usual, left the key with my married sister (it had been one of my father's crotchets—he had several—to anticipate all possible contingencies, and I carried on the custom of the house), and he had magically wheedled it from her: it turned out he had somehow persuaded her that she would earn the gratitude of his posterity by allowing him to attain the kind of shelter commensurate with his qualities.

"Commensurate with your qualities," I sing-songed at him. "When I heard that, I knew she had it verbatim. All right, Elia, you've sucked the place dry. That's all. Out." Every teacup was dirty and he had emptied the whiskey. "You've had parties," I concluded.

"I couldn't help it, Edmund. I've developed so many friendships recently."

"Get out."

"Ah, don't be harsh. You know the little rooms upstairs? The ones that have the skylight? I bet those were maids' rooms once. You wouldn't know I was there, I promise you. Where can I go where there's so much good light? Over at the precinct house it's even worse than the cellar was, they use only forty-watt bulbs. The municipality is prodigiously parsimonious. What have I got if I haven't got my eyesight?

Take my pen and still
I sing. But deny
My eye
And Will
Departs the quill."

"My reply remains Nil," I said. "Just go."

He obliged me with a patronizing laugh. "That's very good. Deny, Reply. Quill, Nil."

"No, I mean it. You can't stay. Besides," I said sourly, "I thought you gave up rhymes long ago."

"You think I'm making it up about my eyes," he said. "Well, look." He darted a thick fist into a pocket and whipped out a pair of glasses and put them on. "While you were gone I had to get these. They're pretty strong for a person of my age. I'm not supposed to abuse my irises. These peepers cost me equal to nearly a month's rent at my old place."

The gesture forced me to study him. He had spoken of his qualities, but they were all quantities: he had grown some more, not upward exactly, and not particularly outward, but in some textural way, as though his bigness required one to assure oneself of it by testing it with the nerve in the fingertip. He was walking around in his underwear. For the first time I took it in how extraordinarily hairy a man he was. His shoulders and his chest were a forest, and the muscles in his arms were globes darkened by brush. I observed that he was thoroughly aware of himself; he held his torso like a bit of classical rubble, but he captured the warrior lines of it with a certain prideful agility.

"Go ahead, put on your clothes," I yelled at him.

"It's not cold in the house, Edmund."

"It is in the street. Go on, get out. With or without your clothes. Go."

He lowered his head, and I noted in surprise the gross stems of his ears. "It would be mean."

"I can take it. Stop worrying about my feelings."

"I'm not referring just to you. I left Sylvia alone upstairs when you came in."

"Are you telling me you've got a *girl* in this house right now?"

"Sure," he said meekly. "But you don't mind, Edmund. I know you don't. It's only what you do yourself, isn't it?"

I went to the foot of the staircase and shouted: "That's enough! Come down! Get out!"

Nothing stirred.

"You've scared her," he said.

"Get rid of her, Elia, or I'll call the police."

"That would be nice," he said wistfully. "*They* like my poems. I always read them aloud down at the station house. Look, if you really want me to go I'll go, and you can get rid of Sylvia yourself. You certainly have a beautiful spacious house here. Nice furniture. I certainly did enjoy it. Your sister told me a few things about it—it was very interesting. Your sister's a rather religious person, isn't she? Moral, like your father. What a funny man your father was, to put a thing like that in his will. Fornication on premises." "What's this all about?" But I knew, and felt the heat of my wariness.

"What your sister mentioned. She just mentioned that your father left you this house only on condition you'd never do anything to defame or defile it, and if you did do anything like that the house would go straight to her. Not that she really needs it for herself, but it would be convenient, with all those children of hers—naturally I'm only quoting. I guess you wouldn't want me to let on to her about Regina last Easter, would you?—You see, Edmund, you're even sweating a little bit yourself, look at your collar, so why be unfair and ask me to put on my clothes?"

I said hoarsely, "How do you know about Regina?"

"Well, I don't really, do I? It's just that I found this bunch of notes from somebody by that name—Regina—and in one or two of them she says how she stayed here with you over Easter and all about the two of you. Actually, your sister might be a little strait-laced, but she's pretty nice, I mean she wouldn't think the family mansion was being desecrated and so on if I stayed here, would she? So in view of all that don't you want to give your consent to my moving in for a little while, Edmund?"

Bitterly I gave it, though consent was academic: he had already installed all his belongings—his dictionary (what was left of it: a poor skeleton, gluey spine and a few of the more infrequent vocabularies, such as K, X, and Z), his suit, and a cigar box filled with thin letters from Liverpool, mostly unopened. I wormed from him a promise that he would keep to the upper part of the house; in return I let him take my typewriter up with him.

What amazed me was that he kept it tapping almost every evening. I had really believed him to be indolent; instead it emerged that he was glib. But I was astonished when

I occasionally saw him turn away visitors—it was more usual for him to grab, squeeze, tease and kiss them. They came often, girls with hats brimmed and plumed, and fur muffs, and brave quick little boots; they followed him up the stairs with crowds of poems stuffed into their muffs—their own, or his, or both—throwing past me jagged hillocks and troughs of laughter, their .chins hidden in stanzas. Then, though the space of a floor was between us, I heard him declaim: then received a zephyr of shrieks; then further laughter, ebbing; then a scuffle like a herd of zoo antelope, until, in the pure zeal of fury, I floundered into the drawing room and violently clapped the doors to. I sat with my book of maps in my father's heavy creaking chair near a stagnant grate and wondered how I could get him out. I thought of carrying the whole rude tale of his licentiousness to my sister —but anything I might say against a person who was plainly my own guest would undoubtedly tell doubly against myself (so wholesome was my father's whim, and so completely had he disliked me), and since all the money had gone to my sister, and only this gigantic curio of a house to me, I had the warmest desire to hold onto it. Room for room I hated the place; it smelled of the wizened scrupulousness of my burdensome childhood, and my dream was to put it on the market at precisely the right time and make off with a fortune. Luckily I had cozy advice from real-estate friends: the right hour was certainly not yet. But for this house and these hopes I owned nothing, not counting my salary, which was, as my sister liked to affirm, beggar's pay in the light of what she called our "background." Her appearances were now unhappily common. She arrived with five or six of her children, and always without her husband, so that she puffed out the effect of having plucked her offspring out of a cloud. She was a small, exact woman, with large, exact views, made in the exact image of a pious bird, with a cautious jewel of an eye, an excessively arched and fussy breast, and two very tiny and exact nostril-points. She admired Elia and used to ascend to his rooms, trailing progeny, at his bedtime, which is to say at nine o'clock in the morning, when I would be just departing the house for my office; whereas the poetesses, to their credit, did not become visible until romantic dusk. Sometimes she would telephone me and recommend that I move such-and-such a desk—or this ottoman or that highboy —into his attic to supply him with the comforts due his gifts.

"Margaret," I answered her, "have you seen his stuff? It's all pointless. It's all trash."

"He's very young," she declared—"you wait and see," which she reproduced in his idiom so mimetically that she nearly sounded like a Glusker herself. "At your age he'll be a man of the world, not a house-hugging eunuch."

I could not protest at this abusive epithet, vibrantly meant for me; to disclaim my celibacy would have been to disclaim my house. Elia, it appeared, was teaching her subtlety as well as ornamental scurrility—"eunuch" had never before alighted on Margaret's austere tongue. But it was true that since I no longer dared to see poor Regina under our old terms—I was too perilously subject to my guest's surveillance —she had dropped me in pique, and though I was not yet in love, I had been fonder of Regina than of almost anyone. "All right," I cried, "then let him be what he can."

"Why that's *everything*," said Margaret; "you don't realize what a find you've got in that young man."

"He's told you his designs on fame."

"Dear, he doesn't have to tell me. I can *see* it. He's unbelievable. He's an artist."

"A cheap little immigrant," I said. "Uncultivated. He never reads anything."

"Well, that's perfectly true, he's *not* effete. And about being a foreigner, do you know that terrible story, what they did to his whole family over there? When you survive a thing like that it turns you into a man. A fighter. Heroic," she ended. Then, with the solemnity of a codicil: "Don't call him little. He's big. He's enormous. His blood hasn't been thinned."

"He didn't *survive* it," I said wearily. "He wasn't even there when it happened. He was safe in England, he was in Liverpool, for God's sake, living with his aunt."

"Dear, please don't exaggerate and *please* don't swear. I see in him what I'm afraid I'll never see in you: because it isn't there. Genuine manliness. You have no tenderness for the children, Edmund, you walk right by them. Your own nieces and nephews. Elia is remarkable with them. That's just a single example."

I recited, "Gentleness Is the True Soul of Virility."

"That's in very bad taste, Edmund, that's a very journalistic way to express it," she said sadly, as though I had shamed her with an indelicacy: so I assumed Elia had not yet educated her to the enunciation of this potent word.

"You don't like it? Neither do I. It's just that it happens to be the title of the manly artist's latest ode," which was a fact. He had imposed it on me only the night before, whereupon I ritually informed him that it was his worst banality yet.

But Margaret was unvanquishable; she had her own point to bring up. "Look here, Edmund, can't you do something about getting him a better job? What he's doing now doesn't come near to being worthy of him. After all, a police station. And the hours!—"

"I take it you don't think the police force an influence suitable to genuine manliness," I said, and reflected that he had, after all, managed to prove his virility at the cost of my demonstrating mine. I had lost Regina; but he still had all his poetesses.

Yet he did, as I have already noted, now and then send them away, and these times, when he was alone in his rooms, I would listen most particularly for the unrelenting clack of the typewriter. He was keeping at it; he was engrossed; he was serious. It seemed to me the most paralyzing sign of all

that this hollow chattering of his machine was so consistent,
so reliable, so intelligible, so without stutter or modest hesitation—it made me sigh. He was deeply deadly purposeful.
The tapping went on and on, and since he never stopped, it was
clear that he never thought. He never daydreamed, meandered,
imagined, meditated, sucked, picked, smoked, scratched
or loafed. He simply tapped, forefinger over forefinger, as
though these sole active digits of his were the legs of a conscientious and dogged errand boy. His investment in self-
belief was absolute in its ambition, and I nearly pitied him
for it. What he struck off the page was spew and offal, and
he called it his career. He mailed three dozen poems a week
to this and that magazine, and when the known periodicals
turned him down he dredged up the unknown ones, shadowy
quarterlies and gazettes printed on hand-presses in dubious
basements and devoted to matters anatomic, astronomic, gas-
tronomic, political, or atheist. To the publication of the
Vegetarian Party he offered a pastoral verse in earthy tro-
chees, and he tried the organ of a ladies' tonic manufacturing
firm with fragile dactyls on the subject of corsets. He sub-
mitted everywhere, and I suppose there was finally no editor
alive who did not clutch his head at the sight of his name.
He clattered out barrage after barrage; he was a scourge to
every idealist who had ever hoped to promote the dim cause
of numbers. And leaf by leaf, travel journals shoulder to
shoulder with Marxist tracts, paramilitarists alongside Seventh-
Day Adventists, suffragettes hand in hand with nudists—to
a man and to a woman they turned him down, they denied
him print, they begged him at last to cease and desist, they
folded their pamphlets like Arab tents and fled when they
saw him brandishing so much as an iamb.

Meanwhile the feet of his fingers ran; he never gave up.
My fright for him began almost to match my contempt. I
was pitying him now in earnest, though his confidence remained as unmoved and oafish as ever. "Wait and see," he
said, sounding like a copy of my sister copying him. The

two of them put their heads together over me, but I had
done all I could for him. He had no prospects. It even
horribly developed that I was looked upon by my colleagues
as his special protector, because when I left for the trenches
my absence was immediately seized on and he was fired.
This, of course, did not reach me until I returned after a
year, missing an earlobe and with a dark and ugly declivity
slashed across the back of my neck. My house guest had been
excused from the draft by virtue of his bad eyesight, or
perhaps more accurately by virtue of the ponderous thick-
ness of his lenses; eight or ten of his poetesses tendered him a
party in celebration of both his exemption and his myopia,
at which he unflinchingly threw a dart into the bull's-eye of
a target-shaped cake. But I was myself no soldier, and went
only as a correspondent to that ancient and so primitive war,
naïvely pretending to encompass the world, but Neanderthal
according to our later and more expansive appetites for anni-
hilation. Someone had merely shot a prince (a nobody—I
myself cannot recall his name), and then, in illogical consequence, various patches of territory had sprung up to occupy
and individualize a former empire. In the same way, I discovered, had Elia sprung up—or, as I must now consistently
call him (lest I seem to stand apart from the miraculous
change in his history), Edmund Gate. What I mean by this
is that he stepped out of his attic and with democratic huge-
ness took over the house. His great form had by now entirely
flattened my father's august chair, and, like a vast male
Goldilocks, he was sleeping in my mother's bed—that shrine
which my father had long ago consecrated to disuse and awe:
a piety my sister and I had soberly perpetuated. I came home
and found him in the drawing room, barefoot and in his
underwear, his dirty socks strewn over the floor, and my
sister in attendance mending the holes he had worn through
the heels, invigilated by a knot of her children. It presently
emerged that she had all along been providing him with an
allowance to suit his tastes, but in that first unwitting moment

when he leaped up to embrace me, at the same time dragging on his shirt (because he knew how I disliked to see him undressed), I was stunned to catch the flash of his initials —"E.G."—embroidered in scarlet silk on a pair of magnificent cuffs.

"Edmund!" he howled. "Not one, not two—two *dozen!* Two dozen in the past two months alone!"

"Two dozen what?" I said, blinking at what had become of him. He was now twenty-one, and taller, larger, and hairier than ever. He wore new glasses (far less formidable than the awful weights his little nose had carried to the draft board), and these, predictably, had matured his expression, especially in the area of the cheekbones: their elderly silver frames very cleverly contradicted that inevitable boyishness which a big face is wont to radiate when it is committed to surrounding the nose of a cherub. I saw plainly, and saw it for myself, without the mesmerizing influence of his preening (for he was standing before me very simply, diligently buttoning up his shirt), that he had been increased and transformed: his fantastic body had made a simile out of him. The element in him that partook of the heathen colossus had swelled to drive out everything callow —with his blunt and balding skull he looked (I am willing to dare the vulgar godliness inherent in the term) like a giant lingam: one of those curious phallic monuments one may suddenly encounter, wreathed with bright chains of leaves, on a dusty wayside in India. His broad hands wheeled, his shirttail flicked; it was clear that his scalp was not going to be friends for long with his follicles—stars of dandruff fluttered from him. He had apparently taken up smoking, because his teeth were already a brown ruin. And with all that, he was somehow a ceremonial and touching spectacle. He was massive and dramatic; he had turned majestic.

"Poems, man, poems!" he roared. "Two dozen poems sold, and to all the best magazines!" He would have pulled

my ear like a comrade had I had a lobe to pull by, but instead
he struck me down into a chair (all the while my sister went
on peacefully darning), and heaped into my arms a jumble
of the most important periodicals of the hour.

"Ah, there's more to it than just that," my sister said.
"How did you manage all this?" I said. "My God, here's
one in *The Centennial!* You mean Fielding accepted? Fielding actually?"

"The sheaf of horrors man, that's right. He's really a
very nice old fellow, you know that, Edmund? I've lunched
with him three times now. He can't stop apologizing for the
way he embarrassed himself—remember, the time he wrote
you that terrible letter about me? He's always saying how
ashamed he is over it."

"Fielding?" I said. "I can't imagine Fielding—"

"Tell the rest," Margaret said complacently.

"Well, tomorrow we're having lunch again—Fielding
and Margaret and me, and he's going to introduce me to this
book publisher who's very interested in my things and wants
to put them between, how did he say it, Margaret?—between
something."

"Boards. A collection, all the poems of Edmund Gate.
You see?" said Margaret.

"I *don't* see," I burst out.

"You never did. You haven't the vigor. I doubt whether
you've ever really *penetrated* Edmund." This confused me,
until I understood that she now habitually addressed him by
the name he had pinched from me. "Edmund," she chal-
lenged—which of us was this? from her scowl I took it as a
finger at myself—"you don't realize his level. It's his *level*
you don't realize."

"I realize it," I said darkly, and let go a landslide of
magazines: but *The Centennial* I retained. "I suppose poor
Fielding's gone senile by now. Wasn't he at least ten years

older than Father even? I suppose he's off his head and they
just don't have the heart to ship him out."

"That won't do," Margaret said. "This boy is getting
his recognition at last, that's all there is to it."

"I know what he means, though," Edmund said. "I tell
them the same thing, I tell them exactly that—all those editors, I tell them they're crazy to carry on the way they do.
You ought to hear—"

"Praise," Margaret intervened with a snap: "praise and
more praise," as if this would spite me.

"I never thought myself those poems were *that* good,"
he said. "It's funny, they were just an experiment at first, but
then I got the hang of it."

"An experiment?" I asked him. His diffidence was novel,
it was even radical; he seemed almost abashed. I had to marvel:
he was as bemused over his good luck as I was.

Not so Margaret, who let it appear that she had read the
cosmic will. "Edmund is working in a new vein," she explained.

"Hasn't he always worked in vain?" I said, and dived into
The Centennial to see.

Edmund slapped his shins at this, but "He who laughs
last," said Margaret, and beat her thimble on the head of the
nearest child: "What a callous man your uncle is. Read!" she
commanded me.

"He has a hole in the back of his neck and only a little
piece of ear left," said the child in a voice of astute assent.

"Ssh," said Margaret. "We don't speak of deformities."

"Unless they turn up as poems," I corrected; and read; and
was startled by a dilation of the lungs, like a horse lashed out
of the blue and made to race beyond its impulse. Was it his,
this clean stupendous stuff? But there was his name, manifest
in print: it was his, according to *The Centennial*, and Fielding
had not gone senile.

"Well?"

"I don't know," I said, feeling muddled.

"He doesn't know! Edmund"—this was to Edmund—
"he doesn't know!"

"I can't believe it."

"He can't believe it, Edmund!"

"Well, neither could I at first," he admitted.
But my sister jumped up and pointed her needle in my
face. "Say it's good."

"Oh, it's good. I can see it's good," I said. "He's hit it for
once."

"They're *all* like that," she expanded. "Look for yourself."

I looked, I looked insatiably, I looked fanatically, I looked
frenetically, I looked incredulously—I went from magazine to
magazine, riffling and rifling, looking and looting and shuffling,
until I had plundered them all of his work. My booty dumb-
founded me: there was nothing to discard. I was transfixed; I
was exhausted; in the end it was an exorcism of my stupefac-
tion. I was converted, I believed; he had hit it every time. And
not with ease—I could trace the wonderful risks he took. It
was a new vein; more, it was an artery, it had a pump and a kick;
it was a robust ineluctable fountain. And when his book came
out half a year later, my proselytization was sealed. Here were
all the poems of the periodicals, already as familiar as solid old
columns, uniquely graven; and layered over them like dazzling
slabs of dappled marble, immovable because of the perfection
of their weight and the inexorability of their balance, was the
aftermath of that early work, those more recent productions to
which I soon became a reverential witness. Or, if not witness,
then auditor: for out of habit he still liked to compose in the
attic, and I would hear him type a poem straight out, without
so much as stopping to breathe. And right afterward he came
down and presented it to me. It seemed, then, that nothing had
changed: only his gift and a single feature of his manner. Unerringly it was a work of—yet who or what was I to declare
him genius?—accept instead the modest judgment of merit. It
was a work of merit he gave me unerringly, but he gave it to

me—this was strangest of all—with a quiescence, a passivity.
All his old arrogance had vanished. So had his vanity. A kind
of tranquillity kept him taut and still, like a man leashed; and
he went up the stairs, on those days when he was seized by the
need for a poem, with a languidness unlike anything I had ever
noticed in him before; he typed, from start to finish, with no
falterings or emendations; then he thumped on the stairs again,
loomed like a thug, and handed the glorious sheet over to my
exulting grasp. I supposed it was a sort of trance he had to
endure—in those dim times we were only just beginning to
know Freud, but even then it was clear that, with the bursting
forth of the latent thing, he had fallen into a relief as deep and
curative as the sleep of ether. If he lacked—or skipped—what
enthusiastic people call the creative exaltation, it was because he
had compressed it all, without the exhibitionism of prelude,
into that singular moment of power—six minutes, or eight
minutes, however long it took him, forefinger over forefinger,
to turn vision into alphabet.

He had become, by the way, a notably fast typist.

I asked him once—this was after he had surrendered a
new-hatched sheet not a quarter of an hour from the typewriter
—how he could account for what had happened in him.

"You used to be awful," I reminded him. "You used to be
unspeakable. My God, you were vile."

"Oh, I don't know," he said in that ennui, or blandness,
that he always displayed after one of his remarkable trips to
the attic, "I don't know if I was *that* bad."

"Well, even if you weren't," I said—in view of what I
had in my hand I could no longer rely on my idea of what he
had been—"this! This!" and fanned the wondrous page like
a triumphant flag. "How do you explain *this*, coming after
what you were?"

He grinned a row of brown incisors at me and gave me a
hearty smack on the ankle. "Plagiarism."

"No, tell me really."

"The plangent plagiarism," he said accommodatingly, "of

the plantigrade persona.—Admit it, Edmund, you don't like the Ps, you never did and you never will."

"For instance," I said, "you don't do *that* any more."

"Do what?" He rubbed the end of a cigarette across his teeth and yawned. "I still do persiflage, don't I? I do it out of my pate, without periwig, pugree, or peril."

"That. Cram grotesque words in every line."

"No, I don't do that any more. A pity, my dictionary's practically all gone."

"Why?" I persisted.

"I used it up, that's why. I *finished* it."

"Be serious. What I'm getting at is why you're different. Your stuff *is* different. I've never seen such a difference."

He sat up suddenly and with inspiration, and it came to me that I was observing the revival of passion. "Margaret's given that a lot of thought, Edmund. *She* attributes it to maturity."

"That's not very perspicacious," I said—for the sake of the Ps, and to show him I no longer minded anything.

But he said shortly, "She means virility."

This made me scoff. "She can't even get herself to say the word."

"Well, maybe there's a difference in Margaret too," he said.

"She's the same silly woman she ever was, and her husband's the same silly stockbroker, the two of them a pair of fertile prudes—she wouldn't recognize so-called virility if she tripped over it. She hates the whole concept—"

"She likes it," he said.

"What she likes is euphemisms for it. She can't face it, so she covers it up. Tenderness! Manliness! Maturity! Heroics! She hasn't got a brain in her head," I said, "and she's never gotten anything done in the world but those silly babies, I've lost count of how many she's done of *those*—"

"The next one's mine," he said.

"That's an imbecile joke."

"Not a joke."

"Look here, joke about plagiarism all you want but don't waste your breath on fairy tales."

"Nursery tales," he amended. "I never waste anything, I told you. That's just it, I've gone and plagiarized Margaret. I've purloined her, if you want to stick to the Ps."—Here he enumerated several other Ps impossible to print, which I am obliged to leave to my reader's experience, though not of the parlor. "And you're plenty wrong about your sister's brains, Edmund. She's a very capable businesswoman—she's simply never had the opportunity. You know since my book's out I have to admit I'm a bit in demand, and what she's done is she's booked me solid for six months' worth of recitations. And the fees! She's getting me more than Edna St. Vincent Millay, if you want the whole truth," he said proudly. "And why not? The only time that dame ever writes a good poem is when she signs her name."

All at once, and against his laughter and its storm of smoke, I understood who was behind the title of his collected poems. I was confounded. It was Margaret. His book was called *Virility*.

A week after this conversation he left with my sister for Chicago, for the inauguration of his reading series.

I went up to his attic and searched it. I was in a boil of distrust; I was outraged. I had lost Regina to Margaret's principles, and now Margaret had lost her principles, and in both cases Edmund Gate had stood to profit. He gained from her morality and he gained from her immorality. I began to hate him again. It would have rejoiced me to believe his quip: nothing could have made me merrier than to think him a thief of words, if only for the revenge of catching him at it—but he could not even be relied on for something so plausible as plagiarism. The place revealed nothing. There was not so much as an anthology of poetry, say, which might account for his extraordinary burgeoning; there was not a single book of any kind—that sparse and pitiful wreck of his dictionary, thrown into a corner together with a cigar box, hardly signified. For the rest, there were only an old desk with his—no, my—typewriter on it, an ottoman, a chair or two, an empty chest, a hot bare floor (the heat pounded upward), and his primordial suit slowly revolving in the sluggish airs on a hanger suspended from the skylight, moths nesting openly on the lapels. It brought to mind Mohammed and the Koran; Joseph Smith and the golden plates. Some mysterious dictation recurred in these rooms: his gift came to him out of the light and out of the dark. I sat myself down at his desk and piecemeal typed out an agonized letter to Regina. I offered to change the terms of our relationship. I said I hoped we could take up again, not as before (my house was in use). I said I would marry her.

She answered immediately, enclosing a wedding announcement six months old.

On that same day Margaret returned. "I left him, of *course* I left him. I had to, not that he can take care of himself under the circumstances, but I sent him on to Detroit anyhow. If I'm going to be his manager, after all, I have to *manage* things. I can't do all that from the provinces, you know—I have to *be* here, I have to see people . . . ah, you can't imagine it, Edmund, they want him everywhere! I have to set up a regular office, just a *little* switchboard to start with—"

"It's going well?"

"Going well! What a way to put it! Edmund, he's a phenomenon. It's supernatural. He has *charisma*, in Chicago they had to arrest three girls, they made a human chain and lowered themselves from a chandelier right over the lectern, and the lowest-hanging one reached down for a hair of his head and nearly tore the poor boy's scalp off—"

"What a pity," I said.

"What do you *mean* what a pity, you don't follow, Edmund, he's a celebrity!"

"But he has so few hairs and he thinks so much of them," I said, and wondered bitterly whether Regina had married a bald man.

"You have no right to take that tone," Margaret said. "You have no idea how modest he is. I suppose that's part of his appeal—he simply has no ego at all. He takes it as innocently as a baby. In Chicago he practically looked over his shoulder to see if they really meant *him*. And they *do* mean him, you can't imagine the screaming, and the shoving for autographs, and people calling bravo and fainting if they happen to meet his eyes—"

"Fainting?" I said doubtfully.

"Fainting! My goodness, Edmund, don't you read the headlines in your own paper? His audiences are three times as big as Caruso's. Oh, you're hard, Edmund, you admit he's good but I say there's a terrible wall in you if you don't see the power in this boy—"

"I see it over you," I said.

"Over me! Over the world, Edmund, it's the world he's got now—I've already booked him for London and Manchester, and here's this cable from Johannesburg pleading for him—oh, he's through with the backwoods, believe you me. And look here, I've just settled up this fine generous contract for his next book, with the reviews still piling in from the first one!" She crackled open her briefcase, and flung out a mass of files, lists, letterheads, schedules, torn envelopes with exotic stamps on them, fat legal-looking portfolios, documents in tiny type—she danced them all noisily upon her pouting lap.

"His second book?" I asked. "Is it ready?"

"Of course it's ready. He's remarkably productive, you know. Fecund."

"He pullulates," I suggested.

"His own word exactly, how did you hit it? He can come up with a poem practically at will. Sometimes right after a reading, when he's exhausted—you know it's his shyness that exhausts him that way—anyhow, there he is all fussed and worried about whether the next performance will be as good, and he'll suddenly get this—well, *fit*, and hide out in the remotest part of the hotel and fumble in his wallet for bits of paper—he's always carrying bits of folded paper, with notes or ideas in them I suppose, and shoo everyone away, even me, and *type* (he's awfully fond of his new typewriter, by the way)—he just types the glory right out of his soul!" she crowed. "It's the energy of genius. He's *authentic*, Edmund, a profoundly energetic man is profoundly energetic in all directions at once. I hope at least you've been following the reviews?"

It was an assault, and I shut myself against it. "What will he call the new book?"

"Oh, he leaves little things like the titles to me, and I'm all for simplicity. —*Virility II*," she announced in her shocking business-magnate voice. "And the one after that will be *Virility III*. And the one after that—"

"Ah, fecund," I said.

"Fecund," she gleamed.

"A bottomless well?"

She marveled at this. "How is it you always hit on Edmund's words exactly?"

"I know how he talks," I said.

"A bottomless well, he said it himself. Wait and see!" she warned me.

She was not mistaken. After *Virility* came *Virility II*, and after that *Virility III*, and after that an infant boy. Margaret named him Edmund—she said it was after me—and her husband the stockbroker, though somewhat puzzled at this human production in the midst of so much literary fertility, was all the same a little cheered. Of late it had seemed to him, now that Margaret's first simple switchboard had expanded to accommodate three secretaries, that he saw her less than ever, or at least that she was noticing him less than ever. This youngest Edmund struck him as proof (though it embarrassed him to think about it even for a minute) that perhaps she had noticed him more than he happened to remember. Margaret, meanwhile, was gay and busy—she slipped the new little Edmund ("Let's call *him* III," she laughed) into her packed nursery and went on about her business, which had grown formidable. Besides the three secretaries, she had two assistants: poets, poetasters, tenors, altos, mystics, rationalists, rightists, leftists, memoirists, fortune-tellers, peddlers, everyone with an *idée fixe* and therefore suitable to the lecture circuit clamored to be bundled into her clientele. Edmund she ran ragged. She ran him to Paris, to Lisbon, to Stockholm, to Moscow; nobody understood him in any of these places, but the title of his books translated impressively into all languages. He developed a sort of growl—it was from always being hoarse; he smoked day and night—and she made him cultivate it. Together with his accent it caused an international shudder among the best of women. She got rid of his initialed cuffs and dressed him like a prize fighter, in high laced black brogans and tight shining T-shirts, out of which his hairiness coiled. A long bladder of smoke was always trailing out of his mouth. In Paris they pursued him into the Place de la Concorde yelling *"Virilité! Virilité!" "Die Manneskraft!"* they howled in Munich. The reviews were an avalanche, a cataclysm. In the rotogravure sections his picture vied with the beribboned bosoms of duchesses. In New Delhi glossy versions of his torso were hawked like an avatar in the streets. He had long since been catapulted out of the hands of the serious literary critics—but it was the serious critics who had begun it. "The Masculine Principle personified, verified, and illuminated." "The bite of Pope, the sensuality of Keats." "The quality, in little, of the very greatest novels. Tolstoyan." "Seminal and hard." "Robust, lusty, male." "Erotic."

Margaret was ecstatic, and slipped a new infant into her bursting nursery. This time the stockbroker helped her choose its name: they decided on Gate, and hired another nanny to take care of the overflow.

After *Virility IV* came *Virility V*. The quality of his work had not diminished, yet it was extraordinary that he could continue to produce at all. Occasionally he came to see me between trips, and then he always went upstairs and took a turn around the sighing floors of his old rooms. He descended haggard and slouching; his pockets looked puffy, but it seemed to be only his huge fists he kept there. Somehow his fame had intensified that curious self-effacement. He had divined that I was privately soured by his success, and he tried bashfully to remind me of the days when he had written badly.

"That only makes it worse," I told him. "It shows what a poor prophet I was."

"No," he said, "you weren't such a bad prophet, Edmund."

"I said you'd never get anywhere with your stuff."

"I haven't."

I hated him for that—Margaret had not long before shown me his bank statement. He was one of the richest men in the country; my paper was always printing human-interest stories about him—"Prosperous Poet Visits Fabulous Patagonia." I said, "What do you mean you haven't gotten anywhere? What more do you want from the world? What else do you think it can give you?"

"Oh, I don't know," he said. He was gloomy and sullen. "I just feel I'm running short on things."

"On triumphs? They're all the time comparing you to Keats. Your pal Fielding wrote in *The Centennial* just the other day that you're practically as great as the Early Milton."

"Fielding's senile. They should have put him away a long time ago."

"And in sales you're next to the Bible."

"I was brought up on the Bible," he said suddenly.

"Aha. It's a fit of conscience? Then look, Elia, why don't you take Margaret and get her divorced and get those babies of yours legitimized, if that's what's worrying you."

"They're legitimate enough. The old man's not a bad father. Besides, they're all mixed up in there, I can't tell one from the other."

"Yours are the ones named after you. You were right about Margaret, she's an efficient woman."

"I don't worry about that," he insisted.

"*Some*thing's worrying you." This satisfied me considerably.

"As a matter of fact—" He trundled himself down into my father's decaying chair. He had just returned from a tour of Italy; he had gone with a wardrobe of thirty-seven satin T-shirts and not one of them had survived intact. His torn-off sleeves sold for twenty lira each. They had stolen his glasses right off his celebrated nose. "I like it here, Edmund," he said. "I like your house. I like the way you've never bothered about my old things up there. A man likes to hang on to his past."

It always bewildered me that the style of his talk had not changed. He was still devoted to the insufferably hackneyed. He still came upon his clichés like Columbus. Yet his poems . . . but how odd, how remiss! I observe that I have not even attempted to describe them. That is because they ought certainly to be *presented*—read aloud, as Edmund was doing all over the world. Short of that, I might of course reproduce them here; but I must not let my narrative falter in order to make room for any of them, even though, it is true, they would not require a great deal of space. They were notably small and spare, in conventional stanza-form. They rhymed consistently and scanned regularly. They were, besides, amazingly simple. Unlike the productions of Edmund's early phase, their language was pristine. There were no unusual words. His poems had the ordinary vocabulary of ordinary men. At the same time they were immensely vigorous. It was astonishingly easy to memorize them—they literally could not be forgotten. Some told stories, like ballads, and they were exhilarating yet shocking stories. Others were strangely explicit love lyrics, of a kind that no Western poet had ever yet dared—but the effect was one of health and purity rather than scandal. It was remarked by everyone who read or heard Edmund Gate's work that only a person who had had great and large experience of the world could have written it. People speculated about his life. If the Borgias, privy to all forms of foulness, had been poets, someone said, they would have written poems like that. If Teddy Roosevelt's Rough Riders had been poets, they would have written poems like that. If Genghis Khan and Napoleon had been poets, they would have written poems like that. They were masculine poems. They were political and personal, public and private. They were full of both passion and ennui, they were youthful and elderly, they were green and wise. But they were not beautiful and they were not dull, the way a well-used, faintly gnarled, but superbly controlled muscle is neither beautiful nor dull. They were, in fact, very much like Margaret's vision of Edmund Gate himself. The poet and the poems were indistinguishable.

She sent her vision to Yugoslavia, she sent it to Egypt, she sent it to Japan. In Warsaw girls ran after him in the street to pick his pockets for souvenirs—they came near to picking his teeth. In Copenhagen they formed an orgiastic club named "The Forbidden Gate" and gathered around a gatepost to read him. In Hong Kong they tore off his underwear and stared giggling at his nakedness. He was now twenty-five; it began to wear him out.

When he returned from Brazil he came to see me. He seemed more morose than ever. He slammed up the stairs, kicked heavily over the floors, and slammed down again. He had brought down with him his old cigar box.

"My aunt's dead," he said.

As usual he took my father's chair. His burly baby's-head lolled.

"The one in Liverpool?"

"Yeah."

"I'm sorry to hear that. Though she must have gotten to be a pretty old lady by now."

"She was seventy-four."

He appeared to be taking it hard. An unmistakable misery creased his giant neck.

"Still," I said, "you must have been providing for her nicely these last few years. At least before she went she had her little comforts."

"No. I never did a thing. I never sent her a penny."

I looked at him. He seemed to be nearly sick. His lips were black. "You always meant to, I suppose. You just never got around to it," I ventured; I thought it was remorse that had darkened him.

"No," he said. "I couldn't. I didn't have it then. I couldn't afford to. Besides, she was always very self-reliant."

He was a worse scoundrel than I had imagined. "Damn you, Elia," I said. "She took you in, if not for her you'd be murdered with your whole family back there—"

"Well, I never had as much as you used to think. That police station job wasn't much."

"Police station!" I yelled.

He gave me an eye full of hurt. "You don't follow, Edmund. My aunt died before all this fuss. She died three years ago."

"Three years ago?"

"Three and a half maybe."

I tried to adjust. "You just got the news, you mean? You just heard?"

"Oh, no. I found out about it right after it happened."

Confusion roiled in me. "You never mentioned it."

"There wasn't any point. It's not as though you *knew* her. Nobody knew her. I hardly knew her myself. She wasn't anybody. She was just this old woman."

"Ah," I said meanly, "so the grief is only just catching up with you, is that it? You've been too busy to find the time to mourn?"

"I never liked her," he admitted. "She was an old nuisance. She talked and talked at me. Then when I got away from her and came here she wrote me and wrote me. After a while I just stopped opening her letters. I figured she must have written me two hundred letters. I saved them. I save everything, even junk.

When you start out poor, you always save everything. You never know when you might need it. I never waste anything." He said portentously, "Waste Not, Want Not."
"If you never answered her how is it she kept on writing?"
"She didn't have anybody else to write to. I guess she had to write and she didn't have anybody. All I've got left are the ones in here. This is the last bunch of letters of hers I've got." He showed me his big scratched cigar box.
"But you say you saved them—"
"Sure, but I used them up. Listen," he said. "I've got to go now, Edmund, I've got to meet Margaret. It's going to be one hell of a fight, I tell you."
"What?" I said.
"I'm not going anywhere else, I don't care how much she squawks. I've had my last trip. I've got to stay home from now on and do poems. I'm going to get a room somewhere, maybe my old room across town, *you* remember—where you came to see me that time?"
"Where I knocked you down. You can stay here," I said.
"Nah," he said. "Nowhere your sister can get at me. I've got to work."
"But you've *been* working," I said. "You've been turning out new poems all along! That's been the amazing thing."
He hefted all his flesh and stood up, clutching the cigar box to his dinosaurish ribs.
"I haven't," he said.
"You've done those five collections—"
"All I've done are those two babies. Edmund and Gate. And they're not even my real names. That's all I've done. The reviews did the rest. Margaret did the rest."
He was suddenly weeping.
"I can't tell it to Margaret—"
"Tell what?"
"There's only one bundle left. No more. After this no more. It's finished."
"Elia, what in God's name *is* this?"

"I'm afraid to tell. I don't know what else to do. I've *tried* to write new stuff. I've tried. It's terrible. It's not the same. It's not the same, Edmund. I can't do it. I've told Margaret that. I've told her I can't write any more. She says it's a block, it happens to all writers. She says don't worry, it'll come back. It always comes back to genius."

He was sobbing wildly; I could scarcely seize his words. He had thrown himself back into my father's chair, and the tears were making brooks of its old leather cracks.

"I'm afraid to tell," he said.

"Elia, for God's sake. Straighten up like a man. Afraid of what?"

"Well, I told you once. I told you because I knew you wouldn't believe me, but I *did* tell you, you can't deny it. You could've stopped me. It's your fault too." He kept his face hidden.

He had made me impatient. "What's my fault?"

"I'm a plagiarist."

"If you mean Margaret again—"

He answered with a whimper: "No, no, don't be a fool, I'm through with Margaret."

"Aren't those collections yours? They're not yours?"

"They're mine," he said. "They came in the mail, so if you mean are they mine *that* way—"

I caught his agitation. "Elia, you're out of your mind—"

"She wrote every last one," he said. "In Liverpool. Every last line of every last one. Tante Rivka. There's only enough left for one more book. Margaret's going to call it *Virility VI*," he bawled.

"Your aunt?" I said. "She wrote them all?"

He moaned.

"Even the one—not the one about the—"

"All," he broke in; his voice was nearly gone.

He stayed with me for three weeks. To fend her off I telephoned Margaret and said that Edmund had come down with the mumps. "But I've just had a cable from Southern Rhodesia!" she wailed. "They need him like mad down there!"

"You'd better keep away, Margaret," I warned. "You don't want to carry the fever back to the nursery. All those babies in there—"

"Why should he get an infant's disease?" she wondered; I heard her fidget.

"It's just the sort of disease that corresponds to his mentality."

"Now stop that. You know that's a terrible sickness for a grown man to get. You know what it does. It's awful."

I had no idea what she could be thinking of; I had chosen this fabrication for its innocence. "Why?" I said. "Children recover beautifully—"

"Don't be an imbecile, Edmund," she rebuked me in my father's familiar tone—my father had often called me a scientific idiot. "He might come out of it as sterile as a stone. Stop it, Edmund, it's nothing to laugh at, you're a brute."

"Then you'll have to call his next book *Sterility*," I said.

He hid out with me, as I have already noted, for nearly a month, and much of the time he cried.

"It's all up with me."

I said coldly, "You knew it was coming."

"I've dreaded it and dreaded it. After this last batch I'm finished. I don't know what to do. I don't know what's going to happen."

"You ought to confess," I advised finally.

"To Margaret?"

"To everyone. To the world."

He gave me a teary smirk. "Sure. The Collected Works of Edmund Gate, by Tante Rivka."

"Vice versa's the case," I said, struck again by a shadow of my first shock. "And since it's true, you ought to make it up to her."

"You can't make anything up to the dead." He was wiping

the river that fell from his nose. "My reputation. My poor
about-to-be-mutilated reputation. No, I'll just go ahead and get
myself a little place to live in and produce new things. What
comes now will be *really* mine. Integrity," he whined. "I'll
save myself that way."

"You'll ruin yourself. You'll be the man of the century
who fizzled before he made it to thirty. There's nothing more
foolish-looking than a poet who loses his gift. Pitiful. They'll
laugh at you. Look how people laugh at the Later Wordsworth.
The Later Gate will be a fiasco at twenty-six. You'd better
confess, Elia."

Moodily he considered it. "What would it get me?"

"Wonder and awe. Admiration. You'll be a great sacri-
ficial figure. You can say your aunt was reticent but a tyrant,
she made you stand in her place. Gate the Lamb. You can say
anything."

This seemed to attract him. "It *was* a sacrifice," he said.
"Believe me it was hell going through all of that. I kept getting
diarrhea from the water in all those different places. I never
could stand the screaming anywhere. Half the time my life was
in danger. In Hong Kong when they stole my shorts I practically got pneumonia." He popped his cigarette out of his
mouth and began to cough. "You really think I ought to do
that, Edmund? Margaret wouldn't like it. She's always hated
sterile men. It'll be an admission of my own poetic sterility,
that's how she'll look at it."

"I thought you're through with her anyhow."

Courage suddenly puffed him out. "You bet I am. I don't
think much of people who exploit other people. She built that
business up right out of my flesh and blood. Right out of my
marrow."

He sat at the typewriter in the attic, at which I had ham-
mered out my futile proposal to Regina, and wrote a letter to
his publisher. It was a complete confession. I went with him to
the drugstore to get it notarized. I felt the ease of the perfect
confidant, the perfect counsel, the perfect avenger. He had

spilled me the cup of humiliation, he had lost me Regina; I would lose him the world.

Meanwhile I assured him he would regain it. "You'll go down," I said, "as the impresario of the nearly-lost. You'll go down as the man who bestowed a hidden genius. You'll go down as the savior who restored to perpetual light what might have wandered a mute inglorious ghost in the eternal dark."

On my paper they had fired better men than I for that sort of prose.

"I'd rather have been the real thing myself," he said. The remark seemed to leap from his heart; it almost touched me.

"Caesar is born, not made," I said. "But who notices Caesar's nephew? Unless he performs a vast deep act. To be Edmund Gate was nothing. But to shed the power of Edmund Gate before the whole watching world, to become little in oneself in order to give away one's potency to another—*that* is an act of profound reverberation."

He said wistfully, "I guess you've got a point there," and emerged to tell Margaret.

She was wrathful. She was furious. She was vicious. "A lady wrote 'em?" she cried. "An old Jewish immigrant lady who never even made it to America?"

"My Tante Rivka," he said bravely.

"Now Margaret," I said. "Don't be obtuse. The next book will be every bit as good as the ones that preceded it. The quality is exactly the same. He picked those poems at random out of a box and one's as good as another. They're all good. They're brilliant, you know that. The book won't be different so its reception won't be different. The profits will be the same."

She screwed up a doubtful scowl. "It'll be the last one. He says *he* can't write. There won't be any more after this."

"The canon closes," I agreed, "when the poet dies."

"This poet's dead all right," she said, and threw him a spiteful laugh. Edmund Gate rubbed his glasses, sucked his cigarette, rented a room, and disappeared.

Margaret grappled in vain with the publisher. "Why not *Virility* again? It was good enough for the other five. It's a selling title."

"This one's by a woman," he said. "Call it *Muliebrity*, no one'll understand you." The publisher was a wit who was proud of his Latin, but he had an abstract and wholesome belief in the stupidity of his readers.

The book appeared under the name *Flowers from Liverpool*. It had a pretty cover, the color of a daisy's petal, with a picture of Tante Rivka on it. The picture was a daguerrotype that Edmund had kept flat at the bottom of the cigar box. It showed his aunt as a young woman in Russia, not very handsome, with large lips, a circular nose, and minuscule light eyes—the handle of what looked strangely like a pistol stuck out of her undistinguished bosom.

The collection itself was sublime. By some accident of the unplanned gesture the last poems left in Edmund Gate's cracked cigar box had turned out to be the crest of the poet's vitality. They were as clear and hard as all the others, but somehow rougher and thicker, perhaps more intellectual. I read and marveled myself into shame—if I had believed I would dash his career by inducing him to drop his connection with it, I had been worse than misled. I had been criminal. Nothing could damage the career of these poems. They would soar and soar beyond petty revenges. If Shakespeare was really Bacon, what difference? If Edmund Gate was really Tante Rivka of Liverpool, what difference? Since nothing can betray a good poem, it is pointless to betray a bad poet.

With a prepublication copy in my hand I knocked at his door. He opened it in his underwear: a stink came out of him. One lens was gone from his glasses.

"Well, here it is," I said. "The last one."

He hiccuped with a mournful drunken spasm.

"The last shall be first," I said with a grin of disgust; the smell of his room made me want to run.

"The first shall be last," he contradicted, flagging me

down with an old newspaper. "You want to come in here, Edmund? Come in, sure."

But there was no chair. I sat on the bed. The floor was splintered and his toenails scraped on it. They were long filthy crescents. I put the book down. "I brought this for you to have first thing."

He looked at the cover. "What a mug on her."

"What a mind," I said. "You were lucky to have known her."

"An old nuisance. If not for her I'd still be what I was. If she didn't run out on me."

"Elia," I began; I had come to tell him a horror. "The publisher did a little biographical investigation. They found where your aunt was living when she died. It seems," I said, "she was just what you've always described. Self-sufficient."

"Always blah blah at me. Old nuisance. I ran out on her, couldn't stand it."

"She got too feeble to work and never let on to a soul. They found her body, all washed clean for burial, in her bed. She'd put on clean linens herself and she'd washed herself. Then she climbed into the bed and starved to death. She just waited it out that way. There wasn't a crumb in the place."

"She never asked me for anything," he said.

"How about the one called 'Hunger'? The one everybody thought was a battle poem?"

"It was only a poem. Besides, she was already dead when I got to it."

"If you'd sent her something," I said, "you might have kept Edmund Gate going a few years more. A hardy old bird like that could live to be a hundred. All she needed was bread."

"Who cares? The stuff would've petered out sooner or later anyhow, wouldn't it? The death of Edmund Gate was unavoidable. I wish you'd go away, Edmund. I'm not used to feeling this drunk. I'm trying to get proficient at it. It's killing my stomach. My bladder's giving out. Go away."

"All right."

"Take that damn book with you."

"It's yours."

"Take it away. It's your fault they've turned me into a woman. I'm a man," he said; he gripped himself between the legs; he was really very drunk.

All the same I left it there, tangled in his dirty quilt.

Margaret was in Mexico with a young client of hers, a baritone. She was arranging bookings for him in hotels. She sent back a photograph of him in a swimming pool. I sat in the clamorous nursery with the stockbroker and together we rattled through the journals, looking for reviews.

"Here's one. 'Thin feminine art,' it says."

"Here's another. 'A lovely girlish voice reflecting a fragile girlish soul: a lace valentine.' "

" 'Limited, as all domestic verse must be. A spinster's one-dimensional vision.' "

" 'Choked with female inwardness. Flat. The typical unimaginativeness of her sex.' "

" 'Distaff talent, secondary by nature. Lacks masculine energy.' "

" 'The fine womanly intuition of a competent poetess.' "

The two youngest children began to yowl. "Now, now Gatey boy," said the stockbroker, "now, now, Edmund. Why can't you be good? Your brothers and sisters are good, *they* don't cry." He turned to me with a shy beam. "Do you know we're having another?"

"No," I said. "I didn't know that. Congratulations."

"She's the New Woman," the stockbroker said. "Runs a business all by herself, just like a man."

"Has babies like a woman."

He laughed proudly. "Well, she doesn't do that one by herself, I'll tell you that."

"Read some more."

"Not much use to it. They all say the same thing, don't

they? By the way, Edmund, did you happen to notice they've already got a new man in *The Centennial*? Poor Fielding, but the funeral was worthy of him. Your father would have wept if he'd been there."

"Read the one in *The Centennial*," I said.

" 'There is something in the feminine mind which resists largeness and depth. Perhaps it is that a woman does not get the chance to sleep under bridges. Even if she got the chance, she would start polishing the piles. Experience is the stuff of art, but experience is not something God made woman for . . .' It's just the same as the others," he said.

"So is the book."

"The title's different," he said wisely. "This one's by a woman, they all point that out. All the rest of 'em were called *Virility*. What happened to that fellow, by the way? He doesn't come around."

The babies howled down the ghost of my reply.

I explained at the outset that only last week I visited the grave of Edmund Gate, but I neglected to describe a curious incident that occurred on that spot.

I also explained the kind of cameraderie elderly people in our modern society feel for one another. We know we are declining together, but we also recognize that our memories are a kind of national treasury, being living repositories for such long-extinct customs as burial and intra-uterine embryo-development.

At Edmund Gate's grave stood an extraordinary person —a frazzled old woman, I thought at first. Then I saw it was a very aged man. His teeth had not been trans-rooted and his vision seemed faint. I was amazed that he did not salute me —like myself, he certainly appeared to be a centagenerian —but I attributed this to the incompetence of his eyes, which wore their lids like hunched capes.

"Not many folks around here nowadays," I said. "People keep away from the old Preserved Cemeteries. My view is these youngsters are morbid. Afraid of the waste. They have to use everything. We weren't morbid in our time, hah?"

He did not answer. I suspected it was deliberate.

"Take this one," I said, in my most cordial manner, inviting his friendship. "This thing right here." I gave the little stone a good knock, taking the risk of arrest by the Outdoor Museum Force Apparently no one saw. I knocked it again with the side of my knuckle. "I actually knew this fellow. He was famous in his day. A big celebrity. That young Chinese fellow, the one who just came back from flying around the edge of the Milky Way, well, the fuss they made over *him*, that's how it was with this fellow. This one was literary, though."

He did not answer; he spat on the part of the stone I had touched, as if to wash it.

"You knew him too?" I said.

He gave me his back—it was shaking horribly—and minced away. He looked shriveled but of a good size still; he was uncommonly ragged. His clothing dragged behind him as though the covering over the legs hobbled him; yet there was a hint of threadbare flare at his ankle. It almost gave me the sense that he was wearing an ancient woman's garment, of the kind in fashion seventy years ago. He had on queer old-fashioned woman's shoes with long thin heels like poles. I took off after him—I am not slow, considering my years—and slid my gaze all over his face. It was a kettle of decay. He was carrying a red stick—it seemed to be a denuded lady's umbrella (an apparatus no longer known among us)—and he held it up to strike.

"Listen here," I said hotly, "what's the matter with you? Can't you pass a companionable word? I'll just yell for the Museum Force, you and that stick, if you don't watch it—"

"I watch it," he said. His voice burst up and broke like boiling water—it sounded vaguely foreign. "I watch it all

the time. That's my monument, and believe you me I watch
it. I won't have anyone else watch it either. See what it
says there? 'I am a man.' You keep away from it."
"I'll watch what I please. You're no more qualified than
I am," I said.
"To be a man? I'll show you," he retorted, full of
malice, his stick still high. "Name's Gate, same as on that
stone. That's my stone. They don't make 'em any more.
You'll do without."
Now this was a sight: madness has not appeared in our
society for over two generations. All forms of such illness
have vanished these days, and if any pops up through some
genetic mishap it is soon eliminated by Electromed Procedure.
I had not met a madman since I was sixty years old.
"Who do you say you are?" I asked him.
"Gate, born Gatoff. Edmund, born Elia."
This startled me: it was a refinement of information
not on the monument.
"Edmund Gate's dead," I said. "You must be a literary
historian to know a point like that. I knew him personally
myself. Nobody's heard of him now, but he was a celebrated
man in my day. A poet."
"Don't tell me," the madman said.
"He jumped off a bridge dead drunk."
"That's what you think. That so, where's the body? I
ask you."
"Under that stone. Pile of bones by now."
"I thought it was in the river. Did anybody ever pull
it out of the river, hah? You've got a rotten memory, and you
look roughly my age, boy. My memory is perfect: I can
remember perfectly and I can forget perfectly. That's my
stone, boy. I survived to see it. That stone's all there's left
of Edmund Gate." He peered at me as though it pained him.
"He's dead, y'know."
"Then you can't be him," I told the madman; genuine
madmen always contradict themselves.

"Oh yes I can! I'm no dead poet, believe you me. I'm what survived him. He was succeeded by a woman, y'know. Crazy old woman. Don't tell *me*."

He raised his bright stick and cracked it down on my shoulder. Then he slipped off, trembling and wobbling in his funny shoes, among the other monuments of the Preserved Cemetery.

He had never once recognized me. If it had really been Elia, he would certainly have known my face. That is why I am sure I have actually met a genuine madman for the first time in over forty years. The Museum Force at my request has made an indefatigable search of the Cemetery area, but up to this writing not so much as his pointed heel-print has been discovered. They do not doubt my word, however, despite my heavy age; senility has been eliminated from our modern society.